DREAMSHORES

MONSTER ISLAND

MIKE ROBINSON

SEVERED PRESS
HOBART TASMANIA

DREAMSHORES

"If we reverse the outer shell and the essence—in other words, consider the outer shell the essence and the essence the outer shell—our lives might be a whole lot easier to understand."
Haruki Murakami, *Kafka on the Shore*

"I exist in your imagination, and your imagination is part of nature, which means that I, too, exist in nature."
Anton Chekhov, *The Black Monk*

"How was it possible that something I'd created from my own being was now larger than my own being?"
Alan Lightman, *Mr. g*

I
MONSTROUS STIRRINGS

1

RUSSELL BOYLAN GOES EXTINCT

After so many millions of years, after so much gestation in the human psyche, dinosaurs had finally been reborn. Real muscles bulged beneath real flesh, which was slicked and dirtied by real elements. The winds once more carried their ancient bellows. Our soil now knew their footprints. Our noses now knew the stink of their breath, our nerves the awful grandeur of their proximity.

In theaters the world over they ran, roared, hunted, stampeded, and millions of people took their popcorn to the prehistoric. Ten years before the start of the twenty-first century, the blockbuster *Cretaceous Crater* had done it, had turned inside-out the dream of every child, had exhumed the childhoods of their parents and elders.

In one such showing, however, sat a man who experienced this triumphant return with an unflinching expression. Nearby eyes would whip in his direction. Some people whispered about him. Newspapers and magazines had, with caution and respect, speculated about his attendance that evening. Others, sadly, eschewed such respect.

Dinosaurs May Be Back, But Russell Boylan Is Going Extinct.

Eras before their digital resurrection, such behemoths had drawn life from Boylan's exacting fingers, their spirits awakened one frame at a time, their eighteen-to-twenty-inch bodies of steel and rubber becoming titans of lost islands, ravagers of cities, sinkers of ships, abductors of damsels. It was the roar of his two-headed Cyclops, its rickety, unearthly gait as it fought off the claws of the Giant Crab, that in 1971 had sparked the imagination of one Joey Cranston, who twenty years on would be touted as Joseph Cranston, the wizard-behind-the-curtain of *Cretaceous Crater*, the new computer-generated milestone in moviemaking.

That night, when the credits rolled, the chatter began, and the held breaths loosed, Russell Boylan made his way quietly out of the theater. His expression had not changed. He watched others speak. Though it was late spring, the Santa Monica air was chilly, and words left fleeting stains on the night.

Then, someone approached—a young, sallow-faced journalist whose imminent, five-second interview would for months, even years, be repeated across many papers and screens.

"Mr. Boylan," said the journalist. "What did you think?"

"Of what?"

"Of the movie. Pretty impressive, huh?" Then, in a slightly lower tone, "Pretty real, huh?"

Boylan regarded the young man. "They're *too* real."

"What do you mean?"

"People want to dream," Boylan said. "Not wake up. We're being woken up."

And he turned and he left.

NIGHT OF THE TERROR

The moment Russell Boylan offered what many dubbed the cantankerous "dream" quote, a ten-year-old girl named Sierra Nevada Smith sat by the backyard campfire of her trailer home, five-hundred miles north of Santa Monica in the Northern California town of Dale, though she herself would later refrain from calling it a true *town*. "It's a splatter of trailer and mobile homes," she'd say in a future interview. "It looks like the droppings of a giant seagull."

The Night of the Terror, as it came to be called, began with her loading BBs into her rifle by the pulsing light of the fire, her dusky hair tied back in a ponytail, which brushed the hood of a black sweatshirt too big for her. Duty tightened her sharp-featured face.

Seated across from her on the log opposite was a boy named Jake Wilcox, waving his hands over the flames that reflected like red banshees in his glasses.

"You're serious," he said. His voice was tinny, almost artificial-sounding, every word like a flick against metal pipes. That wasn't the reason, though, that Jake Wilcox was called "Keyboard," or KB for short: his teeth, at least those in front, were spaced inordinately apart, black slivers visible between each one.

"About what?" Sierra said, focus unbroken.

"You're not going to find anything."

"It's the woods, KB. We'll find something. And if it's there," she looked up, readied the rifle, "we'll get it."

"With a BB gun?"

The forest chirped and whooped and buzzed.

"Here," Sierra said, pulling out a smaller flashlight from her sweatshirt and chucking it to KB. "I got my own."

Startled, KB nearly fumbled the light, but managed to hold onto it.

"How do we know this thing if we see it?" he asked.

No one, of course, was sure what the "thing" was supposed to be. Andy Duncan had seen it scurrying away from his trashcans, though that might well have been a raccoon or deer. High-schoolers named Tom Ratliff and Meredith Stevens said something "like a skinny deformed midget with glowing eyes" had spoiled their first date by jumping onto the hood of Tom's pickup. Many had seen the dents and scratches. Others started talking of scratches left on doors and fleeting green eyes and then Gary Baxter's trail cam had snapped that eerie humanoid blur in the middle of the night, only a few hundred yards from Sierra's trailer.

And somewhere, sometime, in the expanding shockwave of media, it was christened the "Dale Devil."

Earlier playfulness had dimmed in KB's eyes, which Sierra observed with a twinge of something like mourning. Distantly, she was afraid to lose KB's interest. No one else she knew would be such a ready partner in her escapades.

"Come on," Sierra said, cocking her BB gun as she stood to face the great wall of wood.

These were the latter years of what her grandmother Josephine, or Gran-Jo, her legal guardian since she was six, would come to call Sierra's "pure period."

Two years from now, a gleaming stud would take its lifetime perch on her nose, which she herself would pierce with a pin. Three years from then, her backside would see the first of her many tattoos: a snarling likeness of Medusa, as seen in the Russell Boylan film *The Perils of Perseus*.

No matter what she added to herself, permanently or not, little could diminish the pretty girl nature had made. Sharpest were her green eyes, accented by dark eyebrows afloat in pale skin, all framed by a rich cosmos of black hair which many assumed was dyed, probably because the same many assumed her emo, or goth, or hipster, all of which she roundly dismissed.

"I just like folding myself inside-out," she'd say, after her tenth tattoo, this one a green Kraken tentacle coiling around her right ankle.

At this point, Gran-Jo kept the TV away from her, and Sierra would not even set foot in a movie theater until she was fifteen. But she read. By that soon-to-be-infamous night in the woods with KB, she had ingested the biological abominations of Verne and Lovecraft, licked clean the canon of Wells, noshed on a smidgen of Stephen King. Their creations kneaded her brain, flooded its cracks. Such was the reality at odds with any grandmotherly notion of "purity."

Sierra approached the edge of the forest, BB gun in one hand, her flashlight pooling across the trees, KB in cautious tow.

While a fellow Dale native, KB seemed to react to the forest as though it were some foreign thing, dropped in from space. Kind of understandable, she supposed. Dale woods certainly had its share of strange occurrences, the Devil merely being the most current. These forests were a repository of lore, dispensing more legend than oxygen, providing the outlet for collective imagining in a town whose nearest movie theater was a twenty-three-mile drive. Bigfoot had been through here, on several occasions, as had a half-lizard, half-man beast allegedly witnessed by three teenagers. Then there was Mavis Buckner's backyard village of psychic gnomes—the less said about *that* ongoing "situation," the better.

Without looking back, Sierra charged into the woods. They now both had flashlights, after all, and she had a gun. Anything that dared take more than two steps toward them she could easily stun, then pop between the eyes. Whim-bam-boom. Her father had taught her to shoot when she was only seven, half a year before his heart had had enough of him. His boozy evenings had left plenty of empty cans and bottles to set up for target practice. Very often she'd fixed in her crosshairs the bottle of her namesake pale ale.

Sea-blown wind swirled in the canopy. The moon traced vague outlines of the highest leaves. For several minutes, Sierra trained the light toward the upper reaches of the pines, seeing what sorts of eyes she might catch.

"Sierra?" KB called from what seemed like a mile away. "Where the hell're we going?"

"You'll see."

"Not too far, I hope."

How could anyone *not* go far? Sierra had a theory that if one went far enough into the woods, one could find anything.

"It's okay, you wuss," Sierra replied, still not looking back. "We're going to the ruins."

"Is that where the Devil is?"

"Wouldn't you be there, if you were the Devil?" she said. "I think that's where it came into the world. And it might be trying to get back out."

"How do you know?"

Sierra smiled. "Just come on."

Referred to by Dale folks as simply "the ruins," the site sat in the middle of the woods about a third of a mile from Sierra's trailer, on the edge of a steep incline toward a brook. The remains of an old building, presumably a house, it was thought to have been built around the turn of the century. No one was sure what had happened to it, though the totality of the damage suggested a fire. All that remained now was a cement foundation, a rusted claw-footed bathtub and fractured stone columns that made of it a pipsqueak Parthenon. Or, as Sierra saw it, an ancient altar—a place where robed characters out of H.P. Lovecraft might convene to pray to or enliven primordial monsters. Summon gods.

They walked in silence, their lights and eyes recreating the forest, tree-by-tree, out of the dark. Sierra could hear KB's breathing and could smell the fine salty perfume of his fear. She kept the BB gun upright. Every fifteen yards or so, she would glance back and gauge how far they'd traveled, until she could no longer see the dim light of her trailer, and only the whites of KB's peepers greeted her.

Ahead, the babble of the stream, the tinny belching choir of frogs. The ruins were close.

Another few minutes and they were there. A sense of lonesomeness, almost apocalyptic in scope, pervaded this place.

"We made it," KB said. "It's not here. We can turn back."

Sierra whipped her flashlight at him. He winced, recoiled a little. In petty vengeance he shone his own light directly at her.

"I heard it likes to sleep in the creek sometimes," Sierra said. "It half-lives in the water. Like a frog."

"Who said that?"

Blinking away the afterimages left by the flashlight duel, Sierra turned in the direction of the incline. The stream gurgled at the bottom, the water looking oily and viscous in the moonlight.

"I'll check the ruins," Sierra said. "You check the stream. Just be careful going down. There's rocks and twigs and crap."

"Sierra…"

Sierra swung the light back on him. "Are you for serious? You'll be fine. Want this?"

She held up the BB gun toward him.

"No."

KB began his descent, standing sideways, clutching exposed tree roots. For a moment Sierra watched him, before turning back to the ruins. They were undeniably creepy, but in an intoxicating way. Tingling *what-ifs* and *maybes* filled her mind. Would they actually run into the Devil? Would they be the ones to really see it, maybe even shoot it?

She thought of Gran-Jo, who'd fallen asleep in her armchair and, while permissive, would probably have a mini-stroke knowing where her granddaughter was right now.

A snap. Her throat closed, pulse quickened. Against the light glinted eyes, peering through the trees at her. They weren't green, though, nor did they glow.

When the animal moved off, Sierra could tell it was a deer, though her heart still beat fast and hard.

"I'm down here," KB called. "Don't see anything."

Sierra didn't reply. A delicious prospect brewed in her brain. If she couldn't find the Devil, she could *become* it. How would that be any less legitimate? The Devil was something—even if just a story it still existed in the world, floating around like airborne debris. And she could give it a form, a place. She could become a whole other thing, take a timeout from this body called "Sierra." Become a goddamn legend. No beginning and no end. Just an always.

Then, she cried out.

#

According to the story KB would later tell her at her bedside in Monroe County Hospital—of which she would recall only the first part—he turned immediately at her sudden cry for help. His flashlight zipping all around. He called out for her, but received no reply. The fear was turning his flesh a chilled porcelain and it was difficult for him to move.

"Sierra?" he called out, the 'S' beginning squeaky, the "a" ending on little more than a forced exhale.

Nothing.

"Sierra?"

Motionless, he began to feel increasingly vulnerable. He walked forward, up the steep incline, every crunching step like a bright red arrow betraying his position for whatever salivating shadows might be edging in through the trees. Come and get it! Had something taken Sierra? Had the Devil snatched her into its otherworld or underground lair?

Stopping by the ruins, KB listened. The flashlight threw pale light on the decrepit stones, lending them an eerie magical illumination against the dark. Spirits could be in there, he thought, spirits ready to spew forth like volcanic lava.

Then—a footstep. Not his own.

"Sierra?"

KB experienced then a vicarious life review, though not of his life, per se, but his life thus far in monster movies, choice scenes spooling through the projector of his nine-year-old brain. "I was in a scary movie," he said later. "I was in every scary movie I'd seen. All the people who got axed, I was gonna be just like them."

More footsteps. Heavy, spaced well apart, the sounds of a large thing taking long strides.

Getting close. Closer.

KB thought perhaps he could blind whatever it was with the flashlight then make a getaway. But if he started running, death felt guaranteed. The forest would descend on him, engulf him.

"Sierra?"

His voice, gaining decibel, coincided with the next sound, a rapid succession of footfalls charging straight for him. All muscles pinched tight, sucked themselves against bone, and in the second before KB heeded the reflex to run a figure loomed over him, a dark apparition that leapt onto one of the altar's stone columns, arms outstretched, all nighttime billowing behind it as if to show itself as the very face of all midnight terrors.

The Devil!

For the first time in his life, KB screamed, and screamed for real. These few seconds passed like a knife drawn slowly across his brain. It was a seizure of time, a moment when absolutely everything was possible—including, truly, his own death.

Then there was the second of girlish chuckling.

Followed by the second where he saw the black sweatshirt, and the hood drawn tight over the pretty face he could never seem to get away from.

Another second: the stone column beneath her trembled and crumbled away, Sierra along with it.

She gave a startled yelp as she hit the edge of the incline, becoming gravity's chew toy, rolling in a scatter of loosed rocks and gravel down the embankment beyond the reach of the flashlight. Down, down. Crackling, snapping, crumbling down. Toward the stream.

Then—a punctuating *splash*.

It took another short while for those last few seconds to register in KB, to form a picture of what had just happened.

Again he called Sierra's name and again he got no reply. He ran down the hill, nearly stumbling over the stones and jutting roots. The flashlight shone on Sierra lying prostrate in the stream, the current tugging at her clothes. Blood stippled the exposed rocks. More trickled out beneath her hood.

KB screamed her name. He would later tell her he thought she was dead, even if some part of him thought her death an even more impossible notion than his own.

He rustled her, shook her, splashed water on her. Sierra didn't move. He pried off her hood. Glaring there in the full bath of light was a gash down the left side of her forehead.

"Your eyes were weird," he would tell her, "they were closed, but they fluttered, like you were trying to open them."

Squatting in the water about his ankles, KB moved cautiously forward and placed his pale hand on her neck where he felt the reassuring kiss of her pulse against his palm.

They'd entered the woods that night prompted by a strange phenomenon, a mystery, and would emerge later having known a new, more impressive enigma: that of noodle-bodied Jake "KB" Wilcox, who sported bruises on his knuckles from so many arm-wrestling losses to Sierra, having lifted her up and sprinted through the woods to her trailer, she hung limp over his shoulder like a caveman's hide.

He would emerge at Gran-Jo's trailer, his breathing ragged, his eyes wild and panicked. And he would call for Grandma Josephine, righting her from a nap in her armchair.

Even more incredible: he had dropped the flashlight near the bank of the stream.

"I dunno how I made it back," KB would say. "I just had to."

AWAKENING

There was a sensation of cold, and a gentle tugging, a thousand cool hands ushering her away from where she was, toward some greater unknown and she relinquished and allowed them to take her.

She floated up, buoyed by shadows. Could see a small body in the water below, receding from her. Mine? She wasn't immediately sure. The body was the only light thing in her vision, as the canopy and the drifting fog began to envelope her.

This fog fascinated her, distracting her from the frightened shouts far below, where another body had come running down to the one possibly hers that lay still in the dark waters.

The sense of cold retreated. She felt growing warmth.

Where am I, exactly?

She was someone, but didn't particularly remember who.

I'm everything.

The space around her grew foggier. The sights of the trees, the water and the body below, and the sounds of the fearful cries fading all disappeared until there was nothing but clouds. Gray nebulas encircled her, like some infant cosmos yet to choose its colors.

Forms evolved out of the murk, fleeting, strokes of electricity like tiny bolts of lightning inside of them. These were quiet storms around her, drifting, gathering. As one peering upon clouds with Rorschach fancy, she would decide their shapes for them, resolve their elemental indecision.

She imagined a dinosaur, pinching from this fog a grand brontosaurus that snaked its neck at the rest of all unformed.

A sense of power filled her; she felt gifted with God's Play-Doh.

Elsewhere she sculpted a dragon, wings wide and claws out. She felt as a dragon, too, swollen with heat, a sense of lordly airborne liberation. Like she could do anything, be anything. Anything she wanted.

#

She opened her eyes.

For a moment, she was no one, merely a set of dispassionate eyes. A vaporous awareness hovering in front of the figures clustered here, whose faces all peered in the same direction.

Then, in an onslaught, her Sierra-ness broke through the fog, recent moments lighting up harsh across her mind. She knew a brief sense of having made something, of having pressed upon a surface normally hard that was suddenly soft and shapeable.

First impression: Gran-Jo was crying. Sitting. Sitting and crying. A stranger in a white coat—a doctor—loomed a thousand feet tall at her bedside. Bedside?

Yes, she was lying down. In a … hospital. Yes, *hospital*. Her head throbbed, her brain like a stress ball squeezed in a calloused hand.

The others in the room: KB's mother, Joselyn Wilcox, stood by a seated KB, his arms and legs crossed so tight a "No Trespassing" sign ought to have been hung from his nose. All goofiness had evaporated from his face, now carved up by tear streaks. He gazed nowhere.

"Sierra, baby," said Gran-Jo, leaning toward her, the old woman's big round butt lifting the chair forward on its front legs. "How are you feeling?"

Another person entered. Husky frame, doughy with decades. A cowboy hat. Sheriff McCoy.

Oh God.

There were too many people around her. Sierra felt like a turkey on the Thanksgiving table, a vulnerable hunk of meat and the unfortunate center of attention.

The doctor, whose name she saw was Ackerman, patted her left forearm with mechanical repetition. Gran-Jo held her right hand.

"You took a hard spill, Sierra," said Dr. Ackerman. "You hit your head, knocked yourself out. We stitched it back up." He sighed, looked briefly at Gran-Jo. "We found a little bit of bleeding in your brain, too, which we were able to take care of."

"You're going to be all right, though," Gran-Jo interjected.

"Yes, you're going to be just fine," said Dr. Ackerman.

Gran-Jo continued sobbing. "Sierra, I'm not going to lose you, too. This has to stop. No more running around the woods, especially at night. No more going out at night. No more. Got it?"

What to say to that? Sierra wasn't sure. Especially as recollection of what she had done, what had put her here, rose in her. It was all her fault, all her stupidity. She had to be a prankster, to scare poor KB. And he had saved her, certainly. Who else could have?

"KB," she said. Speech felt like a strange new indulgence for her throat. "You went for help?"

"This young man here carried you back to safety," said Sheriff McCoy, his meaty hand clasping KB's shoulder. The kid jumped at the forceful contact. "He's a real hero, this boy."

Mrs. Wilcox stroked her son's hair.

"Do you remember who attacked you?" Gran-Jo asked.

Attacked me?

Then, she understood. She caught KB's gaze, noted the reflex on his part to look away—or maybe that was only because Sierra felt that reflex, too. She resisted it, though, and they shared a wordless discussion. Did her eyes convey apology and gratitude? Sierra didn't know, but figured neither would be enough.

She felt she might have to apologize, not for scaring KB, but for something deeper, for effectively rendering him her slave. He would do anything for her, it seemed. Cover for her. He was hopeless.

Tell them I was being stupid, KB. Tell them I was being mean and got exactly what I deserved.

"He was saying he thought maybe you were attacked by someone," said Sheriff McCoy, skepticism thickening with each word. "Or some thing. Do you remember what happened?"

"I heard you scream," KB said to Sierra and everyone else. "I heard this weird noise and then you falling, and I ran to you and found you lying in the brook. I looked up with my flashlight and saw these crazy green eyes glowing between the trees. Then they were gone."

Crazy green eyes, she thought. Like mine?

"Sierra?" Gran-Jo prodded.

"Uh, yeah," Sierra said. "I don't remember too much."

"It's okay," said Gran-Jo, squeezing her hand. To Sierra, it felt like poisons being pumped into her system. She wanted to cry, and even though tears might well be expected, she imagined they would instantly betray the idiocy of the truth, which was the idiocy of her.

Quickly she drew on the scattered knowledge of Dale Devil lore. The gears and pistons in her skull went to creaking work, their revolutions almost painful. She'd bled in there, Dr. Ackerman had said. Bled in her brain? The idea was terrifying, but also weirdly fascinating—the blood that sustained her, rushing free from around her skull, free from her brain…

"We went out to the ruins," she said. "KB… he was by the stream. I was on the other side of the ruins when I heard this…"

Out poured the lie, a story no more grounded than the breath it rode. As Sierra spoke, an internal rift occurred between the part weaving this fiction and the part utterly incredulous, the part that stepped back and wanted nothing of the former. Not now.

"You're sure this wasn't a person that attacked you?" said the sheriff.

"Pretty sure, I think," she said. *They're all going to jump me right now, pound on me, pound out the truth.* "I don't know exactly what it was. It smelled rotten and it was small. It had long teeth, I think."

Many imaginative excursions under her belt, the hunting halls of her mind adorned with thousands of heads of vanquished monstrosities from T-Rexes to the squid-god Cthulhu, Sierra had made of herself an Instant Creature Feature, quick when called upon to patch together some fantastically ghastly foe.

She would not go into much detail here, though. In her experience, grown-ups were more credulous when given ambiguity.

"I can't believe you carried me," Sierra said to KB.

KB remained quiet as admiring eyes drifted back to him. He tried to avoid them. His mother continued running wiry fingers through his hair, a motion as loving as it was protective, especially given her soft, disapproving scowl. Sierra had sensed that Mrs. Wilcox didn't like her, but had never actually broached the topic with KB. Now there was no need. The answer would be forever clear.

\#

Toward eleven o'clock, the movement and the life of the hospital simmered, then became silent and still. Sierra felt like the last person alive.

Gran-Jo had brought her a few books to read, all of them taken from her nightstand. Sierra appreciated the gesture even if she hated the idea of her grandmother entering her room without her being there and she'd already read all the included books—*Selected Horror Stories* by H.P. Lovecraft, Wells' *The Time Machine* and Clive Barker's *The Thief of Always*.

She opened the Lovecraft book and started some of the stories she hadn't read in a while. She absorbed no more than two or three paragraphs of each tale before abandoning the book. She went on to the Barker novel, but encountered the same problem, making it only two pages in. The words were not coming to life, instead draining straight through her without materializing into vast landscapes and characters that would normally swell beyond page and skin and eclipse all the silence and the loneliness.

Sierra remembered the TV bolted up in the corner. As Gran-Jo kept the trailer's only TV in her bedroom, Sierra had only really watched it at KB's house. Mrs. Wilcox put few limits on her son's viewing habits and, were Sierra inclined, she could probably get away with bingeing anytime she was over there. But KB usually just wanted to watch dumb cartoons, and she would always grow antsy.

But, of course, where could she go now?

Fortunately, she had not broken anything in her fall. Still, a great feeling of vulnerability overcame her. She felt as flimsy as snakeskin, easily shed, flung away. Except the snakeskin was not the snake. Was there an actual "snake" beneath this disposable skin of hers?

Sometimes, she would wonder where the zipper was located on her head, that place she could grab, pinch between thumb and forefinger and proceed to open, to unravel, this "Sierra" costume she'd been given without her full permission. It wasn't a bad costume, per se—but there had to be other things she was barred from feeling, seeing, tasting, knowing. And that bothered her.

With something close to desperation, Sierra tried to remember anything from the time she was unconscious, but there was nothing. She saw grayness, like soupy fog. Is that actual nothingness? Lacking even darkness? The falling, the crash of pain and then… the hospital. An awkward sequence cut together in her mind.

With death, there's nothing on the other side, she thought, *no other side. You just sail off the edge and keep going and going and going.*

Drifting across the Big Dumb.

"We're on a crazy island," her father used to say. "Shipwrecked on life. On both sides is a big dumb sea. Dumb before, dumb after. All we know," he would gesture vaguely with his arms, "is this."

Yes, the Big Dumb. How could that be, though? To her, it was impossible. There had to be a snake beneath the skin. Somehow, "me-ness" had to be immortal. Her flesh would die, but it was incomprehensible that she wouldn't wake up somewhere else, just as she'd woken up safe here in the hospital.

Thoroughly unsettled, she took the remote control and turned on the TV.

#

"I think that was the first time God intervened in my life," she'd later say, referring to that specific moment when the TV blinked on, an instant Genesis of a tiny universe, and she saw the man with the sword, buff and glistening, and the many other armed men scurrying and swinging and scrambling about him as they weathered a storm of massive tentacles making violent love to the ship, coiling the mast from bottom to top, entrapping the hull, smashing into cabins, plucking up the men like weeds.

The *movement* of those tentacles… she had never seen anything like it. They looked real, but clearly were not. They borrowed from reality, mimicked it, mocked it, while remaining yet loyal to some other reality, whatever it was. They seemed to shiver, appearing just out of synch with the fluid motion of the live-action men. A true meeting of dimensions. This was how the multi-limbed beasties of Lovecraft would look, or the Martians from *War of the Worlds*. Things marginally familiar, though made of totally exotic ingredients.

If the tentacles plucked men from the ship, they plucked from Sierra all sense of time, all the seconds and minutes she lay there. The dull throb in her head receded.

That night, Sierra watched a cumulative seven hours of what the commercials called a "Russell Boylan Marathon!" with the volume kept low but audible. At the time the name meant nothing to her, of course, nor did the names of the headlining cast. The monsters were the show. Past the tentacled beast, the men battled a three-headed dragon, a giant crab, and a behemoth bird, all of which stuttered across the screen in that wonderfully alien and oddly agile way. These were *The Untold Trials of Ulysses*. Only later would Sierra come to appreciate the sheer license taken with one of Western civilization's foundational texts.

Other titles drunk through her eyes: *The Perils of Perseus*, *Flying Saucers From the Sea*, *Prehistoric Valley*, *Titan Rises!*, and *The Scourge of Camelot*. The redeye hours overflowed with monsters and the bustle and screams of their tiny victims. These monsters existed, forever and irrefutably.

Yet while so large and so epic, the beasts were also somehow vulnerable. Zealous hands were evident in their locomotion, some symphony of life conducted in every snarl or strut or tail swipe. Their glistening, rippling skin was so tantalizingly touchable, like fancy, fairy-dusted toys. Sierra wanted to be the one playing with them, to be the divine craftsman lording over the tiny sprawl of desert or jungle or sea where these great animals chased the tiny actors in some vicious theater of her make.

Although she would never describe it aloud as such, the movies were like a hug to her, a welcoming and understanding embrace. Through the hammy, outdated lines, through the contrived suspense, the bombastic music, the shrill damsels, a livening energy reached Sierra that she had never felt before, and it had everything to do with the monsters, so hauntingly vivacious.

Something had reached out from this chaotic world and found her. Got her. Two like-hands had clutched one another.

For the first time in her young life, Sierra Nevada Smith was in love.

Between *Titan Rises!* and *Prehistoric Valley*, a short documentary came on, kicked off with a black and white photo of the latter film's Tyrannosaurus Rex, backdropped by the greater giant of an intense-looking man tweaking it into position.

"Before movie magic could be computer-generated," said the narrator, with boyish pride, "it required the painstaking finesse of Russell Boylan, who, frame-by-frame, gave the breath of life to our dreams.

"Boylan started under the tutelage of John Terwiliger," continued the TV, unrolling shots of the intense-looking man as a youth, slick-haired and conferring with another man before a wall of drawings. "Terwiliger, whose best-known work remains the classic *The Great Kundo*, is commonly seen as the father of the art of stop motion animation, which requires precise and gradual movement of a three-dimensional model. Just as hand-drawn animation is a series of still pictures, stop motion is a series of still poses, all marginally different from the last."

Then they showed a video—an older Boylan in grainy color, alone in the studio. Dinosaurs stood fixed in primal combat on a worktable of twisted Jurassic geology. Eyes firm and tongue bulging his lower lip, Boylan knelt and pinched a limb of the Tyrannosaur, free hand steadying the rest of the body, and shifted it slightly. Then he moved away, only to return a second later to move the same limb again, ever-so-slightly.

Toward the end of the clip, a man's voice came on, a lead-in to an interview with a mustached bigshot (or "mucky-muck", as Gran-Jo would say) whose name was Errol Maybury. Under his name were the words, *Producer, Prehistoric Valley*.

"He sucked up all energy to get his work done," Maybury said. "He'd drink blood. You think I'm the shark, being the producer. Not compared to Russ. And he's still that way, even though he's retired. But there'd been no stopping him when he was young. You wonder why his monsters disturbed so many dreams and sent so many under the seats? They were chips off the old block. That fearsomeness, that all came from Russ.

"He came in soft," Maybury went on. "His trademark line was 'I've got a few ideas I want to run by you.' So innocent. But you knew, hearing that phrase, that you were in for a creative tidal wave. Things were gonna change."

I've gotta make my own *monster*, Sierra thought. The idea was utterly religious, the greatest notion in all the history of the world.

Maybury continued: "'Feed them your dreams,' is what Terwiliger told Russ. And he did. Boy, he did. I was never quite sure if he meant the monsters or the audience, but either way it works."

Feed them your dreams, Sierra repeated in her mind, tasting the phrase.

A VISIT FROM BEYOND

Following the Night of the Terror, and her return from the hospital, Sierra was never to go outside for very long, and certainly not at night—Gran-Jo would make sure of that. Sierra understood, even then, that her grandmother's vigilance came from embarrassment at the viral nature of the account, which started in the hospital and eventually led to much of Dale flapping their lips about what might have attacked Alvin Smith's daughter.

"You used to be so pure," Gran-Jo said, to Sierra's utter mystification. "Not this rambunctious risk-taker."

To ease the new restrictions, Gran-Jo brought out the television from her bedroom and put it by the kitchen table, so that Sierra might watch, as well. But Sierra seldom took advantage of the newfound TV access, only flipping through the hazy sampling of channels in her eternal quest for more Russell Boylan-ness. She found one film, once, *The Crown of the World*, playing on a Friday night on Channel 4. Per cosmic law, though, by then only twenty minutes of the movie was left.

She walked often with Gran-Jo to the Dale Library, a building nearly the size of her 5th-grade classroom, where she tried to scrape up what she could of anything Boylan. The Film/Cinema section consisted of a single, half-empty shelf bearing maybe seven books, only two of which listed "Russell Boylan" or "stop motion animation" in their Indexes, and the information was always minimal.

Instead, Sierra browsed her regular literature, as well as the Occult section, where her fingers ran along spines like *Real-Life Monsters!* or *The Enigma of the Bermuda Triangle* or *Mysteries of the Past*. Gran-Jo frequented the same section, pulling out mildewed books on ghost research, an interest stemming back to when she was a child and her late father, in her words, "Tried to carry me outta my bed till I screamed, and Mama threw on the light."

"Why did you scream," Sierra asked, "if you knew it was your father?"

Here Gran-Jo shrugged. "I didn't know that in the moment. Not till I smelled his cologne."

Her grandmother had theorized that her father was trying to "carry her back over the hill of the living," a notion which gave Sierra the creeps. Clearly, if that was the case, for Gran-Jo's dad 'heaven' had proven unsatisfying. Incomplete without his daughter. And if heaven could be unsatisfying, what was the point of the whole business?

One afternoon, while Sierra sat on her bed facing the window, a broken-spined edition of Verne's *The Mysterious Island* on her lap, there was a knock at the front door. She followed the sounds of Gran-Jo responding to it, overheard the mostly inaudible exchange between her and the visitor.

Please don't be for me, she thought.

She heard Gran-Jo's maddeningly polite words, "Come on in," and part of her deflated.

She listened glumly as Gran-Jo led the mystery guest closer and closer to her room. As they neared, bits of their awkward exchange reached Sierra's ears.

"I search for everything," said a male voice. "Well, everything not-of-this-world."

"Have you ever seen spirits?" Gran-Jo asked.

The man sounded hesitant to answer. Sierra was surprised at the directness of her grandmother's question. For the last few months, Gran-Jo had amassed from the library a collection of aged, browned books like *Paranormal Visions* and *True-Life Ghost Stories*. Sierra's hunch was that her grandmother, spurred by her experience as a kid and now in her seventh decade, might be hoping for a sneak preview of what to expect over the earthly hill.

Like her granddaughter, it seemed Josephine Smith also refused to believe in the Big Dumb.

Just outside Sierra's door, they stopped.

"Sierra?" Gran Jo creaked the door open.

"Yeah?" Sierra said, closing her book. She turned to face them, to be polite. To be "pure."

Gran-Jo stood there. Behind her was a stocky man, maybe mid-thirties.

"There's someone here who would like to speak with you about what you might've... seen."

The man stepped forward. Sierra first noticed the black fisherman's hat, and the bright green symbol embroidered on the front. She recognized the symbol's bulbous head, its squiggly beard of tentacles and its raised gargoyle wings. The same insignia graced her anthology of H.P. Lovecraft. The demon lord Cthulhu.

She smiled. She would be "pure," all right.

The man's name was Dwayne. He never gave a last name, or, if he did, neither Sierra nor her grandmother remembered it. By his restless, bohemian air, and his nomadic existence in a decades-old VW van, that he kept a moniker at all was impressive.

He was jittery, his skin like a tarp in the wind, constantly restraining the gust of a new idea or sudden urge. While the Cthulhu logo may have quickly put her at ease, Sierra recognized deeper kinship with this Dwayne.

"I was passing through here," Dwayne said, taking a seat on the end of her bed. In the other room, Gran-Jo cleared her throat. Dwayne's eyes shot curiously to the door, then back to Sierra. "And I picked up some town-talk of you having an encounter with what might be the Dale Devil."

"Oh."

"You know what I'm talking about, right?"

Sierra nodded.

From his pocket, Dwayne brought out a Xerox of what appeared to be a child's sketch of a dwarfish, spiny creature on all-fours. He handed it to her, obviously trying to stray his eyes from the healing gash on her forehead.

"This was drawn just over here by Petersville," Dwayne said. "By a kid your age."

Sierra looked at the drawing. Crude. Stilted.

"It look familiar?"

Slowly, she shook her head. "I don't know."

"I'm a paranormal investigator," Dwayne said. "You know what that means?" He glanced at the Jules Verne book still in her hand, bookmarked by her thumb, and at the *Real-Life Monsters!* tome lying by her pillow. "Of course you know what that means."

"You look for ghosts and aliens and stuff?" she said.

Dwayne cracked a smile. "It's the 'and stuff' that really interests me."

He pressed her more on her encounter with the Devil. With every response, guilt pinched her tighter.

"Nasty cut you got there," he said. "I'm sorry."

Sierra shrugged.

"Can I see where it happened?" he asked.

Sierra nodded, led him toward the backyard. They passed the kitchen, where Gran-Jo stood preparing a grilled cheese sandwich, her t-shirt sleeves rolled up to her shoulders.

"Where're you going?" Gran-Jo asked.

Dwayne explained.

"Sierra stays here," Gran-Jo said. "If you don't mind."

Sierra whipped a glare at her grandmother, but Dwayne just smiled and said, "Sure thing."

All three went out the back screen door, walking across the weedy backyard, passing the ashen campfire toward the woods.

"How do I get to the ruins?" Dwayne said. "Just walk straight?"

"Pretty much," Sierra said, pointing. "There's kind of a trail. Follow it out there. It's by a stream."

From the pocket of his windbreaker, Dwayne brought out a chunky, old-looking camera.

"I'll be back," he said, and started off crunching into the forest. He strode further into the woods, a human punctuation mark in the towering scrawl of trees. His footfalls grew dim and the woods swallowed him in their twilight.

Sierra returned with Gran-Jo to the trailer and dove back into her book. When she heard Dwayne come back, she waited until his face appeared in her doorway again.

"Last question," Dwayne said. "Think you could draw it for me?"

Having no specific art paper, or even plain blank paper as they had no fax machine or printer and it'd been years since Gran-Jo had used her typewriter, Sierra asked if she could use stationary to draw the Devil she never saw.

"No," Gran-Jo said, munching on her second grilled cheese of the day. Beside her on the dinette table sat a pile of unopened mail and forms. She dug through them and brought out a white sheet. "Just use this."

On one side was a splatter of numbers, dollar signs and medical terms. The backside was empty. Sierra shrugged and took it, then brought out her shoebox of art supplies.

"Thanks, Sierra," said Dwayne, sitting next to Gran-Jo. "I'll give you some space."

On her bed, and using the hardcover *Real-Life Monsters!* as a surface, Sierra began to draw.

And something happened.

The world of the blank page enveloped her, only now she had complete control. Her hand carved out the beastly contours. The flowery, chemical smell of the markers intoxicated her. All faculties angled like gravity-bent buildings toward the white 8.5x11 vacuum. The creature now her own. She forgot that she had not *actually* seen it, that all this was really serving a lie.

Did it have horns? Sure, long spiraling ones, big and crusted yellow.

And huge feet like a pterodactyl's.

And burning, bulbous eyes.

And a tentacle beard—that would be gnarly. Literally. Like baleen. Feasting on the plankton that is us.

I can do anything, be anything.

Pinching and pulling something out of non-existence.

Anything I want.

Drawing finished, she returned to the living room. Gran-Jo and Dwayne had been talking, and her presence curtly interrupted them. She held out the half-medical bill, half-Devil.

"Here."

Dwayne smiled and took the drawing. Looked at it. Squinted. His brow furrowed.

"This is what you saw, Sierra?" he said.

"Sierra, sweetie," said Gran-Jo, peering over. "I don't remember you or Jake telling me all that. Good Lord, that thing is hideous."

"Is this what you think you saw?" Dwayne said. "Are you sure?"

"Well, it was weird," she said. She jammed her tongue into the space behind her bottom lip. "It was almost as if the trees themselves came alive."

"Sweetie, come on," Gran-Jo said. "Trees don't come alive."

Why not? she thought. Weren't trees living things? Or were they like rocks? What made something move and live, anyway? What made something grow and change and speak and make noise? Why couldn't her drawing move?

Hell, maybe she was wrong—maybe rocks, too, were alive.

"Well I certainly appreciate the drawing," Dwayne said, folding it in half. "And your time." He looked at Gran-Jo too, who waved him off. Turning back to Sierra, he said, "Would you like to see the van?"

"Van?"

"My van, my office," he said, grinning. "My museum of monsters."

Sierra turned to Gran-Jo.

"Go ahead," said her grandmother, rising to follow.

They followed Dwayne across the front lawn to the Twinkie-shaped blue-and-white van. Curtained plaid covered the windows. Tiny continents of rust and chipped paint spotted the body, which was old and had drunk its fair share of road.

Gran-Jo came out a few paces behind Sierra, her face genial, her arms crossed as she watched Dwayne go around to the back and part the double doors.

For Sierra just then, the fabric of reality altered, if only a bit. Suddenly there was this *other* world before her, encapsulated in the van: large strutting simians and swamp-wading dinosaurs and scythe-like beasts soaring through murky air and white phantoms floating like humanoid dandelion dust. Between them bulged hundreds of cutout articles, correspondence, and maps.

"Holy shit," Sierra said.

"Sierra!" Gran-Jo hissed.

Dwayne chuckled. Sierra was too entranced to apologize, her eyes careening from one image to another.

She stopped, her gaze caught not by any mysterious photo or drawing, but by a small stack of VHS tapes rising above the disarray on the floor. In fat red letters, one of the spines read: *The Untold Trials of Ulysses*.

Sierra dove at the tapes, wonder-eyed. "You have his *movies*?"

Again, Dwayne chuckled. "Not all. But a good chunk. I grew up on Russell Boylan movies. I'm impressed you know about him. Never thought anyone below my generation would know of him."

She rifled through the tapes. Besides "Ulysses," there was *The Scourge of Camelot* (highlight: the big Dragon, snatching up screaming the red-headed Princess Rama), *Prehistoric Valley* (headliner: the T-Rex fight with the triceratops), *The Crown of the World* (all about the forty-foot Yeti, at least the twenty minutes she'd seen), *Knightmares of Old* (those badass warrior skeletons), and...

"What's your favorite?" Dwayne asked.

Sierra stopped. In the hospital, she'd received a hearty dose of Russell Boylan. Individual opinions had yet to settle and form. So she went with the one that had initially sucked her in.

"This one," she said, holding up *The Untold Trials of Ulysses*. "The one where the two-headed cyclops fights the giant crab."

"That's a classic fight, right there."

"I wish I could find them again on TV," Sierra said. "They were all so cool. How many has he made?"

"Movies? Boylan? Geez, not sure. Something like twenty-five or thirty."

Thirty!

Dwayne pointed at her. "You and your grandmother don't have a VCR?"

"A tape-player? No."

After a second-long deliberation, Dwayne ducked down and entered the van. He was on a mission. Sierra released the tapes and scooted out of his way, watching as he dug around the TV set and uprooted a VCR, color-tipped wires dangling, which he presented to her like a birthday present.

"Here, take it," he said. "Still works."

"Whoa. Are you sure?"

"I'm sure. I could use the space." Dwayne sat on the mattress and picked up the pile of Boylan videos. He sifted through them, a wistful smirk playing at the corner of his lips. Then he placed them carefully atop the VCR that Sierra now held between her two scrawny arms.

At this, her face bloomed.

"Are you for serious?" she said.

Dwayne laughed. "Yes, I'm for serious. It's time I pass the torch. Enjoy them."

"Holy shit, thank you!"

"Thank you." Dwayne cocked his head. "You don't think grandma will mind?"

Sierra turned to face Gran-Jo, who still stood with her arms crossed. The woman shrugged resignedly.

"All right then," Dwayne said.

After a pause, she asked, "Where are you going now?"

Dwayne sighed. "I'm sticking around this area for another day or so, then heading up by Eugene, Oregon. Elf sightings."

Sierra blinked. "Elf? Like, pointy ears? Pointy hat?"

"You got it."

"They exist?"

Dwayne made a non-committal shrug. "Maybe."

"You really think all this," Sierra said, surveying the monstrous illustrations and photos plastered over the van, "you think all this stuff is really out there?"

She didn't mean for the question to be skeptical. It was hopeful. Thankfully, Dwayne appeared to take it as such.

"As far as I'm concerned, it's all out there," Dwayne said. "Lots of us like to think everything stops at the edge of the touchable, hearable, smell-able universe. But that's just material, or matter. There's still the whole overlapping world of the mind, of our dreams. To me, saying *this* is all there is like assuming that the seashore is where the earth stops, where life stops. Well, there's obviously the ocean, and the ocean is much bigger, darker, more unknown. We can penetrate it, but not to the extent that it penetrates us. It runs in our veins. It rains on our towns. It floods our towns. And," Dwayne smiled, "and, once in a while, it sweeps us out there."

2
TEN YEARS LATER

ANCIENT APOCALYPSE

Russell Boylan leaned toward the television, watching. Hilly pastures and scattered woods, tinted an afternoon gold. Odd, prerecorded organ music played.

From this wide, panoramic shot, the video cut jarringly to a fuzzy close-up of some young boy, ostensibly one of the "actors." There was a self-conscious smarminess about him, and Russell was distracted by the inordinate spaces between his teeth.

But the boy quickly joined a roster of overreaching, teenaged non-actors. The film quality was poor—it had been shot with a regular camcorder, it looked like, causing Russell to half-expect it to switch to some wedding reception's drunken testimonial.

The phone rang. He paused the video.

"Hello?"

"Russy!" said Errol Maybury on the other end. In the decades since Russell had known the man, since that first day they'd met—in church, of all places—and consummated their mutual cinematic love of dinosaurs and monsters and aliens, Maybury had never lost his verve. His voice was as boisterous as it'd been almost forty years ago. "How're things shaking?"

"Pretty good." Russell leaned back in the chair, smirking at the TV's paused image of the young wide-toothed actor in the middle of a scream. "You'd get a kick out of what I'm watching right now."

"What's that?"

"A fan film someone gave me at a convention not long ago. Young teenagers. They're ambitious, I gotta hand them that."

"I see. No good?" Even into his eightieth year, Maybury's producer feelers were always out.

"Maybe give them another few years," Russell said. He was struck with unexpected regret for talking behind the back of the tattooed girl who'd given him the video. "How's Australia?"

"You can find out for yourself," Maybury said. "That's why I called. You gonna come out this year?"

Maybury, bless him, was still making movies. Now five years a widower, he did it all over the goddamn world. In particular, he'd always wanted to go to Australia, and what began as a film project in the outback soon became a settled lifestyle. The Aussie film industry, it turned out, proved quite welcoming of the one and only Errol Maybury, noted producer of *The Untold Trials of Ulysses*, *Terror B.C.*, and so many others.

After a year or so spent convincing, Maybury had managed to break not only Russell's routine, but also his chronic fear of airplanes. It was never so bad that he couldn't fly when necessary, but in his retirement, Russell had come to require greater and greater excuses to strap himself into an aircraft. At first the prospect of Maybury's Sydney beach house had not passed muster. The man was persistent, though, exercising all Hollywood knack for negotiation and persuasion, and since that first visit three years ago Russell had gone annually. At his age, he figured the trip substantial enough to compensate for being a homebody (to some people, practically a hermit) most of the rest of the year.

"I'm still planning to come, yes," Russell said.

"Great." Maybury muttered to someone nearby. "I'm on set, so I should probably bonk off for a bit. Just wanted to check in. Let's chat later."

They hung up. Russell fell into a momentary daze, studied from his armchair the stretched screaming face of the kid on the TV. Static flickered at the bottom of the screen. Sometimes, in certain moments, he would wonder how he'd gotten to wherever he was. Life became nothing but the present, his past like some ghostly illusion and the name "Russell Boylan" meaning nothing beyond the body he was right then.

He picked up the remote and un-paused the video. The kid sprang back to life and finished his scream.

The plot of this schlock—*Ancient Apocalypse*, it was apparently called—involved a group of college students on a scientific excursion into some generic forest, in order to uncover... a story, Russell guessed. The film was not cohesive, but rather a series of incomplete or isolated scenes, some connected with title cards and, to his surprise, impressively drawn storyboards.

Then, the first monster appeared. And, as with many, many efforts in this tradition, very nearly redeemed the whole show.

He assumed the creatures, versatile in both movement and conception, had been conceived by the girl he'd met at the convention. Russell knew nothing of anyone else involved, but knew intuitively that only her eclectic spirit could have birthed the tentacle-legged, green-eyed demon-thing and the prehistoric beasts it resurrected and recruited into its apocalyptic army.

The girl floated back into his mind. Thin and pale, her height aided by thick-heeled boots. She had looked about eighteen. She may have still been in high school, for all he knew. She had that tenuous confidence, her eyes making statements about who she was, but always with a last-minute question mark. Sierra, was her name. Or Sienna? No, it was Sierra. "Like the mountains," she'd said.

Russell had been sitting behind his booth at the Realms of Magic Convention in San Francisco, waiting to receive requests for autographs, taking occasional sips from his flask. Despite slim enthusiasm for L.A.'s northern, foggier cousin, he went nearly every year, because the convention treated him well. And, loathe as he was to admit it, even to himself, he needed that revitalizing knowledge that people still remembered who he was.

This Sierra girl had sported familiar tattoos. *Terror B.C.*'s elasmosaurus around her wrist. *Prehistoric Valley's* pterodactyl peeking above her shirt. And those were the only ones openly visible. She was a walking gallery of more— much more. A skin-wrapped cosmology of his creatures.

"I want to get them all, eventually," she boasted, rolling down her pant leg after a quick exhibition. The people behind her stared wide-eyed, some laughing and whispering. Furtively Sierra glanced at them, her lips pursing.

Looking at Sierra's inked skin, it was the first time in Russell's life that he approved of a tattoo, to say nothing of four or five and the prospect of many more. He found himself wary and excited. Here was a new kind of fan, a stand-out even from the decidedly weird and devoted masses, the shifting pool of ponytailed Laurels and shirt-stained Hardys.

This girl was different.

From her backpack, she unfurled two posters—one for *The Untold Trials of Ulysses* and *The Crown of the World*—and two older cassette editions of *Prehistoric Valley* and *Horror from the Abyss*, in transparent plastic covers. She wanted him to sign them all.

"What's your name, dear?" Russell asked.

"Sierra," she said. Her eyes glittered so that he imagined he might find constellations in there, if he looked long enough. "Like the mountains."

"Pretty." With his Sharpie pen, growing fainter by the signature, he scrawled his name across the merchandise.

When he looked up, she was handing him another tape.

"This is for you," she said. "It's my... well, movie, I guess. It's not done yet. It's like a test reel. But it's got some badass shots."

Badass? He didn't like the phrase. But there was an energy about her. An obvious passion, which Russell regarded with a stew of emotion: proud and hopeful and relieved to see such creative vibrancy in a member of a generation he knew pittance about and had all but written off. But worried, too—worried what the gauntlet of what the coming years might do to such passion, and if she could develop the muscle to power through it.

Russell took the tape. "Ancient Apocalypse," he read aloud, off the handwritten label.

Sierra seemed suddenly bashful. "I probably don't have to tell you that it's stop-motion animation. My friend and my aunt helped me get the stuff for it. I worked in my aunt's garage." Her tongue pressed out her bottom lip. "It lives on, right?"

Russell leaned forward. He noted the fidgeting of the folks behind her, the fast-blinking, unbelieving eyes. They can wait, he thought.

"You're not into all the computer stuff?" Russell said.

Sierra made the face of one confronted by a sour odor. "No. No, no. Nobody touches anything in the computer. Nothing is there. It's all holed up in microchips. The animators don't touch them and actors don't touch them and so neither does the audience. There's no soul. It's noisy wind."

Only when she finished did Russell Boylan become aware of the giddy width of his grin. Though it well could have partly been the whiskey, something very much like love spun through him, and it was a new kind of love, a strange hybrid of grandfatherly affection and juvenile excitement. Thank God, he found in her no sexual appeal, though he did crave engagement with her, a meeting of minds, an intercourse of spirit past the smoothness and roughness of their respective skins.

Dramatic though it was, she seemed the first green bud in an apocalyptic wasteland. He wanted to nourish her. Protect her.

With every passing of yet another alleged "golden" year, Russell noticed something unsettling about himself. Good memories of recent, pleasant events did not *stick* as they used to. It wasn't senility—if prompted, he could recall anything he wanted, could trace with impressive detail each happy moment. But such happiness did not resonate much. In younger years, a good dinner, a womanly touch, a great new picture might make his week. Now, it was as if he'd involuntarily shrugged it all off by the following morning. It felt like unwilling detachment. Russell could not hold goodness in his hands for too long before it was put up in unreachable display.

So it was that, in returning from Realms of Magic, he came to forget about Sierra and her video, at least for a while. By the end of that day he had taken in too many eyes, spoken too many words, shaken too many clammy hands. He was exhausted, mildly drunk, and flirted with the idea of canceling the next day's panel appearance, though he knew he never would.

Convention staff helped him pack up the booth, as well as store and transfer the items or trinkets fans had gifted to him. They were to either toss them or haul them to a storage locker, with one last-minute exception: the tape of *Ancient Apocalypse*.

He'd taken the tape home, but it'd remained unwatched for about a year. After some scrounging, he'd stumbled upon it, and, on a whim, slid it into the VCR in his den.

Monster-wise, thus far the video featured only the demon-thing, a Tyrannosaur, a Brontosaur and a cave bear, the storyboards suggesting more to come: a mammoth, a Stegosaur, a giant ape.

Certainly ambitious. Maybe overly so. But it was always good to start out trying to fit the entire ocean in a glass. Anyone could simply dip a glass into the ocean. Over-ambition tested limits, the very boundaries of potential, the only place where you could find that elusive firefly of genius.

While an appropriately far cry from genius, Sierra's craftsmanship was evident. Her creatures rippled with personality. They had quirks. You got the sense they saw, they tasted, they thought. They foamed with life. And that shone through any technical glitch.

"Feed them your dreams," said John Terwiliger, Russell's mentor and the first great animator of that first great stop-motion animated movie, *The Great Kundo*.

In a wave of static, the tape abruptly stopped. Russell ejected it, looked at it in his hands. Despite its questionable quality, he felt as if he held something very precious. He was taken with her handwriting on the label—feminine yet forceful. I'm *here*! *Remember*! it said between every loopy, confident stroke. And don't try to get rid of me.

Beneath the title and her name, and a smaller credit that read *Produced by Jake "KB" Wilcox*, an address was written, somewhere in Sacramento.

Russell poured himself a glass of scotch, went to his desk and unearthed stationary and a fountain pen. He sat poised, ready to write.

What to say? He took a sip. Why on God's green earth was he, veteran master animator, actually a little nervous about the prospect of contacting her?

Maybe it was youth—youth intimidated him, as did any other inexorable force of nature. He would be honest, of course. He would acknowledge the roughness, the amateur hiccups, the flaws, but above all he would encourage her, because she was the only thing he felt like encouraging.

He sipped more of his drink.

He wrote *Dear*. He started to write *Sierra* when something of an electric high suddenly broke over him.

He stopped. The pen fell from his hand. His mouth filled with a gray, ozone-like taste. His pulse quickened, faster. His bones vibrated. His vitals crackled. His flesh stiffened. He twitched.

The Lightning was coming.

He was discovered several hours later, trembling on the floor, having knocked his head against the corner of the desk. He spent the next two days under surveillance at the hospital. He would never finish the letter to Sierra.

3
THE WANDERER

During the night, Sierra had a dream that, lucid as it was, she would forget come dawn. When she awoke it would hover over her elusively, an island of color and sensation receding fast over the misty horizon of memory.

In the dream she stood in a spacious warehouse. She felt exposed, as hundreds of others milled around her and passed her. They seemed to pay her no mind, though. Sierra wasn't sure but she assumed she'd drifted onto a movie set, a sound stage where tool-belted teamsters bustled by next to actors in costumes, the most notable of which were those of generic and politically-incorrect natives, feathered, painted visages out of some older film where the square-jawed hero might refer to them as "babbling savages" or "birds."

A show was being born. A grand production in development. A vision in gestation.

And someone did recognize her. Out of the forest of faces came Russell Boylan. Russell Boylan! In the flesh! He was creased and dapper and smiling that same smile as when she'd approached him for the first and only time in person, at the Realms of Magic Convention in San Francisco. That moment of meeting him had been so long in coming, so anticipated, conceived so many different ways that, once it happened, the real encounter had seemed to bleed into all the prior, imagined ones.

Sierra had come away from his booth remembering little of the finer moments of their interaction, as if she'd stepped temporarily out of her body. He'd smiled, though, and she had made sure to give him the early tape for *Ancient Apocalypse*, her (yes, and KB's) movie.

Still, she was convinced she must have made a fool of herself. He never wrote to her, or reached out to her. Not that that should be expected, of course, but…

Either he hated me, or my movie.

This dream version of Boylan before her, though, hardly appeared to hate her.

"You're here," he said. "I was hoping to find you."

A sudden heaviness came over Sierra. She looked down.

She was naked, her illustrated skin all aglow. But while exposed, she was not self-conscious or embarrassed. She was being admired.

Boylan took her hand. Oddly, their hands seemed to meld into one another, as if their bodies were softer here.

Boylan led her through the crowds to a section of the warehouse where the miniatures had been set up: the impeccable sets of primordial volcanoes; fern-choked jungle cliffs; and craggy Cretaceous canyons; archaic Grecian temples; the howling mountain passes of the Yeti; and the forests and castles of Camelot. All impressive, if she were the tiny moviegoer sucked into them. But right now, she wasn't. She was behind it all, big as a god and mingling with the very gods of illusion.

Peppering the sets were the models of all the beasts reflected across her flesh.

"You know it all, Sierra," said Boylan. "You've ingested it all, as much as I have. You'll help me with my masterpiece, right?"

It was then the dream began to evaporate, becoming mist through which only vague forms were visible, until there was nothing left.

Sierra awoke the following dawn, the face lingering in her mind that of Russell Boylan, though she couldn't say exactly why. A hangover drummed her skull.

Where am I? The ceiling was right above her, pressing down on her like a coffin, her bedspace confined, her room swaying. In the window beside her the ocean sprawled to infinity.

My cabin. Steadily, the memories pooled back into the mental vacuum. She was on *The Wanderer*, the yacht—technically *super*-yacht—that KB had told her about when he was in L.A. last summer, and which she'd now been working on for several months.

She looked at the clock and, to her dismay, saw it was forty minutes till her alarm. Just below, her bunkmate Anna turned, groaned softly in her sleep.

She was exhausted, her bones cement. Her head felt like a bowling ball depressing the pillow. Squirming deep in her was the eerily unshakable sense that something had been taken from her.

#

She stared at the passing ocean. Before joining the crew of *The Wanderer*, Sierra had seen the ocean only twice before. The second time, of course, had been while in San Francisco for the Realms of Magic convention.

The first, however, was a dimmer memory, dim enough that she wondered if it might've been some lucid dream in her early childhood. But it had been real— her father had taken her to the Big Sur area, where he'd met with an old friend. There, on a wet, log-strewn beach, her eyes had taken their first gulp of the Pacific.

She'd long imagined the ocean a frightening place to be. As a woods girl, she needed a sense of enclosure, of hard things nearby. The ocean seemed like one big, inviolable illusion.

But no—the sea, it turned out, was intoxicating. Suddenly, she got *Moby Dick*, or at least its first few pages, which was all she'd ever read. The sea replenished. You had a sense that it was a giant liquid brain, constantly changing its mind, tumbling around new ideas for new lands and new organisms.

There's still the whole overlapping world of the mind, of our dreams, the VW guy Dwayne had said. *To me, saying* this *is all there is, is like assuming that the seashore is where the earth stops, where life stops. Well, there's obviously the ocean, and the ocean is much bigger, darker, and more unknown.*

Slowly, she took a sip of her scotch. She sat alone at the lounge area bar, poised over one of the communal tablets issued to the crew. A thin film of tears covered her eyes, which didn't stray from the window and the ocean's infinite miles beyond.

We can penetrate it, Dwayne had said, but not to the extent that it penetrates us. It runs in our veins. *It rains on our towns. It floods our towns. And… and, once in a while, it sweeps us out there.*

Sierra had come to see the world not as "hard material," but more fluid, malleable. Nature was not the land, but the sea. It could do anything, go anywhere. Make anything. But there were so many arrogant people who thought that all that nature had made was fixed, and had more or less been seen and classified.

Sure, they'd say, there might be a new species of bird here and there. Or a new strain of bacterium. But all the big stuff—lost beasts, lost worlds—all those had all been found and checked off. At least on this earth.

Sierra sometimes thought human beings, for their sake, should've left just one land or continent pristine and untouched, so that we might always have the privilege of wondering about it. It would be the place to channel all childhood, a reservoir of potential. As everything else was dissected, catalogued, boxed, we could still say, well, there's still *that* place.

There's still Dream Country.

Before her lay the tablet, glaring the news headline she simultaneously refused to look at again, yet could not bring herself to click off. It was the last lingering piece of him, it felt like. The world's hasty and final utterance of his existence.

Taking another large sip of scotch, Sierra closed her eyes, brought them down to the tablet screen again. Opening them, she hoped the words had changed somehow. They hadn't.

757 CRASHES IN PACIFIC
208 Estimated Dead; Legendary Effects Artist Russell Boylan Among Them

II
THE EDGE OF THE OCEAN

1
THE FOG

The scissors rested closed in her hand. She was supposed to be on her knees, on the rug of the dining room, snipping long or stray threads. Such was one of many mind-numbing, miscellaneous jobs aboard *The Wanderer*. Comparatively, serving meals to the owner's family, and their guests, was a task full of noble meaning.

Sierra hadn't started cutting, unable to stop thinking about Russell Boylan. How disastrously, violently, absurdly he'd been ripped from the fabric of this world. He had lived seventy-three years, she nineteen. Even now, she felt she had too much life under her belt that a sudden death would be ridiculously unwarranted. So she could hardly imagine it for Boylan, who had accomplished so much. Envisioned so much.

The longer you live, she thought, the better the excuse God needs for wiping you so quickly off the map.

No good excuse. Boylan had not done a film in almost a decade, sure, but his existence, his *there*-ness, assured her the dreams still thrived, the dreams that would feed her own.

The previous night, while her crewmates took drinks and pipes into the top deck jacuzzi, Sierra had bundled herself up in her cabin, alone with a bottle of some Malaysian beer KB had bought her, and watched a taped documentary on Boylan.

"Russell was always in charge," the producer Errol Maybury had said, in one of his many interview snippets. "Even if no one really knew that, even if he didn't really know that, he always was. His monsters were the stars, and he was their god."

"Film is one of the few ways we can get beyond the limits of our sad flesh," Boylan said in the documentary. "Where we can make something wondrous and transcendent and alive."

His death had also, perhaps pretentiously on Sierra's part, dumped a load of responsibility on her shoulders. *You're the last one*, said a voice inside her. *You've got to carry on the torch.*

How?

Though she sometimes chastised herself for being an overreaching fan, and while she knew this tendency was hardly unique toward a given idol, Sierra sensed a much deeper connection with Boylan, one beyond the marauding beasts onscreen.

In some ways, their lives overlapped, her years brushing his in a realm outside time. She imagined that whoever or whatever agent of fate had threaded Russell Boylan's life had reused some of those strands on her own. Both had grown up under the watch of one person, their fathers having died when they were about seven. Boylan's mother had been a boozer, as had Alvin Smith. They'd suffered hospitalizing traumas, at similar ages, on either side of seeing their first Big Movie: Sierra had seen *The Untold Trials of Ulysses* hours after her near-death in Dale, and in 1942 Boylan had suffered his first epileptic seizure (which he'd referred to in interviews as "the Lightning," and which, as he also claimed, filled him with a brief sense of "electric godliness") when strolling from the Grauman's Chinese Theater on Hollywood Boulevard, not an hour after his inaugural taste of *The Great Kundo*.

The way she saw it, she had lost the other half of her upbringing. Gran-Jo had died two years ago, suffering a heart attack in her armchair, a half-eaten grilled cheese in her hand. Sierra, then a high school senior, had found her that evening, after an afternoon of supposedly studying for finals at KB's. Really, they'd been working on the script and logistics for *Ancient Apocalypse*.

"Gran-Jo?" she had said, nudging her. Sierra had tried a few more times to rouse her, even though she'd known the situation as soon as she saw her grandmother. Death had cast its ashen net over the old woman's face.

Right up to her demise, Gran-Jo had accumulated books on spirits and the afterlife, and as Sierra had cleared them out, with the aid of KB and her neighbors, she wondered if the Big Dumb had lived up to Gran-Jo's expectations.

"What did you and Dwayne talk about, by the way?" Sierra had asked days after Dwayne's visit.

"I asked him about spirits," Gran-Jo had said. "About heaven."

"What did he say?"

Gran-Jo had paused, sighed, and closed her eyes as if trying to remember all she'd been told. "He said," her grandmother finally answered, "he thinks that, when we get to the other side, we can make up our own world. Here, in this world, we can make things, but only by the sweat of our brow. Over there, it's a snap. If we want to live in the house we grew up in, or our own palace, we can create it on the spot. *Poof*!"

"That's weird," Sierra said. "What about ghosts?"

"I don't know. Dwayne thinks maybe ghosts are dead people whose created worlds are bumping into ours. They have trouble detaching from here, so they want to take some of it with them, or affect our world to their liking."

Sierra wasn't sure she understood all this. "They don't like heaven?"

"Seems like heaven lets you make your own," she said. "Even if you have to borrow from earth."

Sierra imagined Russell Boylan "up there," or on the other side, confronting God, that ultimate of domineering executive producers. Boylan would shake his hand, would nod and smile through all the Deity's wisdom, the booming praise on exploiting the talents with which Boylan had been gifted. Boylan would listen with hard eyes and, when it was his turn to speak, he would clap God on the arm and tell him, "Right. I've got a few ideas I want to run by you."

#

Sierra awoke in her bunk to laughter down the hallway. A headache ricocheted between her temples. The room floated, wobbled. Rain accumulated on the window. On her bedside shelf stood the bottle of Irish whiskey she'd gotten in London. A few coin-sized drops left in her glass. She downed the rest.

She hadn't meant to fall asleep, and the unexpected nap disoriented her.

The book she'd been reading, a yellowed paperback of Doyle's *The Lost World*, lay creased on her breast. She set it aside, amidst a slew of loose sketches of dinosaurs—mostly T-Rexes, her own conception of which she'd been trying to perfect—as well as half-drawn or doodled ideas for aqua-creatures inspired by her time at sea. Currently, her pet goal was to construct some perfect water-beast combining the grandeur of whales, the terror of sharks, and the alien exoticism of cephalopods.

Carefully she sat up, listening to the laughter, to the voices.

They're having a good time. Why would they need me?

And, dammit, how could they have a good time without *me?*

She climbed down from her bunk, checked her cabin-mate Anna's bunk, which was empty, and made her way into the hall. The ship swayed and she put up steadying arms to catch the walls. They were somewhere on the Indian Ocean, crossing uneasy waters. It'd taken a few months for Sierra to perfect her sea legs.

The voices grew louder. They came from the crew's break room. She heard Tom's boisterous Aussie accent and Maxine's giggling and Kasey's sultry sarcasm. All their attention seemed directed at something playing on the TV.

Screams. Lines she knew. Choppy music. Monstrous roars.

Something that sounded very familiar.

They're watching a movie, Sierra thought. Without me.

And the resentment fell away to terror when she finally recognized what they were watching.

Ancient Apocalypse.

Her movie.

She froze, refusing to continue the remaining twenty or so feet into the break room. She shut her eyes, put her palms over her ears. *Don't want to hear. No, don't want to.* How had they found it? Who'd rooted around in her belongings? Anna wouldn't dare, or care, to do that.

The pool of suspects drained fast toward one central face, smiling that gap-toothed smile in her mind's eye.

KB.

She started forward when Maxine, crossing the break room toward the toilet, appeared in her line of sight. Maxine stopped, cheeks flushed as red as her hair. She tried to betray casual good humor, raising to Sierra a stiff thumbs-up.

"We like your movie," Maxine said, in her lilting British accent. She was a pretty, pale girl with a cutely long nose, from a town called Something-shire. "It's funny. Fun."

"See!" KB shouted. "Fun! Focus group approves!"

Maxine turned and winked at him.

Fun? Sierra thought.

Funny?

Against her every impulse, Sierra walked forth into the break room, where eyes whipped at her, some of them beer-misted. Tom the Aussie watched her. His Melbourne girlfriend Marla watched her. Paul, KB's cabin-mate, watched her. To her right, Maxine watched her. Kasey, the arguable 'it' girl of the crew, a

Houston-born blonde with a body honed by cheerleading and swimming, sat peering at Sierra with her seamless legs crossed. And farthest away, sitting by the TV flashing her stuttering creations and pieces of her ultimate vision, was KB, who gazed at her behind his glasses, whose keyboard smile shone in full.

"The Monster Girl!" Tom said, raising his can of beer. "In the flesh!"

Sierra noted the moment in KB's expression when he recognized her humiliated disapproval. He snapped, "Hey, shut up, Tom."

"KB," Sierra said, trying to control the quiver in her voice. The Monster Girl, a nickname she'd garnered not a week into her career aboard *The Wanderer*, was not prone to outward emotion, was someone who prided herself on remaining above the petty drama that ensnared the rest of her young, hot-blooded crewmates. "What are you doing?"

On the screen, the tentacle-legged demon, Azulus, filled a low-angle shot, tendrils coiling like serpents, his shivering mouth issuing a silent roar not yet dubbed.

Then, a shot of KB himself, screaming, "Let's get *out* of here!"

"I thought I'd show them our mystery project," KB said. "Get a little focus group going. You made me producer, right? This is what a producer does. I'm just doing my thing. You all liked it, right? It was cool, right?"

You were caught, jackass, Sierra thought. She could just see how it might've played out: the crew's cumulative taunts, jabs, curious remarks, and genuine inquiries regarding their "Monster Movie Project" had finally broken KB, to the point where he'd snuck into her cabin and stolen her copy.

"I didn't take your copy," said KB. "I made my own. I'm the producer, remember?"

"It looks kinda crazy," Kasey said. Her throaty voice irritated Sierra. "Like, kinda cheap. No offense."

"Well, this is just the stepping stone," KB said. "We're gonna perfect this version. Then, we'll use it to try and generate interest in a big-budget version, with computer animation and everything."

"Dude!" Sierra said.

KB peered at her. "What?"

She darted from the room.

"Sierra!" KB called after her.

The brief idea of returning to her cabin nauseated her. She would only box herself in there, leave herself vulnerable for everyone to walk by and to laugh at her and to laugh at her movie. Why were people such dicks?

They can't do what I do. Yes. She'd fucking *made* something. Made something that moved and breathed and lived and what had they done?

Nothing. Fucking *nothing*.

Sierra ran through the corridors and, still lopsided from the liquor, brushed up against the walls. Her thoughts raged, blending with her emotions, becoming a kind of flowing crashing acid inside her.

KB and others—Maxine, she thought—continued to call after her, but she needed to escape, to fly and right now she felt too imprisoned, too suffocated.

She made it outside, barreling toward the staircase there leading to lower decks. The platforms were wet and her feet slipped on the first couple rungs. She stumbled before catching herself on the railing and carrying herself farther down.

Halfway on her descent, she stopped.

There was no bottom. A soupy cauldron of fog had gathered around *The Wanderer*, absorbing it totally. She looked beyond.

There was no sea.

Instantly the world fell in line, her dizziness straightening. A primal clarity sobered her. The whizzing din of her emotions ebbed, as did the thunder of her pulse and even her headache.

KB and Maxine emerged behind her, uttering brief snippets of what Sierra imagined were loaded apologies, explanations, or excuses. Until they, too, fell silent at the sight before them.

The mist not only looked wrong, but felt wrong.

Since living on *The Wanderer*, since spending periods under tropical and Mediterranean sun, Sierra had developed a regrettable vulnerability to the damp cold, and so comfort in dense fog meant at least two layers of clothing. Not here, though. Here, coldness was moot, even with strengthening rain. Temperature, non-existent.

The air was faintly electric, too. Crackly currents she could not see but could feel danced between her hairs, erecting them in static charge. She tasted ozone, and wasn't sure how, or why she knew that.

Tendrils of fog twisted, swirled, rendered themselves in shapes and motions of life-like verve. A mesmerizing circus of phantoms.

"What is this?" Maxine said.

"It's… fog," KB replied.

"No, it's not. That's not normal fog." Maxine backed up. "Are we even moving?"

"Sierra?" KB said. "Are you okay?"

It took a moment for Sierra to respond. "Um, yeah, I think so."

"We should go back inside."

Sierra returned up the staircase and joined them as they headed back toward the doorway.

"Wait," Sierra said. She touched KB's shoulder and felt a static shock.

"What?"

"Listen."

"What?" KB said again. "What are we hearing?"

"Nothing," she said. "I don't hear the ship's engine. Do you?"

#

The engine is off.

No sound. No guttural hum of *The Wanderer's* metal innards.

But we're still moving.

Or at least it appeared they were. She felt the forward momentum of the boat, heard the chop of the ocean licking at the hull. Eyes couldn't confirm any of this, however, as the water was obscured by the thick fog that had engulfed them, clouding the windowpane like giant's breath.

Sierra watched from her cabin window, put her hand on the glass. She imagined it sulfurous or, worse yet, radioactive. But she smelled nothing unusual and figured, if they'd drifted into some nuclear fog, she likely wouldn't have had an easy time waking up this morning.

Clambering from her bunk, Sierra trotted out into the dark hallway and down to KB's cabin, which he shared with a thin Georgian smoker named Paul.

The door was already open a crack and Sierra knocked.

"Hey," Sierra said.

"Hey," KB said, perched on the edge of his lower bunk, tying his shoes.

"Where's Paul?"

"Think he's in the break room." KB stood up. He tried to look calm but she knew him—he was scared. He was in the Dale woods again. "All power's off."

"Kinda looks like that."

He threw her his cell phone. "Can't even turn on my phone."

The screen was a lifeless pupil. She noted the digital clock, too, blank and ignorant of all hours and minutes. Icy ants marched through her veins. Wrongness scented the air. Some deeper—higher?—part of her knew exactly what was wrong, too, or so she sensed. But this all-knowing Sierra was unwilling to clue in the lesser, flesh-and-blood Sierra.

Others began to gather in the hall: Tom, red-eyed in a tank-top and clutching his girlfriend Marla; Kasey, dressed in baggy sleepwear; Maxine, affecting a little-girl concern with big eyes and the nibbling of her lime-painted fingernails. She approached KB.

"I have a weird feeling," Maxine said to him, as if he were the only one around.

KB rubbed her arm. Sierra saw right through the more masculine image he was trying to betray, and, though tempted, she said nothing.

A voice boomed from down the hallway: "Everyone!"

The baritone voice of *The Wanderer's* wide-framed First Mate. Sierra, on first meeting him and hearing his name, had been convinced he wasn't real, maybe some caricature that had taken a wrong turn out of the panels of action comics. "Yes, my last name really is Maverick," he'd said, "but it's spelled 'Maverique'." Then, with a smile that grew more flirtatious with every recollection, this John Maverique had added, "Is Sierra Nevada really *your* name?"

The crew filed toward the break room, where Maverique stood wearing a *Wanderer* windbreaker and scratching the back of his neck in a repeated motion less necessary and more nervous. The climate of confusion thickened with every new pair of eyes Sierra met.

"Everyone," Maverique said again, at a lower tone. Others stood behind him. Seated already in the break room were the cooks, the chef—a rail-thin French culinary graduate—and the two Finnish engineers who occupied the front table. Three fog-shrouded windows provided the only light. A sickly hue tinted everyone's complexion.

Questions murmured about.

"What the hell's going on?"

"Where are we?"

"Why is everything… off?"

Sierra took a seat with KB and Maxine at a table near the refrigerator. She could see the fog dancing in the window, and thought she could make out a variety of faces briefly shaped, fleetingly snuffed. She thought of the early scene in *The Great Kundo*, the first major stop-motion movie animated by Russell Boylan's idol and mentor, John Terwiliger (to her, no match for anything Boylan) where the vessel drifts through a misty purgatory before seeing the island that harbors what turns out to be the Temple of Kundo.

While unsettled, Sierra was also undeniably titillated. Very seldom did life dare mimic fantastic adventure tales, and, if it did, it was usually in watered-down spurts, charitable change in the outstretched cup of her beggar soul, just enough to feed her and keep her going.

Once everyone settled, Maverique spoke.

"So, I can only be straight with everyone," he said. "Captain Adams, all of us, are at a loss to explain what's happened, or what's happening. As you've no doubt realized, we've lost all power. Our navigational equipment is down. Our radios are unusable. We can't see anything through this fog. It's as though we've been removed from the grid."

Several questions flew at once, the most predominant of which was, "How are we moving if there's no power?"

Maverique resumed scratching the back of his neck. He grimaced. Sierra realized she had never seen him so vulnerable-looking.

"I mean," continued the questioner, a half-Brazilian, aspiring med student named Michael, "we *are* still moving, right? It feels like it."

"We are, yes, still moving," Maverique replied. "But we don't know how. We just had Ross and Jonah down in the engine room," he gestured to the two Finnish engineers, "but the whole place is as dead as a goddamn junkyard."

"Maybe a current is pulling us," ventured Paul.

Maverique nodded half-heartedly, in an "anything is possible" manner.

Tom, in a bark of his thick accent, said, "No radio, I gather?"

"No radio," Maverique said.

Sierra spoke up. "The compass?"

Maverique's eyes, already so fattened with defeat, appeared to subtly plead for any and all further questions to stop. He was a man who enjoyed a reputation of giving answers, because leaders answered. But he was now another child among children.

"The compass," said Maverique. "The compasses are, um, going haywire. Spinning. Like I said, at this stage we're going to continue working on it, and hoping this fog clears—"

"It's not normal fog, is it?" Sierra said.

Hardening somewhere between incredulity and exasperation, Maverique's demeanor unleashed another wordless plea that Sierra read as, *Please stop. Please just shut up.*

"We don't know what kind of fog it is," Maverique said. "It's fog."

"It's warm fog," said Jonah, an engineer. "There's something different about it—"

"—but we know it's not dangerous," Maverique said. "It's nothing to be afraid of. And we'll get through this."

A thought tunneled to light in Sierra. "It's like the Bermuda Triangle," she said.

More heads turned her way this time. Snorts. Stillborn snickers. But primarily a quiet expectancy—she was the Monster Girl, after all.

Beside her, KB said, "What?" His voice was more mocking than probably intended, but nonetheless inspiring in Sierra a furtive 'Fuck You' glance. She noticed Maxine's hand on his wrist tighten protectively. It annoyed her.

"I've read about the Bermuda Triangle," Sierra said, dredging up chapters from old occult books, so many so well-worn (all those hands desperate to understand the other side, or the Big Dumb, she'd thought), that either she or Gran-Jo had plucked from the Dale Library. "People who've survived say they went through a yellowy fog that took them to some other dimension or time or something." She shrugged. "Their compasses go crazy, like you said. Power shuts off." Goosebumps formed on her arms. "I'm just… just saying."

"We'll keep those theories in the corner with the tinfoil hats," Maverique said. He spoke fast, as though trying to override Sierra's statement. "We'll keep you updated. We'll run an emergency drill in a short while. Meantime, lay low, don't panic. Stay calm. And remember," he glanced toward Sierra, "Bermuda's on the other side of the world."

\#

It became very near impossible to tell how long they'd been drifting through the fog. Time had abandoned *The Wanderer*, not only in dead stalled clocks but in the very broad cycles of night and day, for neither noon nor midnight could penetrate the somber opaqueness of this mist.

Only in rare glimpses off immediate port or starboard could one catch brief sight of the white chop of the ocean, some evidence of elsewhere which made Sierra think, *Okay, still on Earth… at least.*

For what felt like the first few days, they underwent periodic emergency drills, which petered off in the assumption that everyone was prepared, and in the general preference of not staying long out in the strange fog.

Personal updates from the navigational crew or Maverique or even Captain Adams himself also tapered off, especially when the reports began bleeding together. Compasses still acted haywire, spinning deliriously toward every route and every adventure possible. All electronics, everything with a screen and everything battery-powered, remained sealed unresponsive in their comas.

And *The Wanderer* carried silently on, deeper into this smoky belly, toward an end some began to think did not exist.

\#

Sierra realized just how much the human body and mind relied on any sense of time. *The Wanderer* moved forward, but there was no sense of forwardness, no telling the time of day, when to be hungry, when to sleep.

They'd been nearing New Zealand, passing over Northern Australia. Academic Sierra said that at any moment the fog would disperse and the ocean and the kiwi shorelines and the sky would exist once more as if nothing had happened.

Animal Sierra, however, assumed nothing would be the same again, that they'd entered some passage, some Bermuda Triangle portal, and that, all this time, the inaudible whispers in the mist conferred about what plane of existence, dimension or time period to ultimately deposit *The Wanderer* and its sad little denizens. The Jurassic Period, one might say? Nah, more modern, say, the last Ice Age? Or the Renaissance? Or right before some trigger-happy World War II battleship? ... No, you're *way* off, let's send them to another planet, or the dimension where pigs make chops of primates...

Strained and haggard, the crew partook judiciously of the yacht's remaining supply of edible food, some taking to the canned meats, beans and vegetables, and the dry food and chips stuffing the cabinets. Drinks came out in greater haste, the warming beer downed first.

Most of the time, they played cards, or board games.

"Sierra," said Tom one day, as he, Marla, KB and Maxine sat by the window bent over a game of *Sorry!* and a bottle of vodka. "Here's something I've always wondered."

"What's that?" Sierra drew a *Sorry!* card and deliberated who to kick off the board. "Sorry, KB," she said, taking her last red pawn and putting it in place of KB's homebound blue one.

"Dammit," said KB. His eyes were red.

Maxine was already pouring another shot of vodka. "All right, Jakey-Jake, open wide." She handed him the wobbling glass and he drank it, winced. The rest of the players, Sierra included, smiled in tipsy approval.

Sierra now had three of her pawns either 'Home' or in the 'Safe Zone.' Switching with KB had now put her only sixteen spaces, and a possible slide, between her and victory.

"What were you wondering, Tom?" she said.

"Ever consider being a stripper?"

Marla stiffened and slapped his arm, hard. Her face was stern and embarrassed, but the vodka had loosened her expression into amusement.

"Tom, honestly," she said, in her own thick Aussie accent. "I'm right here."

"Not asking because I want a lap dance, sweetie." At this, Tom winked at Sierra. "More just curious. Because I'd find it hard to concentrate with all your monster tats. It'd be like watching a movie at the same time."

Sierra chuckled. "No. But that ain't a bad idea. KB, if we need more money after this, ring up a few clubs."

KB smiled, but it was reserved. Maxine gave at most a tentative smirk. Sierra knew Maxine's dislike of her had grown in direct correlation with Maxine's obvious crush on KB. The tether between Sierra and KB was unbreakable. He was her official producer on *Ancient Apocalypse*, after all, her childhood friend and for so long had held another capacity only dreamt of behind his eyes. Maxine knew she had her work cut out for her, to build her way toward some comparable significance. Sierra felt sorry for her.

"You have all the monsters you want on you?" Tom said.

Sierra shook her head. "No. But I'm running out of room."

"I was gonna say… " Maxine said, quietly.

"I do want the Roc," Sierra said.

"What's the Roc?" asked Tom.

"It's a giant bird out of Greek mythology. It was in *The Perils of Perseus*. Big and black and creepy-looking."

"Don't you have something like that?" he said, loosely pointing. "Near your breasts?"

"No. That's a pterodactyl. Flying dinosaur."

Tom shook his head, amused. "One of these days, Monster Girl," he said, "you're going to have to show us all those beasties on you."

Marla unleashed another assault on his arm. "Tom! Honestly…"

"Well we can play strip poker," Sierra said. "I think Kasey and Jenny and some of the others did that the other night."

"They did?" Tom said, bracing himself for another smack. "Where was I?"

The *Sorry!* round continued. Sierra had not played this game since she was eleven or twelve, when Gran-Jo, indulging her protectiveness after the Night of the Terror, had sought to keep her entertained indoors. It was a fun, silly game, but Sierra had forgotten how suspenseful it could be, too. She saw her last pawn, hanging out in the open, vulnerable, her others snug in 'Home,' or in the 'Safe Zone,' and she felt stupidly afraid for it, even though it was a chunk of plastic with no mind of its isolation or the dangers, and relying on her, some towering god, to guide its movement.

2
THE ISLAND

It could have been two days, a week or maybe even a month later. Whatever clocks or calendars would have labeled it, to Sierra and the crew of *The Wanderer* it was the glorious moment when the fog rapidly thinned, and drew apart like the parting of eyelids, when the world woke bright and blue once more.

Some of the crew still slept. Normal rhythms had become tattered, but it was not long before every pair of feet, from every level and cabin and chamber, saw to the outside decks where they took in the cloudless sky, the temperate sun, felt the smooth silken ocean breezes, almost sensual after the electric fog.

At the railing, Sierra stood near Maxine who stood next to KB who was next to Kasey and there was also Paul with a cigarette in his mouth and Tom and Marla and Michael the Brazilian med student.

"We're out of it," KB said. "I hope."

There was hesitation to celebrate, as none of the ship's computers or mechanisms worked. Nor had the compasses settled. Clocks remained lifeless. But at least they would have the day/night cycle.

I hope.

Her gut still trembled. On and on *The Wanderer* cruised. The Pacific's sun-dusted blue hissed and heaved, waves compressing toward the horizon ... where there rose the jagged imprint of land.

"Is that..." Paul said, pointing with several others who'd also spotted it. "Is that... what is that? New Zealand?"

They drew closer. Binoculars made frequent rounds. First Mate Maverique said at one point he watched the land through a telescope and couldn't identify it, but thought maybe it was a small Southeast Asian island. Disoriented as they were, it was anyone's guess which of the many pieces of earth they were being pulled toward.

Pulled, Sierra thought. As if we're caught in some undertow.

#

Gradually, the island took on color and dimension. Through binoculars, Sierra could see thick greenery at its base, out of which rose clusters of sharp, rocky spires, like some earthen temple.

It didn't look real at first.

It looks painted.

"Maybe it's a lost world," KB said, as they sat together on the bow. His tone fell hopelessly lost somewhere between musing and joking.

Sierra was glad she hadn't said it first, even though she knew KB was not serious. Because dammit, from here it certainly *resembled* a lost world, those portrayed in countless films—many, of course, of the Russell Boylan stock. It had that exaggerated primeval look, borne of an imaginative mixture of wonder and fear.

And indeed, they were drawing closer to it, pulled upon some inexorable track. As they approached, the island lost none of the jagged, hyper-real exoticism glimpsed from afar. In fact, it gained more of it. It was a chromatic symphony, every hue and shade the premiere expression of itself, which after the fog proved garishly offensive to the eyes. The trees and flora were all a green choir of bloom, the sands glistening as crushed diamonds, the earth and the hills and the sky varnished like paintings.

That's really what the whole scene resembled, too: a thing ripped from a surrealist canvas, life breathed into it so that it swelled rounded and real, and *there*.

And *The Wanderer* slowed, easing until it drifted, quiet as a breath, to a stopping point hundreds of yards before the shoreline.

We've arrived, Sierra thought, unsure exactly why.

NIGHT OF THE (TENTACLED) TERROR

The sun was moving again, the bright noon that had welcomed them out of the mist waning at regular rhythm toward early evening and eventually into a golden sunset. Hours had resumed their march.

Toward evening, Sierra sat alone on the deck, periodically lifting binoculars to closer inspect the wild panorama across the bay. Her sketchbook lay open in her lap, a two-page spread dressed with pencil drawings of the island. While viewed from afar, there was a fertile charge to the place, an aura of *anything*-ness.

Nature's own sketchbook.

She was entranced, her gaze dissecting the shadows and nooks and hollows at all visible, as if something, a secret, maybe, might be—

What was that?

There was something moving. A large, shambling object, disturbing the trees. Shadowed. She couldn't accept that it would be anything non-human, or non-mechanical, but it seemed to move with awkward sentience. Until the jungle stilled once more, and there was no more sign of it.

"Hey."

A voice behind her. Tinny. Definitely KB. She ignored it for a second.

"Hey, Sierra."

She lowered the binoculars and turned.

"Maverique's calling another meeting."

Sierra waited a few more moments before closing her sketchbook and wrenching herself away.

Descending to the break room, she saw most of the crew assembled there, much as they'd been that first misty day of this surreal detour. Despite the favorable turn in climate, many of their general expressions remained unchanged. People bit their lips, chewed their fingernails, nursed drinks, fidgeted.

Sierra herself was caught between fear and a strangely giddy excitement. She took a seat in the corner, by the sink, three chairs between her and everyone else.

"We're all wondering where we are," Maverique said, arms crossed and pacing back and forth. "But we don't know. Our navigational equipment is still down. Our radios are still out. As far as we can tell, there are no stations or frequencies to speak of on this island. The best we can do," he cleared his throat, violently, "is take the data of our last known position and compare it on the charts, to see where we might be. But it's all speculative."

"So we're stranded," said Kasey. Her head bobbed as she said this, hammering home her point.

"Let's not use the S-word just yet," Maverique said. "We have the engineers down there working out any way to help us get moving again."

"There's no one on the island?" Tom said. "Or no sign of anyone?"

"Not that we've picked up."

"Should we go ashore to see?"

Maverique's machismo could not mask, at least for Sierra, that shadow of trepidation across his face. His complexion lost a little color.

"Not yet," he said. "We still have plenty of supplies aboard, so for now we should keep holding tight."

As the meeting disbanded, Sierra got up and followed Maverique through the corridor and up the spiral staircase leading out of the crew deck. She said nothing to indicate her presence, and moved casually until they were alone by the kitchen. Then she spoke.

"Mr. Maverique."

He acknowledged her, a defeated look about him, facial creases pronounced. His hair looked grayer, too.

"Yes, Sierra?"

"Did you see anything?" she said. "When you were looking through the telescope?"

"Yeah, stars."

"No, I mean on the island. Anything moving."

He glanced out the window. The sun had almost fully set, leaving only a smear of twilight on the horizon. The whole time, Maverique had not uncrossed his arms.

"Get a good rest, Sierra," he said, and proceeded on, at a faster pace.

#

Sierra awoke to startling blackness. Somehow her cabin had grown even darker. Disoriented, she spent the first few seconds struggling to remember where she was, what she was doing. The bed beneath her. *Okay*. The pillow. The boat. *Yes.*

Beyond that, who knows?

She felt around in the direction of the window and touched the cool pane. There was nothing else beyond it. The world was black. She kept her hand on the glass, still wondering if she was dreaming.

The blackness moved.

Yes, this is a dream.

A solid dark thing drew away from the window. There was harsh light behind it, and the moonlit ripples of the ocean. Something had been pressed against the glass. Sierra couldn't tell what it was, but the more she tried to look at it the greater grew her conviction that she was dreaming, or that she had lost her mind.

Because the thing looked undeniably alive.

Thick as a tree trunk, the object finally caught the pale light, unveiling the face-sized suckers down its underside. The massive tentacle—wait, *tentacle?*—quivered and began to sway, in a kind of anticipatory dance. Beyond it, another, smaller appendage coiled with serpentine stealth around the portside railing.

I'm seeing this. I'm fucking seeing this.

Sierra then did something she'd never thought possible of herself.

She screamed.

At once, she could feel the restless stirring of the entire boat. Her bunk quaked with bunkmate Anna's violent awakening. Outside, the tentacle curled instantly, poised itself to drive straight through her window.

Sierra clambered out of bed, or tried, wrestling with the tangles of her own bedsheets until falling to the floor, missing Anna's outstretched head by a nose.

"Sierra! Jesus!" Anna cried. "What is it? What're you doing?"

"Get *out* of here!" Sierra cried, scrambling toward the door. "Get away from the window!"

Anna remained upright in her bunk, uncomprehending. The tentacle rammed into the cabin, becoming the cabin, unscrewing, shattering, billowing, shredding all things within and sending Anna quickly back to rest under its muscled tsunami, which burst across the room toward Sierra, grasping but missing. It spilled into the hallway, flailing and flopping like a shore-ridden fish.

Sierra raced down the hall, straight into more crew as they filed from their quarters. Their eyes were the only things visible, floating like fireflies in the dark. Screams erupted. More screams followed when those at the other end of the hallway saw the writhing monstrosity barring their only way out.

The boat groaned and teetered, throwing everyone off their feet. Candy from a candy bag, Sierra thought. Shaking out the treats.

Not happening this is not happening no not happening—

A vicious percussion of collisions rocked the boat, sending everyone to their knees, some into the wall and some into one another. Tom's head had struck something, lining his brow with blood. People sobbed, shrieked, found other arms and stayed there.

Over the commotion Sierra could hear snatches of the chaos upstairs, heavy with feet and the breaking and shattering destruction, overlaid by the guttural hum of a massive thing all-encompassing. A thing hungry and alive.

The rest of the crew became obstacles to survival. A selfish urge for violence gripped Sierra's bones, but unraveled quickly in meeting eyes with Jenny, whom she didn't know well—dyed-blonde hair, likes Paul, lip-ring, from Missouri—but to whom Sierra became the last sight as a tentacle found the poor girl and ripped her away so fast she might have left a fissure in space.

All at once, Sierra felt distanced from everything, as though part of her, absolutely convinced this was some elaborate production, sought to step off the stage. This simply could not be real. She saw the faces around her. She saw KB down the hallway, slanted against the wall, the veins of his throat punched out in a shrieking wail. Farther down, Maxine made her way toward him when a gelatinous swarm of tentacles burst into the corridor between them. One tentacle snagged her by the waist, and she screamed.

KB turned and ran to her. The appendage tried to pull her back, just as Maxine grasped the nearest doorframe. She cried out. Tom appeared with an emergency axe which he sent twice into the tentacle before it retreated. A weird, rubbery smell filled the hall. Maxine collapsed, kept flat against the floor.

Behind KB, the shadows became gelatinous with swarming tentacles. Ancestral terror clouded the eyes of every crewmate, the return of the first mousy mammal that once shivered beneath the dinosaurs.

In terrible crashes *The Wanderer* imploded. Endless assault. The super-yacht's state-of-the-art construction now little more than aluminum foil.

Tentacles snaked above Sierra, puckering and tasting the panic-suffused air, grasping for any flesh it could and whipping people away one by one, hauling them screaming into darkness or dragging them in a trail of uncomprehending sobs across the devastation.

Sierra made it to KB and they embraced one another between the two sections of hallway yet to collapse. The yacht rocked back and forth. A squeaking groan sounded, difficult to identify as either mechanical or organic.

"What the fuck?" KB screamed. "What the fuck! What the—"

"What is this?" Maxine screamed at their feet, terrified to get up.

The wall before them exploded, spewing nails and shrapnel across their tightly-drawn limbs. A tentacle loomed, interposed itself between them as KB stumbled away and Sierra remained still. The great suckers rippled just over her, sensing her with its array of hungry, white-lipped mouths.

The tentacle wound toward her. It trembled, almost spastic. Before Sierra could maneuver, it coiled her leg, as if tracing her tentacle tattoo.

"Sierra!"

KB lunged—but not in time. As Sierra fought, the tentacle swept up to her knee and yanked, dragging her bumping and thudding toward the falling shattered night until Sierra saw the ship's railing and reached, clutching it, resisting with all her strength.

No.

More great groaning, far below. The tentacle ventured further up Sierra's body, wrapping. Tightening. She gasped. Despair filled her. Defeat filled her.

Just take me. Just take me already.

The moment slowed. Throbbed. The texture of the tentacle was strange—coarser than she would have expected. It moved, clearly, it thrashed and it preyed and it held her yet, distantly, Sierra sensed inauthenticity in it. That its truth was half-truth.

NO.

And then, suddenly, the tentacle unwound from her, whistling back into the sea-sprayed dark and leaving her to clamber over the railing and back through the ragged holes of what she thought used to be the crew's rec room. She looked for KB, for Maxine, but could see neither.

In a scraping metal bellow, the boat tilted sharply, and Sierra tumbled back toward the open air and the gnashing sea below. She managed to slow her descent on the leg of an overturned bed. The yacht continued to tilt, creaking and rotating like a kaleidoscope in the fingers of a furiously fascinated child.

Upside-down—we're going fucking upside-down. Screams and cries tore from unseen throats, from every direction. She thought she heard KB. He's still alive. How many wounded? How many dead?

Don't think about that.

The tilting ceased. The boat shuddered. The bed Sierra clung to shifted; she lost her grip and slid out into the open over the shattered remains of the deck toward the edge. She grabbed the twisted railing once more and hung there, open, primed, legs pumping on nothing but sea-spray. The air stank of salt and marine-rot. The ocean a frothing monster in its own right. A roar thrummed up from depths below, one she knew, one she had heard for the first time when she was ten and lying in a bed in Monroe County Hospital.

Can't be—

Any moment she would be snatched into oblivion, any fucking moment. Sierra hauled herself up, the greatest chin-up she'd ever done in her life, scaling along the twisted spires of the railing. Not far above her another person, a faceless crewmember—a man, judging by the scream—went sailing off in the grasp of a tentacle. She couldn't know who it was. Only that she heard his screams no more.

She swung herself onto the broken deck. The yacht had righted somewhat, but she could now hear devastating splintering sounds, the vessel jerked, rattled as the tentacles began shredding it apart, pulling at it like taffy. Eviscerating. Scouring.

The floor was splitting, a rift widening so fast she could not escape, and so fell amid a rain of debris into a ragged void newly made. Soon cold churning currents enveloped her, stinging every pore, numbing her lower extremities. She was in the sea, in the water with it, its tremendous untold bulk surging just below. Glistening tentacles looped and swayed around her.

Past the suckered storm, when her head wasn't doused by one passing wave or another, Sierra thought she heard her name. A tinny voice. Faraway.

KB! She looked around, water lashing her face, her throat. Every second her imagination prepared her for the sensation of another tentacle around her.

Again: "Sierra!"

The creature's attention was centered on *The Wanderer*. Abruptly, Sierra had a notion it was here less to feed than to actually destroy, to act as a sort of guardian, or a sieve through which objects or people were broken down, distilled, filtered. That it was doing its conscripted duty.

The ocean churned with the beast's growing movement. Through the chaos Sierra tried to gauge the direction of KB's voice. *Just get away.* She couldn't remain in one place. She started swimming, swells pushing at her. Tentacles looping spastically toward her. Beyond everything, the moon shimmered.

She saw it: a dinghy! Riding the chop like a toy boat in bathwater and sparsely occupied. Oars slicing at the sea. Another swimmer grasped and clawed toward them, coughing and crying. Maxine. They dipped into the water and hauled her aboard. Sierra made her way to them and heard her name once again and kept going, still convinced she was not going to live at the same time she knew that at any moment she would wake up.

KB and Tom, the Aussie, were there and ready to receive her. Sierra lifted her arms to them and they took her and pulled her up just as the currents spun the dinghy in a complete circle.

The oars lifted. John Maverique had control of one of them and he shouted things no one heard but tried to heed. Sierra saw Paul the Georgian there and Marla Tom's girlfriend and Kasey the cheer-leader-swimmer and Maxine and Michael, the Brazilian medical student. Sierra joined Maverique, Tom, and Marla at the oars, and they fought for their own fate against the maelstrom of other, worse fates now fighting to claim them.

Go, just go. Go—never had a single thought so preoccupied Sierra, she now an extension of the oar: driving, churning, going dammit *going*. The boat cut across the waters, reached the milestone of the breakers where it bobbed high.

Sierra felt queasy but it was far away, in a body she would come back to. All that mattered now was that beach. Getting to that beach.

Some dared to look back. Though constantly tempted, she looked only once. Crumpled and broken, *The Wanderer* was being lowered into the chop in a clasp of tentacles. Free appendages curled and slid like slimy roller coasters across the surface. One rose at what must have been only fifty yards away.

How big is this thing?

And then there was the eye, a stormy Jupiter looming up from the slosh, pupil narrowed in savage focus. Recessed in a mound of barnacled flesh, the eye alone was at least as big as Sierra, if not the goddamn dinghy.

The beach was closer and closer, only two breakers away. It still doesn't look totally real, Sierra thought. Paranoia whispered that the entire island before them would blink out, leaving them lost and adrift.

She glanced around. No other dinghies had been dispatched. There could still be survivors, but they would be back there, pumping furiously away from the descending wreck, evading by sheer chance the living forest of tentacles.

Closer. The boat rose, dipped. Lulled. Closer.

"I can *swim* faster than this," said Kasey, rising to stand. Her voice was fractured, her eyes panicked, reasonless.

"Kasey what are you doing?" Sierra said. "Don't!"

Others chimed in, sputtering protests. Sierra and John Maverique lunged to grab Kasey, but grasped only her shirt, not enough to break her determination.

The girl plunged in, vanishing briefly before emerging toward the bow as a pair of arms slicing through the surf, gaining fast and passing them, until she was yards ahead and able to stand sopping wet on the sand. She ran to the beach and collapsed, the dinghy moments behind her. All watched with stunned admiration.

Kasey knelt there, a fragile lonesome thing in a wide and empty beach, her head bowed, wet tangled hair drooped around it as she spat and caught her breath. She did not see what everyone else saw until the shadow had enveloped her.

"Holy Christ!" someone cried.

The bird was enormous, a feathery thundercloud, its beak long and hooked like a claw, its eyes acid green. It too moved with odd distinction, shuddering down, oiled and wheeled by mechanics not entirely natural.

Unleashing a triumphant cry, the bird set upon Kasey, who had no time to move except to form a pitiful shield with her hand before the huge talons grasped her and swept her up into the bird's great shadow which cut across the beach and over the stone cliffs and away from all sight, Kasey screaming all throughout until once more there was only the noise of the surf.

It can't be.

No one had processed it. Evolution, in any form, had hardly prepared the human brain to comprehend such things as the last second, the last hour. Yet while most of her faculties now operated under Animal Sierra, and while it was night, she knew she recognized that bird-creature.

It was not an exact match, appearing more aerodynamic and somehow nastier, but in basic design it bore uncanny resemblance to... to...

It can't fucking be.

Most people were crying now, Sierra among them. The dinghy pulled into shore and everyone foamed out and hauled it upon the sand. Some took the oars for weapons. All eyes were on the sky.

The actual beach, wide and long, looked empty. At its terminus stood a jungle, massive swells of green and veined with branches. Jutting from the forest were occasional giant stones, some of which stretched across the beach and segued into wave-battered reefs.

"When the hell *are* we?" Tom said.

The inevitable question.

Sierra's attention was drawn to a dark object on the sand, lying right where Kasey was taken.

A giant feather.

She picked it up.

The Perils of Perseus.

The tentacles? The Kraken?

The Untold Trials of Ulysses.

All eyes, all gazes, creaked around to her, though maybe Sierra just felt like they did. She was in a hot-seat of some kind, so it seemed. About to endure wild and arduous interrogation.

Why?

Because I'm the Monster Girl, she thought. Because I'm the Russell Boylan freak. And right now I'm holding a feather from the Roc.

3
CAMP

That interrogation didn't come, at least not immediately. The un-realness of it all allowed little coherence. Questions began, but were aborted; Sierra would hear from several mouths a "Why" or a "How" or a "What," spoken at no one in particular, and which would trail off into silence.

Everyone drifted and knocked about a shared broken space. Their personalities, their quirks, all that might have distinguished them, leveled. Even Tom's Aussie accent, or Maxine's regal British lilt, seemed to lose all distinction.

Maverique asked if anyone was seriously hurt. He looked at Michael the med student, who stood biting his lip in the mounting realization that he would by default become doctor here. Miraculously, beyond scrapes and bruises, there were no obvious injuries to speak of.

There were now only eight of them, including Sierra and KB. For a while they would be able to subsist on the supplies stored in the dinghy, much of which had been designed for survival at sea, though there were cans of beans and water and spam and a single tent.

"We shouldn't stay on the beach, right?" said Marla, Tom's girlfriend, eyes surveying the treeline and sky. "That... thing... that bird... could easily come back."

As if in reply, a roar sounded from deeper inland. Raw. Primordial.

"What was *that*?" said Maxine.

Sierra knew that roar, felt KB looking at her, but said nothing.

"We should just stay on the beach," Sierra said. "For now. Just keep watch and be vigilant."

"The hell *are* we?" said Paul, bringing out a pack of damp cigarettes from his pocket. "Some fucking Land of the Lost? Some parallel universe?"

"I don't know," Sierra said. "Let's just focus on one thing at a time. Help me set up the tent."

Only a few—Sierra, Maverique, and KB—appeared mobile enough to participate in setting up camp. The rest of the crew remained in a stupor, attention lost in the wall of jungle or the naked night sky or the demoralizing sprawl of the ocean.

The tent erect, with two of its corners stocked with provisions, Sierra and Maverique and KB stood back and looked upon it with glazed resignation.

"Think this'll fit all of us?" KB said.

Maverique shrugged. It was a protracted, existential shrug. "I think it could. It'll be a tight fit, but..." He scanned the skies. "I almost wonder if we shouldn't take shifts with sitting outside, in case any plane or ship drifts by. We have flares..."

Again, he trailed off. Maverique's usual brusque assurance had taken a beating. He was still processing. As they all were and would be, for some time. But Sierra knew several factors muddied his thought about flares. First, they only had two. Second, the flares were the only feasible long-range weapons available, and so might be better used to deter another monstrosity, winged or otherwise.

And third, it was clear, subtly-though-painfully clear, that everyone here was isolated, walled off from the world in a way not even the Swiss Family Robinson could imagine. For some reason, at least to Sierra, the notion of a passerby plane or boat was patently absurd, even more so than a living Roc, or a Kraken.

"Until we see more of this place, we need to monitor our provisions," said Maverique, as if he were the first to have such a thought. "Does anyone want any food or water right now?"

Glances were shared. Some, like Marla, were pale and unplugged and not really paying attention. No one wanted anything. Neither did Sierra. She chalked it up to nerves.

"I can't even begin to understand where we are," Maverique said. "Or what's happened to us. We're all confused and upset and we should let that out. But we also need to work together so that we might get through this. We can't afford to lose it."

"This isn't r-real," Paul stammered, addressing no one in particular. He snapped his fingers. "It'll all end soon, just like that. And we'll be fine."

"It's real for now," said Maverique. "So we deal with it as long as have to." He breathed hard. "Until we wake up."

#

She soared, but it was not her soaring. She watched it all as she would a movie, the screen having enclosed her, entered all her senses. Above her, nighttime heavens glimmered, cut off by the ocean beneath her, where the island sat as a clump of majestic earth.

Somehow, she was flying. Her body immense. Her eyes could penetrate detail at a distance impossible for a human being.

Down below, a round vat of red light throbbed in the center of the island. Lava. A volcanic heat, pumping its Promethean flame through the veins of this place.

She dipped down. Who was she? What was she? Vaguely, she knew it was possible to control her flight, to steer this body, but not yet. She had just arrived on this island, was still getting her feet wet. Along for the ride. Undergoing a test-run.

Test-run.

For what?

She dipped further downward, the island speeding at her, her at it, until it overtook the ocean on either side of her field of vision, a sea of foliage usurping that of water. Her body bent forward and suddenly she noticed the talons, the talons attached to her: great and demon-curled and iron-rod, gnarled open for landing. For grabbing. Claws of death.

The very instruments that had taken Kasey.

I'm the Roc, Sierra thought.

It's a dream. It has to be. Just like all of this. That's all.

She could never control her dreams, had to ride this out.

She set upon a huge nest built of splintered, mutilated trees. Fragments of eggshells littered the floor, pulpy with the remains of meals. Many appeared to be the remains of smaller creatures—maybe juveniles. Oddly, their exposed bones glinted silver. Their skeletons metallic.

Metallic?

One body, though, was very familiar. Very human. Freshly deposited and freshly ravaged. It was into this particular morsel that, to her dread, the bird repeatedly drove its hooked beak. Possessing no control over the instincts of this creature she currently inhabited, Sierra could only shout into the echoing, unhearing chambers of its dumb mind: Kasey, oh God Kasey, screaming and screaming—

—until she snapped awake, and was once more lying in the tent.

Where I've been the whole time.

Right?

Sierra sat up, releasing all possibility of more sleep. The dark mounds of the other crewmates lay around her like ill-fitted puzzle pieces. Some bodies twitched, others turned, violently. Tom mumbled disturbed, inaudible Aussie-speak. They were all disturbed. Fragments of terrible dreams bubbled up in the shared air.

Starting toward the tent flap, a voice, rough with sleep but thick with incredulity, stopped her.

"Sierra?" it said. "The hell're you going?"

KB.

"Go back to sleep," she said, before quickly slinking out into the sand.

She gazed at the breakers. The moon glared down at her. No breeze blew. A haphazard survey of her surroundings was the only respect she paid to the very real possibility of some other airborne assault, by some unfathomable beast.

Sierra began walking down the shoreline, the ocean sighing incoherent secrets in one ear, the island offering its own to the other, distant cries and bellows like she'd never heard before.

You've heard them before.

Someone had once told her that everyone had versions of themselves they had not yet met, all scattered over the globe, holed up in future circumstances, waiting for us to stumble upon, find and incorporate them into some greater picture of identity which could never be finished, only abandoned.

As Sierra understood it, someone from Wisconsin might well find their life's meaning in a rat hole bar in Beijing, or, to get crazier, their ideal soul mate might be locked up in an East Indian peasant 3,000 years ago, or in an alien trillions of light years away. All we had to do was recognize when luck decided to throw us a bone by steering us, when possible, into such opportunities.

What version of herself awaited her on this island?

This place was terrifying. This place was otherworldly, unnatural, impossible and all related adjectives. But—and she hated this feeling, given all that'd happened, all who'd died—it was also, strangely, right, right in some ungraspable, fateful way. At least to her.

She had a sense of having been ushered to these shores, tugged by currents beyond those of the sea. There was a heat here, intoxicating, as if the land were situated closer to the cosmic furnace that thawed all forms into fluid possibility. There was a faint electric taste to the wind, the air almost a malleable tissue— containing things just waiting to be pinched into certain existence.

If she were honest with herself, Sierra recognized a kind of invincibility here, though she did not understand why. She knew such a sensation could be delusional. In deeper regions of her, this place had pried open a door, the light beyond bleeding out.

Something stirred in her.

Something almost god-like.

That's your mind defending itself, she thought. Pulling up childhood dreams of indestructibility in the face of things it can't, and won't, try to understand.

It's all simple—you're in a dream. How else could this happen?

How else could you be living a fucking Russell Boylan *movie?*

She stopped at a dull sparkle down the beach. Reflective. Something large and metallic half-buried in the sand.

Sierra rushed toward it. Broken joints. Bent beams. A hollowed-out ship? It didn't look rusted enough, nor did there appear to be any other debris to indicate a vessel. And its position was too far inland from the waves.

On approaching, she entered a radius of stink, a strengthening odor of rot, but it wasn't organic. The smell was chemical. The smell was plastic. She ascertained the source—gobs of a reddish, clay-like substance lying beneath or hanging from the metal beams. Rubber. Some of it still imprinted with flesh-like designs. With scales.

It hit her in full, the large structure suddenly taking shape. The clawed arm, the halved jaw. The hind leg. The main vertebrate, studded with bolts. It was a skeleton, but an armature skeleton, the decomposing carcass of an artificial creature made of steel and foam rubber.

Except it wasn't twenty inches tall.

More like thirty feet.

She thought of the way the tentacles had moved, their queer stuttering motion. She remembered the oddness of the giant bird's flight.

Stop-motion animation. Christ.

If she'd seen it on a screen, it would have been obvious. But in it, surrounded by it, attacked by it... no room was made for any kind of understanding.

I'm dreaming. This is a delusion. A fantasy. I'm sick. I'm lying in a mental ward right now. I'm asleep.

I'm dead.

Drowned in the Big Dumb.

Intuitively, she turned and confronted a pair of eyes. She cried out.

"Sierra," said KB. He stood tense and rigid, like a person knowing at any moment they might explode. His face scrunched in the odor. "What is this? What's going on?"

Rapidly, Sierra's brain had to relearn the English language, as her gaze went from dead rubber-metal carcass to KB, a creature of flesh and blood. She checked her pulse, felt her tongue, scrutinized her skin, its blue veins carrying what she still hoped was real human blood.

Somehow, by whatever astronomical rule, whatever violation of everything physical or biological, this realm, this impossible realm, could support organic and synthetic life.

But how? Who had made them? Had she dreamed these things into existence, worshipped long enough at the tube or cinematic altar to actually manifest these things of Boylan's films?

Were they super-sophisticated animatronics, built by some rich prankster?

"I don't know…" Sierra said. "I don't know."

"Is that… is that a thing?" he said, pointing at the carcass. "That's a goddamn *thing*, isn't it?"

Sierra said nothing.

"It looks like a giant…"

"Yeah."

"Christ." KB knelt, put his head in his hands as a desperate worshipper in final plea might. "What in fuck's name is going *on* here, Sierra?"

"I don't know. I swear."

He looked up at her, eyes moist, expression loony and terrified and contemptuous and somewhat gone. He put up his hand and Sierra took it and pulled him back upon his feet. He sputtered a long sigh.

"Let's go back," he said. "Just, please."

Sierra nodded.

They walked back in silence, KB scanning the jungle and the stars, Sierra lost in the sand just before her, her mind void and black, flashing with random thoughts. Like a new universe testing unprecedented paradigms, or methods of creation.

"Whatever this is," KB said. "Wherever we are, we'll get through it."

The statement, which she knew desperately awaited affirmation, reached her from afar, dissolved between them.

They returned to camp. Someone's head protruded from the tent flap, watching them. It was Maxine.

"Where did you go?" Maxine said, glancing back and forth between KB and Sierra.

"Just down a ways," said KB, ducking down to re-enter the tent. "This place… doesn't make any sense."

Sierra stopped just outside. KB and Maxine looked back at her, their heads stacked almost totem-like between the parted canvas. By their curious expressions Sierra figured she herself must look curious, perhaps even wistful. She didn't know what to feel, much less how she appeared.

"I'll be in in a moment," said Sierra.

"Just be careful out there," KB said, before retracting his head.

Sierra plopped onto the sand, watched the waves, stared ahead at the ocean now indistinguishable from the night sky. No horizon.

No horizon.

With every groundbreaking discovery, every colorful new tidbit from the science world about the universe, about the very bones and guts and nature, every illuminating new theory that tempted her toward assuming that her species, these oh-so-adorably-rapacious human beings, were actually about to cross the intellectual or scientific finish line, Sierra had to remind herself of the embarrassing arrogance of that kind of thinking, and would watch with compassion each time she saw another discoverer or theorist on TV speaking in excited revelation. Nature showed you one thing, she'd think, but next week it'll erase the blackboard, doodle something new.

In political spheres, people spoke of income or wealth gaps. Likewise, she often thought the cosmos exceedingly imbalanced in its distribution of intellectual wealth. As a human gifted with a human brain, Sierra would look with pity on insects scuttling and hopping and flying through their lives, would think on the billions or even trillions of them and how not a single one would ever know that it shared a universe with Shakespeare, with space shuttles, with Russell Boylan movies, with the Great Pyramids, with the internet, with other distant worlds.

And she would see apes and dolphins, those creatures almost there, so teasingly placed at the threshold of intelligence. Which would be worse? she'd think, before realizing maybe she was a human cursed with a human brain, barred from yet greater Shakespeares, or Boylan films, or shuttles, or Pyramids, or other worlds. And, worse, *knowing* she was barred.

Who stood pitying her? Who stood pitying her pitier?

Maybe the universe was one long chain of sympathy. Maybe that was how any animal was able to make its way up the evolutionary ladder—through a charitable gift from higher sympathizers. Any way to rise above the Big Dumb.

Maybe that's what this island was.

Maybe.

THE CYCLOPS

It had been a long night for everyone, Sierra surmised. Whatever periods weren't spent fighting beneath the weight of nightmares were spent in gloomy meditation, every nudge and shift and toss and turn felt by everyone else. The night was another dark sea they bobbed aimless upon, uncertain what the morning shores might bring. Hints came in the occasional roar, bellow or terrible shriek from the innards of the island.

And then with dawn came the illnesses.

Sierra was the only one to stand erect that morning. Despite having slept what must have been only a few hours, she felt energized, far more than she would have expected. In fact, she felt a surplus of energy radiating from her body. An urge to fly stirred within her, a desire to be swept up with the wind, *become* the wind, to shift and swirl and blow anywhere she might.

I feel less… me here.

John Maverique was the second one to awake, emerging from the tent like an injured dog, propped by his arms, hungry for breath, complexion drained. Eyes closed, he rubbed his forehead.

"I can barely see," he said. The crusty bass of his voice had thinned to a fearful, adolescent whine. "Everything is spinning."

Sierra knelt by him, took his hand and pulled him stand up like a sober friend might with one intoxicated. Maverique groaned, staggered into a hunched Neanderthal posture.

"I'm ill," he said.

In murmurs and grunts, others within the tent began to echo his misery. Anxious, Sierra peeled back the tent flap on KB, who sat halfway up, grimacing as he caressed his stomach. Maxine coughed to the point of gagging. "I feel drunk," she lamented. Tom and Marla lay pale and barely moving. Paul scrambled from his corner and ran toward Sierra, who moved out of the way and watched as he collapsed in the sun and dry-heaved upon the sand. Even the resident "doctor," Michael, groaned unmoving from his position.

Sierra quickly retrieved a canister of water and pried it open. She handed it first to Maverique, who reached for it with what appeared strenuous effort before aborting the motion.

"Hold it for me," he said, exhaling between each word. He blinked slowly, as if he couldn't decide to keep his eyes open or closed. "Think I'd drop it."

She put the canister at his lips and in sloppy sips he drank.

"Paul," Sierra said. "Do you want water?"

"What's wrong with us?" KB said, crawling from the tent.

Sierra stood among the remaining *Wanderer* crew like a nurse amid those wounded on a battlefield. Loneliness swept over her. She felt a gulf separating her from the people around her. She wanted to apologize to them for somehow playing a massive trick on them, for avenging their mockery of her movie, maybe.

Looking at the weakened crew, a thought occurred to her: *Easy pickings.*

"I think I should scout for shelter," Sierra said. "Someplace more secure."

"Why aren't *you* sick?" KB said to her.

Because you fit, right? shouted a dim voice, from some corner in Sierra's mind. Because you're the one right piece and the rest of them are organ transplants, rejected by the host body.

"I don't know," Sierra said. "But I think we should start getting a lay of the land, see what we're dealing with."

Wincing, KB said, "Is this... recognizable? To you?"

Sierra furrowed her brow, even though his insinuation was pretty clear.

"Our boat was destroyed by a fucking Kraken, or whatever," said KB. "Kasey was killed by a damn giant bird. There's a dead metal dinosaur drying out down the beach."

"You want me to tell you why?" Sierra snapped. "Or you think I know when these things are gonna happen or why we're here?"

KB said nothing. A challenging glare bore through the sick cloud in his eyes, and it said, *Well, do you?*

"Again, I have no clue where we are, or why," Sierra said. "Or how."

Those awake watched her, with expressions hard to discern. They might not have been expressions attached to any real mental or emotional understanding. They just were, and unknown even to those who wore them.

"I'm going," Sierra said. She rummaged in the supplies and brought out the flare gun.

"You're taking that? Tom said. "Wouldn't we need it more?"

"Let her take it," KB said. "You won't be gone long, right?"

Sierra gazed off down the beach. Another distinct roar sounded. The screech of the Styracosaur from *Dino Island.*

"I don't know how long I'll be gone," Sierra said.

With moderate effort, more than should be required for his age, KB pushed himself to his feet. "Let me go with you."

Of course, Sierra thought. Of course one of the boys had to gallantly offer his companionship. Of course it's KB.

"You're not feeling well," Sierra said. "You think you'll be okay?"

KB fidgeted. The lull between them indicated he might have been waiting for more out of Sierra, and she knew exactly what. She was supposed to tear up, thank him, and pay homage to his obvious courage in the face of illness and danger. She was supposed to embrace him and say that she couldn't live without him if something were to happen.

"If you want to come, come," Sierra said. "I just want to make sure you're up for it and won't slow me down." She started off. A pang of compassion hit her, and she turned. "I want you to be safe."

\#

KB measured his breathing, and kept decent pace with Sierra across the glittering sands, periodically turning to see how far from camp they'd traveled.

"You doing okay?" Sierra said.

"I think so." He kept a soft hand on his stomach. "I can't tell what's wrong with us. Or me. I feel like all my organs are being rearranged."

"You're adjusting," Sierra said, half-consciously. And adjusting faster. Why? He had been at her side in her fanatical Boylan devotion. He'd been greased, more than the others, for this transition.

"What?" KB said.

She kept quiet.

"Sierra, just cut the shit. It can't be a coincidence that you're the fucking Monster Girl and we're shipwrecked on Monster Island."

"I don't think it is a coincidence," Sierra said. She felt like she was conceding to something huge, but wasn't sure what that could possibly be. "But I can't say why I think that."

Tugging, prying, fiddling somewhere on this island might unearth an explanation, or at least the beginning of one. Still, though, Sierra persisted partly in a stasis of non-acceptance, like one who knows they are dreaming, or a moviegoer aware of the monsters' inability to step off the screen.

The beach curved sharply around, sections of sand divided by loose clusters of rock and reef, none of which had the true density of "real" rocks. The sea tried to out-blue the sky. Encroaching jungle narrowed the shoreline, thinning further against the tide.

"I see something out there," said KB, pointing out past the waves.

Sierra didn't need his finger; she'd spotted it the moment he had. About five hundred yards out was a gray amphibious hump, spotted green and brown and wheeling casually through the water.

"What is that?" KB asked.

She recognized the creature's color scheme, for it also occupied the area by her left hip, where the Pleisiosaur, the long-necked, maritime marauder from *Prehistoric Valley*, remained fixed in the amber of her flesh.

KB's face made a dyspeptic squint.

She stopped at the sight of a massive rocky wall covered partially in foliage, its top steepled like a lighthouse. Sierra peered at the formation and somewhere in the background KB asked what was wrong, but she didn't respond. Excitement churned in her, bolstered by an insatiable curiosity that she guiltily tried to suppress.

If one goes far enough, one could find anything.

She sprinted forward.

"Hey!" KB called.

Her suspicions confirmed: a great cave, stretching up from only a few feet of sand and yawning high and black like the very mouth of the ocean. It had swallowed terrors. It could spit up terrors.

It was the cave of the two-headed Cyclops, from *The Untold Trials of Ulysses*. Well, not exactly. It lacked the smaller hollows that were made for skull-like eye sockets. But that particular feature, Sierra recalled, had been demanded by the director and the art director. Boylan had fought it, thinking it hokey and unnecessary. And so… here they weren't.

Here they aren't.

Finally, KB caught up to her, pale and breathing hard. He suddenly didn't feel real to her, more an illusory pipeline to her old life.

"We're not going in there," KB said.

For him, it was a rare moment of utter authoritativeness. Ignoring it, she walked forward.

"Sierra," KB said. "Son of a bitch."

He was going to follow her, KB. Couldn't be doubted. He always would. Newtonian Law. Just as he had followed her into the woods to find the Dale Devil. But she herself had to obey the gravity of this place, this mysterious cave before her, to heed a hunger gnawing harsher in her breast, one she had not felt in a long time. It was a youthful hunger. A conquering hunger.

"Sierra."

She entered the whistling shade of the cave. She could tell it ran long, deep. Clearly meant to accommodate largeness. She kept going. With a resigned sigh, KB pursued.

Sierra had walked maybe fifty feet in when KB spoke.

"Hey," he said. "This is really weird."

"What?" Sierra said, before taking a moment to turn.

KB stood near the mouth of the cave, hand raised to the rock wall.

"This stone," he said, tapping on it then knocking. "It's so light. I think it's hollow."

Sierra went and touched it. Like papier-mâché, or Styrofoam.

Like what they build sets with.

"This place is... fake," KB murmured. "But..."

Loose sticks and rocks and fragments lay at her feet. Peering closer, she saw they were bones, or supposed to be.

"Somebody built this whole place," KB said.

A rank weedy smell blew through the cavern. Then came the breathing, deep lung-scrapes, heaving inhales and geyser exhales. The dark's respiration. *Come in*, said the foul breeze. *No*, it would change its mind. *Stay out.*

Sierra looked at KB and decided to take the latter advice.

Then, with a snarled hiccup, the breathing stopped.

And they both ran. A roar pounded through the cave, deep and humanoid and gnarled with primitive language. A current of hot noisome wind pushed at Sierra's back. The walls trembled. Thunderous footfalls beat the ground.

In Sierra rose the ten-year-old from Dale—excited, too excited, to turn and see this massive monster, this toy, chasing her. Sierra dared not indulge her, especially as she felt the whistling gust of what could have only been the club— *the bone-club?*—as it swung across the dark and smashed against the wall.

Another roar. Fuller. Madder.

"Split off!" Sierra cried to KB. "You go right, I go left!"

Crash. The club against the cave wall. Showers of bone fragments across her backside.

She emerged onto the beach.

"Run!" she screamed, hoping the camp might hear.

Turning sharply left, Sierra recognized instantly she'd gotten a better deal—maybe. In her direction sat several tide pools, surrounded by huge clusters of sea-slicked volcanic rock, where small craters funneled wave water into geysers spewing high and foamy, like a whale's blowhole. In contrast to the relative openness of the beach to the right of the cave, there were plenty of nooks and crannies she could hide.

The Cyclops issued another roar. It was almost out. *Hide dammit hide.* Plenty of crevices, though most were too tight a fit. Sierra tried not to slip as she made her way down the rocks, but in her caution she moved too slow for her own comfort, and so started to jump down, platform to platform, the Cyclops' roar cresting over the rocks.

It's coming for me.

Her foot struck a loose stone. Pain erupted from her ankle and Sierra tumbled down the rocks. Lying in a shifting sheet of seawater, ears alive with the screeching and impossible tenor of her coming death, she felt squeezed in ache, and for a second cared absolutely nothing about whatever might happen to her.

The bone-club smashed the rocks. Fragments showered down over her. She curled up, eyes fastened shut. Staggering to her feet, pain pulsing, Sierra continued on, not daring to look back.

Then, a giant shadow fell over her, and a large, solid thing struck her body with all the force of what felt like a car. Huge rubbery fingers enclosed her, trapped her in the very fist of the Cyclops and before she had even the wherewithal to resist she was being lifted high, her legs kicking at air.

"No!" she cried, pounding the thing's thumb and forefinger. The fist squeezed her. She gasped.

The monster brought her closer to its two massive heads, both savagely ugly, accented with that much more realness than they'd possessed in their close-ups onscreen. The two faces grunted, rippled with different expressions, brows furrowing as Sierra hung there heaving in its grasp. Were the heads talking to one another? About her?

She took in that monstrous totality. The Cyclops *was* the Cyclops, no mistaking it. The big two-headed, strutting brute of ancient terror, the booming xenophobe that had chased off Ulysses' men on this very beach.

But there were new things, new traits it possessed. The awkward two-toed feet, never good for oversized lumbering, had sprouted several more. The body was leaner, better proportioned, balanced by a tail that had not been there in the film. Bigger eyes roved in its two heads, which were closer together, perhaps on a slow Darwinian path to merging.

That word popped out: *Darwinian.*

"Let me go," she muttered.

The Cyclops stared at her.

Release me.

She sensed a slight loosening of its fingers. She clutched its knuckle, aware of the forty-foot drop. One Cyclops head looked confused. The other, angry.

Then, the Cyclops extended its arm, held her away from its mouth as if to analyze her like a collector would an antique item. She kicked her legs. *It's going to throw me,* she thought, almost certain in that second. She breathed in, held it—

—and the fingers opened and she fell, hurtled down the forty feet straight into the pool where half another bellow from the beast became instantly garbled under the surface. In the chaos, she sensed that it regretted its decision to drop her, as though it'd just blinked from a spell.

A spell I put it in?

Coldness and floating, then swam against the irritable current. The pool was deep, deep, a vertical tunnel leading to dark cavernous fathoms.

How had Ulysses beaten the Cyclops? In Homer's poem, of course, the Trojan War hero cleverly uses an alias, "No Man," when meeting the giant, and proceeds to impale its eye while it sleeps. Boylan's Cyclops, however, couldn't be smartly tricked. Only felled or distracted, as the men in the movie had done by having it chase them to the lair of the Giant Crab, which emerged in pincher-snapping fury at the disturbance and went for the biggest, most obvious culprit. Club on claw ensued—one of the most famous fights from Boylan's films.

Sierra held her breath for what felt like minutes, but which were probably seconds. Clutching the wall of the pool, she dove down, down, where the tunnel stretched away from all light, and the Cyclops' bellow faded.

4
AWAKENING

The images washed upon him, splashing colors and shapes. He couldn't tell which picture or which … thing deserved his attention most. All were significant—scratch that, they were *magnificent*. But what were they? The pictures seemed hazy and capricious.

Distantly, he began to feel each scene. The more he focused on one, the more it moved, responded, and the moving objects became like digits of a new appendage which he was to break in, raising first fingers, wiggling inaugural toes, christening the dialogue between them and his mind.

The only real issue was understanding where to focus first.

In the clearest image were flowers, or what resembled flowers. They were multi-colored, at full bloom, but he recognized none of them. His eyes, if he were looking with his eyes, drifted to this image and it began to grow, seeping up and expanding like smoke across his vision. The flowers and the vegetation took on a harder, more tangible presence. They were there, not just projections. And the more he focused, the stronger the sense of a surrounding density, that something like a body contained him.

Then he moved—involuntarily.

He was a spectator in another's head. Whether human or animal, it was unclear. But wait, what *was* he, exactly? How had he gotten here? Why did he naturally assume himself a 'he'?

At some deep level, he heard the raps of an identity that had been neatly buried and stored away, for safekeeping, maybe, or until he grew accustomed to this particular realm, or being.

He existed now as naked awareness, unblemished by opinion or much knowing.

These eyes he peered through belonged to some kind of creature, ambling low to the ground but still taller than he was used to. It leaned in, ripped away at the vegetation before it and chewed. Foraging.

Slowly, hunger eddied into him. The creature. Its nervous system was connected—connecting—to his own. If he had one.

A tremor in the ground. Ominous, as were almost all tremors. The beast issued a whiny grunt. Its head whipped left to the other, substantially larger behemoth next to it—his mother. No, the *creature's* mother.

He knew this beast.

It stood on elephantine legs, and heaved with breath. A thick tail brushed the weeds. A horned crest fanned over its head, and long pointed horns jutted over its face. Its jaws worked on the foliage, cow-like.

A name came to him, perhaps the first memory to reach him.

Triceratops.

A what? A… a… dinosaur.

This was significant for many big reasons, none of which he could grasp right now.

I'm a baby triceratops.

The more he focused on the mother, however, the more the scene began to change again. He imagined these pictures composed of a pliable substance, like paint, and at no more than the whim of a breeze a solution could be spilled upon the canvas, and that all of it could be cleansed and remade.

Suddenly he was staring down at a baby triceratops. Tiny-horned, grunting, chewing. He knew it to be the one whose head he'd just occupied, but he was no longer inside it, had in fact hopped like a flea into the body of its mother.

And there were others, milling nearby in the forest. He could hear their crunching footfalls and grunty utterances.

The tremors in the ground strengthened. Fear settled like acidic dew on the clearing. The vibrations increased. *Something approaching*. The baby whined, louder, as did the others in the brush. *No, be quiet.*

He rode the mother's eyes as she looked left, toward the ragged corridor of trees. Usually the forest was beautiful, he remembered. Right now, it felt like death.

What's death?

Whatever moved toward them moved fast, carried by its bulky tremendous power. The mother triceratops issued her own cry. He felt the guttural tremble of her voice up from her breast and out her throat.

The kin responded in kind. Time to act. The others came barreling out of the woods, they and their young, and they came together in a fortress around the defenseless and they bellowed and they waited.

The terrible monster came closer. Flashes of its green-brown flesh. It walked with fiendish doggedness. It walked strong with the knowledge that only it decided who, or what, broke its lordly strut.

The triceratops barked and bellowed. From the center of the ring, the infants wailed. Atop his vision the horns remained, poised forward, itching to impale.

He stared, he watched—then, the scene dissolved again, reconstituting in another, even higher set of eyes now moving through the trees. Toward the clearing where the agitated triceratops huddled.

I've jumped again.

He had jumped to the monster, to the head of the beast terrorizing the triceratops. Through the trees he could see the matriarch, where he'd just been. He felt sorry for her, almost as if he had betrayed her and she knew it.

What am I? What am I doing here?

Mother Triceratops lowered to the ground, scraped up dust with her right leg. Preparing to charge. Her movement was rickety. Unreal. But familiar.

He knew great hunger now, and a thundering, overwhelming desperation.

He knew the mind of a tyrant.

ALONE

Already her chest tightened. Shadow-spots on her vision. How far did this pool go? Amid the chaos in her mind one image, one memory, managed to form.

The lagoon from *Prehistoric Valley*. To escape the Tyrannosaur—technically *Allosaur*, as it sported three claws on its puny arms—rampaging through their camp, the survivors make it to the shore, the strutting, gnashing, green-scaled menace at their heels, and they dive into one of the tide pools there which to their fortune becomes a cavernous, underground passage to another section of the valley.

To their *mis*fortune, though, in the tradition of all Saturday-matinee spectacle, they emerge in the lake of a waiting Elasmosaurus.

Nowhere else to go.

If the island's inhabitants were built of movie anatomy, Sierra certainly wasn't. Editors and writers were the gods allowing characters their impossible escapes and liberal lung capacity. Who watched out for her, took liberties with her?

The tunnel curved and she followed it, entering a blackness more absolute than a dreamless sleep. Down here, all reality had truly bottomed out.

She could barely hear the Cyclops and its ruckus above. At the center of her chest, death had begun to tighten, ready to unspool across her system. Everything slowed. Her heart became a dense metal thing, like a wrecking ball in methodic, shattering rhythm against her breast. Sierra felt like she was about to simultaneously implode and explode.

On a whim, she rose her hand up, expecting in inches to touch the constricting rock. But there was room, more room, then even more room. Her whole hand was above the water, then her forearm! And if her forearm—

In a torrent of bubbles, she surfaced. Air! Wonderful and rank and primal air. It was breathable, though. Blood resumed its marathon through her veins. It was *life*. Yet still she was blind.

She floated there, exhausted, thankfully the only thing moving and disturbing the water, at least that she could see, or hear. Relief tempted her to stay longer. What if this was the only pocket of air in a chamber stretching miles? But she couldn't just linger—who knew what pinchered or toothy or multi-appendaged thing might cruise by and delight at a pair of fleshy, kicking legs?

Did these things eat flesh? It was kind of assumed, of course. But if they were all artificial, and, if ostensibly, they ate one another, why assume they would be interested in the taste of "real" meat?

Of course, even if these particular creatures didn't like flesh, though, one aimed to avoid being the inaugural taste-test.

Keeping at the surface, she cautiously swam forward. The chamber appeared to be curving around to the right, but that could have been her imagination. She wondered if she could find her way back, if she wished. She was an insect caught between two clasped palms.

Please, she thought. Just *please*.

Then—a dull light. Very dull. Beneath her feet, toward the bottom. A faint blue glow filtered through what appeared to be an arch. Something visible was on the other side. Even if it proved only phosphorus, or a thousand jellyfish, or (God forbid) a passage of daylight too small to fit through, it would be good for orientation, for her eyes to kiss any sight of anything.

Inhaling once more, Sierra dove. The light grew brighter. There was nothing around her. The ultimate lifelessness of this cavern was almost as unnerving as if it'd been teeming with creatures. It felt like an empty aquarium, awaiting its contents.

In the merciful light, Sierra could see that the pool became shallow, the ground rising steeply toward a bank which, upon surfacing, she could tell offered a way out, one big enough to fit through if she crawled.

She scrambled ashore, haunted by the recent memory of Kasey, that tragic pioneer, grabbed with such grotesque efficiency by those talons the second her soles touched sand. As if it had been anticipated. Orchestrated.

Scripted?

Nothing appeared to dwell amidst the stalactites above, nor did anything inhabit this little twilight beach. In fact, the sand looked utterly immaculate.

In fact...

This place could well prove an ideal camp. There was shelter, water, no visible or audible monsters and too small an entryway for any vengeful Cyclops, gnashing bird or even Kraken tentacle or any other winged or clawed Armageddon. If she could just find the others—

If they're alive.

Lying on the sand, Sierra sniffed, more tears pressing hot at her eyes. She had ditched the others. Abandoned them. And what had happened to KB? Was he—*no, stop.*

Of course, she had merely been trying to save her own life. What kinds of noble decisions can be made when running from a goddamn two-headed *Cyclops*? And yet the guilt she felt came from a strong sense of responsibility, that somehow she had led the whole boat astray, that she in part shouldered blame for those dead, for those stranded.

That the meaning of her tied inexplicably to the meaning of this place.

She approached the small exit, crouched down and began crawling through the passageway, her back scraping against the roof.

The passage widened, and with it increased the whirring static of a waterfall. The walls grew wetter, the ground slicker. The waterfall didn't sound too heavy. She just hoped it didn't presage a fifty-foot plunge.

The passage curved again and brought within view the yawning exit and the glassy sheet of the falls, behind which wobbled the colors of the jungle, nebulous like a thing in flux.

Sierra crawled forth, could see the pond laid out at the center of this rocky grotto. Not too big, thankfully. And, by that logic, hopefully not too deep.

Watery mist increased, billowing at her as she moved forward. Soon water was the world's only sound. She shivered, teeth chattering. The falls were a portal, a liquid gateway. She reached out to it and the water curtained around her fingers.

And then, a great lumbering beast emerged from the trees. Bipedal, it strode toward the pond. Its skin was green-brown. Even as a blurred silhouette there was no mistaking such a thing as the Tyrannosaurus Rex, emperor of meat-eaters, the king in every consciousness, the star of every one of Russell Boylan's dinosaur movies.

At the bank of the pond, it crouched awkwardly on its haunches and lapped at the water.

Jutting like a saber toward the forest behind it, the Rex's tail was high and taut, exactly as more recent scientific illustrations had depicted, but at odds with its dated look in *Prehistoric Valley, Terror B.C., Rampage, Dino Island, Jaws of the Jurassic,* or the tattoo at her navel, where the T-Rex stood more vertical, its tail dragging and writhing on the ground.

Like the Cyclops, the Rex was definitely that of Russell Boylan's, but … tweaked.

Again, the word wafted through her head: *Darwinian.*

They're evolved. They have *evolved.* Natural selection had brought into its fold these unsightly inorganic beings left nowadays to the cold outside all dreams and imaginations, left to grow and to roam and to sprout and to mutate however circumstance saw fit, beyond the constraints of script or screen.

The Rex turned and walked away.

Sierra hesitated, then stuck her head and torso through the waterfall. Across the clearing rose a massive tree, a wooden cyclone twisting up from the soil, swirled in vines and sprouting huge leaves. It looked like the tree of the deadly Wood Gnomes in *The Scourge of Camelot.*

She peered at the pond. No danger she could see. No Elasmosaurus. No Kraken. She hastily dove in and made her way to the shore. Of this place's tremendous hierarchy of strangeness, a small observation now stood out to Sierra—there were no bird calls or bug noises. Only loud, echoing calls haunted the air, sounding from the interior. No small creatures appeared to inhabit the island. While no biologist, Sierra knew that in nature, real nature, the macro could not exist without the micro.

And that rubber and metal cannot come alive.

But this was an experiment, perhaps. The fruition of a long-held vision of some overzealous protégé struggling to impress, or become, the master. A dream-in-waiting, groping toward the real. Nature, the master, had patiently taken its time, understanding its own resources and potential. This creation here, full of so many holes, imbalances, impossibilities, could only be the product of a child who, after a few art lessons, attempts their own Sistine Chapel.

And who was this artist? Russell Boylan?

Who else?

Right?

His whole universe walked here, his spirit breathed here. But was he here?

He died—at sea.

Sierra tried to oust all such useless speculation from her mind. Her curiosity played tug-o-war with her instinct to stay alive, and she couldn't let the former detract from the latter, not now.

She sprinted toward the tree, skipping over the Rex's giant three-toed prints, freshest among the others. There were rounded feet, spindly bird feet, and, most disturbingly, massive humanoid feet.

The body of the tree, and all its furnishings, felt light. It was made of foamboard and fiber-glass. Props. Settings. Life-sized miniatures, if that made any kind of sense. But all of it dense enough to support her as she scaled its vines and sat on one of the higher, thicker branches. She half-anticipated one of those vicious, tree-dwelling Gnomes to pop out.

She gasped. The *view*.

The valley before her was so round, almost too round, as if it had been meticulously made. Sawtooth ridges and peaks lined its borders, earthen uprisings cupping a luminous forest, which while clearly wild, also carried a specter of authorship. Winding through this greenery, heads aloft from the canopy, moved a herd of great gray sauropods, the long-necked dinosaurs for which the catch-all label was usually "Brontosaurus."

And towering above it all: the mountain, ancient-looking yet also fabricated, like a giant science fair project.

The mountain, of course, was not really a mountain but a volcano, sighing up a pillar of smoke. Brimming with an eruption forever imminent.

Sierra had seen this volcano before. She had been airborne. Not totally herself. A dream? Yes. Probably a dream.

She sensed significance in this peak. Leaning against the tree, she watched the smoke curl skyward, listened to the calls and the roars and the cries and the brays of the beasts seen and unseen. Of the beasts once unmade, now made.

REIGNING TYRANT

Much like a shark, the Tyrannosaur had to keep on the move. Fine for him as, dressed in its skin, he enjoyed the shuddering music of its footfalls, felt even giddy at the waves of lesser beasts dispersing at its presence. Sometimes his vision would slip into theirs, even during feasting. But he was improving at controlling where he went, and so would right himself once again behind the eyes of this Lord of the Dinosaurs.

Somehow, somewhere, at some level, he knew all this to be a dream come true.

The longer he remained in the Rex, the more fastened his essence became to its nervous system, eroding the barriers once keeping him from the rawness of its senses, or its hunger, or its ache. Would he eventually lose himself entirely, slip below the surface and be swallowed by this primal sinkhole of mind?

Maybe. Maybe not. The more integrated he was with the Rex, the more he felt *as* the Rex, looming separate and alone and above all others. And the more he was the Rex, the more substantial he found his sway over its movement. It was a fine balance. Dipping in enough to control. Not enough to lose himself.

Even if "he" still didn't know who "he" truly was.

Like a novice pilot tuning dials, he dabbled in his command—testing functions, curling a claw or two here, wagging the tail there. Greater control was evidently and palpably within reach, but he would have to accustom himself toward it, evolve himself within this creature. Often, his thirst for exploration and answers clashed with the dinosaur's loyalty to every blood-scented breeze.

Amid so many charges that animated this thunderstorm of life and teeth, he would have to become the dominant bolt.

When heeding the distress cry of injured prey, or the ripe stink of a fresh carcass, there was little he could do to derail the direction of the Rex. In hunting, its faculties were spear-pointed, leaving no room for him, and he was along for the ride, watching and feeling as the foliage parted to reveal the triceratops prey lying there, leg broken and abandoned by its kind. It yelped when it saw him, its cries desperate.

He jumped again, and assumed the body of the prey, stretched pained across the soil, staring behind watery eyes up at the approaching Rex, that cavern of canines, which had just been his. The pain seared, and he knew utter panic, as well as remorse for the poor creature.

And curiosity stirred him, too—for jutting from the creature's shattered leg was a twisted piece of metallic bone, lightly aglow in the sun. He didn't know why, but this struck him as either unnatural or downright wrong.

Somehow, things here were not as they should be. An error had been made. A rule had been overwritten.

Yet what could he truly know, or care, about how things should be? He knew no other nature. This world was to be acknowledged, was to be filled—and filled by him.

TOWARD DAWN

Sierra didn't know what to do. She wanted to find the rest of her crewmates as much as she wanted to stay in the tree and as much as she wanted to explore every crevice of this island—from a safe distance, of course.

Awaking in the middle of the night, Sierra realized she couldn't have slept for more than a few hours. She actually didn't even remember falling asleep. Yet she wasn't tired, nor was she hungry, despite not having eaten in more than half a day.

What is *there to eat here, anyway?*

Below, foliage crackled. Something lurked underneath, issuing heavy grunts. She kept low to the branch, listening.

Was this the dinosaur section? Did each creature, every "film," abide by its own "zone?" Or did every beast have carte blanche to wander wherever the wind might take it? If the Rex and the Cyclops got into it, it would likely not turn out well for the Rex.

Night sky glimmered through the leaves, as normal as the sky over Dale or Los Angeles or Johannesburg or London or anywhere else in the world, and grinning bright with a thin crescent moon.

The lurking beast below, whatever it was, began to wander off. She couldn't tell what it was. And soon, there was nothing to tell.

She had to make it back. Every minute presented another resolute decision, but returning to the beach was the one that jabbed her fiercest. Even if it offered no answers for the where, why, or how of this place. Even if some magnetic force sought to tug her farther and farther inland.

A howl echoed down the mountains, monstrous though human-like. Sierra recognized it instantly. The Yeti. From *The Crown of the World.* It was up there, stomping about, its grotesque simian face cutting through the icy winds, its shaggy, bulging arms probably thrusting defiance at the warmer world below, beating its leathery chest.

The movie's Yeti model, Sierra knew, had been hung with rabbit fur. How would that work, translated to "life-size?" Like the giant metal armatures and tonnage of rubber, she figured the fur had in size truly become that of the Yeti's. Even if "real" Yetis were hardly the size Boylan had made them.

She had to stop thinking. The more she did, the more her situation discouraged it. The island's ideal visitor would be a child, someone with no interest in picking apart logic and mechanics.

She felt like a hook had been thrown into the pool of her mind, and that the child inside her, the one of Dale, seeking any excuse to show itself, had clamped down on it and that some faceless fisherman, battling the obstacles of intervening adult years, was reeling it to light.

Another bellow. Curdling the dark.

Soon, Sierra fell asleep again.

When she awoke, dawn blazed pink over the peaks. She sat up. She felt no ache, despite having slept on an enormous tree limb. She still wasn't hungry, either, and her mind was alert, freshly branded with a dream she had just been having.

In the dream, she had been walking tall and unencumbered through lush growth. She was imperial. Smells clouded her snout. She could not tell what body she was attached to, but it was not her own and it was a grand body and knew itself so.

And in this body, she had stopped just before a large tree, a rocky grotto and the moonlit pond just beyond it, and she had smelled something new and looked up to see *herself*, the sleeping body of Sierra Nevada Smith draped across the branch, tentacled leg dangling within easy reach of her current jaws.

No, she had thought in the dream. Leave that one alone.

That one.

Climbing down from the tree, she saw fresh three-toed prints, the kind she had seen yesterday when emerging from the pond, that haunt of the Tyrannosaurs Rex.

BACK TO THE BEACH

Looking every which way, Sierra descended the tree and made her way back toward the coast. Walking cautiously at first, the longer she spent in the jungle the more she picked up speed, sprinting, then running, toward the ocean. Periodically, she noted tall twisting trees, easily climbable in case something spotted her.

Nearing the beach, she slowed. Stopped. Dread overcame her. What was she going to see? Who was she going to see smashed to death, flattened into the sand? Strewn in gnawed pieces up and down the coast?

Moving against sudden dizziness, Sierra left the forest and emerged back into the terribly open paradise of the beach. Slight breezes blew.

She looked to the right, way down, where only surf moved.

The same down to the left.

No one.

Sierra noticed the clouds on the horizon, amassed like shapeless white muscles, ready to challenge space itself. They were everywhere in the distance, and that distance was the real world. By contrast, not a single cloud hovered over this island, which existed, maybe, in a zone protected from all unwanted elements.

Sierra walked closer toward the water. The Cyclops cave rose down the beach. Ravages of the chase were still visible in the sand, a pair of massive footprints violently mixed in with those of shoes and normal humans. The Cyclops would have had no trouble catching up to them.

The blood. Dotted here and there. Splashed about. Strips of fabric, some of which she recognized. Depending on one's Murphy tendencies, the scene was either sufficiently grim to suspect mass and total death, or hardly grim enough. Sierra tried to convince herself of the latter.

She took a deep breath and cried out, her voice hustled away with the breezes.

She noticed a large hole in the sand, constantly licked at by the waves. She went to it, following a trail of increasingly erratic prints that had broken off from the others. Her stomach knotted. Toward the edge of the hole, she stopped.

Gasped.

The body had been smashed into its own open grave, which now filled with reddened seawater, pulped with bobbing brain and tissue matter. It didn't look real. It had to be another cinematic fabrication, a fancy illusion.

No.

While facedown, from the hair and the clothes she could tell it was Paul the Georgian—or had been.

His body had been pummeled into something like road kill, so much so it was difficult to imagine a person had ever spoken, walked, or thought inside it.

She saw no other bodies, at least not immediately. She moved in the other direction, toward the Cyclops' cave.

She remembered something.

In *The Untold Trials of Ulysses*, the Cyclops did not merely try to smash the pesky intruders. It had abducted a few as ingredients in a giant stew.

Sierra took deep breaths, gulping the wind. The dizziness came in spurts.

A shoe. Lying on its side, half-buried in sand. Black and white. Nike. She recognized it.

An "Oh God" dribbled from Sierra's lips, though it came out more a choking noise. She knew the sneaker.

"KB!" she shouted.

No reply. With little forethought, she ran toward the Cyclops' cave. Listened. She stuck by the side of the rock wall, easily able to conceal herself should anything emerge.

A wave of emotion struck her and she collapsed to her knees, leaned her back against the stone. She cried. Her spirit here was porous. It could only accept these things with the occasional meltdown, a cleansing cry-out for reason and for mercy.

Tears clearing, Sierra stared at the green tentacle coiled in ink around her right shin. The first tattoo she had gotten, in that dark one-man parlor in Kruegerville, ten miles north of Dale. The image seemed so old, even older than the skin where it'd been painted. Like all her inks and all her monsters, it had been a companion.

Except now they weren't. Now, her skin was a shrine to tragedy and death.

She continued focusing on the tentacle.

Is it… glowing?

And then…

In some deep part of herself, she felt a *snap*—a splintering.

And suddenly, everything was blue. Everything swayed. The world was liquid. She saw rocks below, lit by channels of sunlight through the surface above.

She was underwater. In the ocean.

In the aqua haze before her unfurled a huge, serpentine shape. Greenish and slick. Underside studded with pulsing suction cups.

A tentacle. Joined by many others, propelling her through the sea, ready at any stutter of movement, in any direction, to snatch and to squeeze and to swallow. They were all so big, these culprits that had destroyed *The Wanderer*, taken to most of its passengers like a famished child to McNuggets, and they were all attached to her as she cruised on constant patrol these depths just offshore.

Thoughts of *The Wanderer,* its destruction, its many deaths, touched her with sudden, perverse satisfaction. It had been a purpose fulfilled. Sustenance had.

No, it was senseless. Tragic. Absurd.

Sierra's mind vacillated between remorse and morbid celebration. It was then she knew she was not alone behind the eyes of this beast the Kraken, that another, perhaps the beast's original self was in here with her.

What was there to eat? There seemed not many fish about, the sea barren.

Then, she spotted movement far away. A large shape, though not as large as she. The Kraken darted closer, taking her with it, heaving its whole body into attack mode and homing missile-like at the long-necked silhouette, a creature normally much bigger. A juvenile… what was it? That serpent from *Terror B.C.*, a young… yes… a young Plesiosaur.

Closer.

Then came the distant, echoing scream: "Leave me the fuck alone!"

Snap—and the tentacles froze, became once again the ink on her leg.

Sierra blinked. She was back on the beach, cheeks sticky with tears, nose wet with mucus. She felt pulled from a dream. What had happened?

Who had yelled?

Another scream ripped through the air, boyish and terrified, tearing out of the cave behind her.

KB.

Sierra turned and ran inside.

5
THE BABY GIANT

Sierra realized how differently she now reacted to the Cyclops cave. The thought of the giant presented a much lesser threat. She knew this. Her whole life she had been lapping up this world. It was part of her constitution. She had mastered it. She took from it. That it could take from her seemed an egregious overstepping of this world's natural boundaries.

Shadows fattened in the chilly cave air. Past the collection of bones, the darkness magnified, but there was enough of a light to navigate the winding passage.

"Just *eat* me already," a voice suddenly screamed. The whiny, nasal quality, though choked with terror, was unmistakable.

Definitely KB. Sierra's heart lifted.

A reddish light opened on her eyes.

Ahead of her, drawn in the firelight of large braziers, was a massive rounded den. The lair of the bipedal beast now stuttering about the shadows.

The den of the Cyclops.

"Eat me already!"

And centered in the den was a cage, built of cross-stitched wood and strips of metal that Sierra guessed were the bones of dead creatures. Shelves lined the walls, propping crudely-made pots and tools. From deeper within the lair, the Cyclops uttered a casual pulse of grunts. She could barely see the giant, but it sounded preoccupied, and so she moved closer.

But where was KB? His voice seemed to echo from everywhere. She imagined him lined up on a shelf, anxiously overlooking a bubbling pot.

New voices then. New noises. A rasping, ghoulish kind of cooing. KB cried out again, and this time Sierra caught movement within the cage, the size of which loomed larger and larger. With her every step, the origin of KB's pathetic sobs, the pleas and wails, narrowed to that cage.

He was in there. With something else.

Something much bigger.

While obscured, the thing in the cage began to take shape for Sierra. It was sitting, its arms moving in spirited, fascinated play, its two drooling mouths babbling with infantile merriment. Its eyes were trained on the little living doll it now held by its now sneaker-less feet.

"Just eat me!" KB shouted.

Not a cage, Sierra thought. It was a playpen. For a child Cyclops.

No Boylan film, of course, had featured a baby Cyclops. Sierra began to intuit, though, that that didn't matter. In wisps of memory, she recalled seeing eggshells in the nest of the great Roc bird. Just now, in that brief, bizarre stint as the Kraken, she had chased a juvenile plesiosaur.

They evolved, yes. They grew. And they reproduced.

Watching the little Cyclops, Sierra became aware of a sensation brewing within her, one indeed of fluidness, as though everything in her was preparing to break the dam of her skin and gush forth. Ready to *snap*.

Her "self" was slippery.

Then—*snap*!

And abruptly, once more, she was no longer Sierra. The wave had left, her spirit sloshed over into yet another skull.

She peered before her, at the giant arm holding by the ankle a writhing and weeping KB.

She was inside the playpen. More, she was inside the baby *Cyclops*.

How was this possible? What in God's name was *happening*? The baby Cyclops was a storm of sensation, an electric mind constantly titillated, easily distracted. Nestling into it was like plopping one's self amidst a litter of jittery cats. Thoughts sprang away from her, ill-formed notions, conceits, puffed through its skull. Sierra tried to wrangle control.

She thought back to when the adult Cyclops had grabbed her. For reasons she didn't understand, it had let her go.

Put him down. Her thought-command rippled through the Cyclops brain, but tapered off quickly. The wild intelligence of the baby beast surrounded her, a boggy climate of energy, reflex and faint glimmers of simian reason. Her words were overpowered.

Sierra concentrated, trying not to worry about her own body, if it was well enough hidden. Or if she could safely return to it.

Let him go, she commanded again. It was not the English she hoped would sway the Cyclops, more the sentiment, the command beneath the words.

Suddenly, the baby's paws opened. KB yelped as he plummeted to the ground below, landing awkwardly and violently enough that Sierra was concerned he might've broken something. But he quickly stood up and sprinted to the edge of the cage.

Her control lessened. The energy of the baby giant pushed her along, like a strengthening current. The reins loosening. More, Sierra could feel herself slipping away. She thought of her original body and that seemed the final trigger.

Snap!

She was back in her native, tattooed skin. Shrank down to Sierra Smith. The baby giant made raucous squeaking sounds.

She had to do something, but there seemed little she could do herself. She could... okay, she could enter these things, control them to some extent, take up co-pilot with whatever spirit animated them. Yet here, such a thing felt natural... even, well, necessary.

Glancing toward daddy Cyclops, Sierra recalled the strange way it had obeyed her command to let her go. One second, it had looked at her with hungry rage. The next, bewilderment, then—

She focused.

Snap!

The cavern sprawled out below her, everything like pesky little toys. Papa Cyclops groaned, agitated, as if sending something amiss about itself. Its thoughts were smarter than she might've given it credit for, pushing at her with some simian-level strength of identity. She whirled about, unable to grasp control.

Then she saw: *I'm only in one head.* The other, head glared at its sibling, its one eye narrowing in puzzled anger. She felt like she was standing amid some rush-hour traffic of invisible vehicles, driven by invisible drunks.

A thought struck her: *What if my body dies while I'm in here?* Would she become an orphaned "spirit," if that's what she was? A sentient radio wave, flying endlessly around the island, received by all its inhabitants?

Without even trying—

Snap!

—she was booted from the adult Cyclops, back to her body.

Orienting herself, her mind raced. She needed a distraction, some way of disrupting this rocky domicile.

Claw-on-club?

Yes. One of the more famous monster duels of Boylan films. The Cyclops and the crab were bitter rivals. Territorial beach neighbors.

She found a secluded spot in the grotto, where she hunkered and scoured her skin, forgetting momentarily where her giant crab tattoo was. It was on her foot, by the 'shoreline' of her purple-nailed toes.

She stared at it, as she had the tattoo of the Kraken tentacle. She stared and stared.

Her mind wobbled, the energy grew, and soon—

Snap!

She was somewhere else. A rocky cavern, but different from that of the Cyclops'. This one was more horizontal, stretched like a rugged docking bay, its mouth opening to sun and crashing surf.

It had worked.

This new mind, what she could only surmise was the crab-mind, was more chaotic, a windstorm of instinct and senses. None of its legs, neither of its two oversized pinchers, heeded her input. It was like shouting commands at a river.

But it had worked. The transplant had succeeded. She was here. By cinematic rule, the giant crab was the Cyclops' enemy, its rival ruler of this coastal kingdom. She just had to thrust and hold together the many reins of this crustacean brain, and to steer it properly.

In the crab, she did not feel as much company as she had in the Kraken. Its skull, its shell, whatever, was emptier.

Sierra tried to calm herself, to stay fixed, a statue against floodwaters. She had to assert herself here if she wanted full control, to acquire patience even if she didn't have time.

Concentrating, she wedged out her own groove within the crab, her essence sliding deeper into the beast's, filling its many limbs. She rose and opened the left pincher. A burst of mental resistance from the crab-mind, but this time Sierra overrode it, and by her own volition snapped the pincher shut. Success!

The crab-mind retreated into deeper corners of itself, its chaotic thought subsiding.

Sierra hauled the crab body forward. Movement proved awkward. Turning would be difficult, to say nothing of keeping it on-course. Though she was mostly in charge, constant sensory input pricked the crab, threatening to yank it this way or that.

Emerging from the cavern, the surf exploded over her, yet the only coldness she felt was in her mind. Nor did the water sway her. Effortlessly, she clambered up the reef.

Where am I?

The image of the Cyclops crossed her mind, and suddenly the crab surged, anger flaring from its dark corners. Wild, unknown, unknowable anger. There was little else it could be.

It hates the Cyclops. As written. Scripted!

Sierra pictured the Cyclops again. Like flapping red before a bull, more rage lit up the crab-mind. Its legs moved quicker, and not entirely at Sierra's discretion. She realized that if she just kept imagining the Cyclops, burning it onto the crab-mind, by sheer programming it would take her there itself.

The colossal crustacean hastened over mounds of reef, lashed by waves, until bringing its agile ballet across the beach sands. The Cyclops' cave not much further. The crab's lair, she saw, had the whole time been right near their camp, hidden halfway under the tide.

Go. *Go*! Almost there. The cavern grew larger. Sierra continued feeding the crab's anger with her thoughts of the Cyclops.

A shadow pooled over her. The sun went away.

No!

That cry—triumphant and shrill, the one that had seen Kasey screaming off these sands.

For the first time, Sierra's intent synched with that of the crab-mind's, and the crab halted, raised its pinchers at the black-feathered menace descending, its Roc talons opening as wide as its beak.

GAINING GROUND

More and more, he was spreading across this island, like water spilled onto paper. Seeping. Blooming. He did not feel that he controlled this so much as it was an inevitable process. He was a discoverer, along for the ride. All these animals like some grand, living wardrobe for him.

They were… what? Representations of him?

I made this. I made this happen. Somehow.

Didn't I?

No, that seemed impossible. But it was not impossible that, somehow, this world had been set up for him to enjoy. Continually there unfolded more and more he wanted to see, craved to see, even though he did not fully understand the source of this desire.

Yet it was *clean* desire, without precedent or expectation. The vast buffet of experience was overwhelming, a wonderful gift.

He was like some spiritual fungus, stretching and sprawling wide and far, receiving sensory feeds from every corner and chemical of this island.

In the mountain's rolling tundra, he strutted as a two-legged colossus, bristling with fur as white as the snow depressed by his huge tracks. His roar the very voice of the mountain.

At the same time he was another giant, wielding a club in a cavern, ready to chase down another beast through whose eyes he also saw, and so at once knew the romance of the hunter and the panic of the hunted, a dynamic playing out all over.

He cruised the waters around the island, too, long-necked and casting razor sharp grimaces at the abyss, and he soared in the skies with outstretched wings and reptilian claws, and a breast roiling with fire to unleash upon any pesky adversary.

He was the playground. He had not been put here. He had made here, had grown with it. All things here were his constitution.

In wiggling a toe, he wiggled the grass.

In sighing, he swept rank air from the caverns.

In flexing a muscle, he flooded the river, shook the ground, hastened the death-stomp of some marauding behemoth.

Occupying a permanent seat in them all, he was content to watch, and to feel the tremors of their experience on his own self. If he wished, he could exert more specific control, but why? These creatures operated on the behavioral batteries given them, on the life endowed to them, and it was more entertaining not knowing what might happen next.

Then, there were "those" creatures.

First distinguished by their relative smallness, he came to realize that, of all the animals here, these particular creatures betrayed by far the most intelligence.

To a modest degree, maybe, they could think like him.

What or who were they? They seemed at home here, that was for sure, having erected makeshift dwelling structures across the beach, and toward the fringe of the forest. They had long, hollowed-out objects they rode on the water, and plenty of tools and a language all their own. More or less, all of them wore the same kind of outfit, thin strips of clothing carefully placed across the body, their necks hung with layers of necklaces, their skin painted with abstract designs. While unified by one culture, in physical appearance they ran the gamut: short, tall, wide, thin, pale, dark-skinned, dusk-hued, small eyes, wide eyes, long hair, cropped hair, bald or balding. At a certain level, it was clear they were not one people.

Also clear, though, was that, despite all surface differences, something had brought them here.

Me?

Who is... me?

Most peculiarly, they were the only animals he couldn't inhabit. For he tried to enter these creatures, to see through their eyes, feel through their limbs, to project himself into them and to know their experience.

He bounced right off.

Were they trespassers? No. Intuition told him they weren't. They were supposed to be here.

A word popped out of the darkness: *Natives.*

Given their resources and intellect, he worried that, if they wanted to, they might have the means to take over the entire island. To snatch from him his own creations. Could they, though?

If he couldn't oversee them from within, he'd have to oversee them from without. And if they got out of line, in any way, well... maybe their ground might soon know the thunderous prints of his Tyrannosaurus Rex.

Yet there were signs they served him. Although he'd not been aware of it at the time, it seemed others had come to this island, and that these "natives" had found them. These true trespassers were dressed much differently than the villagers, and they appeared young. He couldn't inhabit them, either.

He did not know how they had found this place of his, his Eden, but they could do little harm, seeing as how the natives had them all bound up in one of the huts—where, on occasion, he could hear their muffled, desperate cries.

CRAWLING BACK

Sierra unleashed a flurry of pincher-snaps. The great bird recoiled, moved in again until meeting another snip at its steel spidery talons. She scuttled around the fluttering shadow, defensive like a boxer, conducting this frenzied dance between sky and sand.

The bird kept squawking, rising frustration in its cry. It swooped down again and she managed to snag in her pincher the avian terror's left ankle. It screeched in disbelieving rage. A storm of beak hailed upon her crab-shell, hammered cracks that sounded worse than they felt. She squeezed and squeezed until—*pop!*—the entire clawed foot, crowned in torn metal, collapsed on the beach.

Exploding in fury, the bird eclipsed her, shrouding the entire crab in feathery nightfall. *Can't get away.* She lunged at the torso, cutting, snipping, pinchers flying. *Fuck.* More screeching. Cracking. Blows and more blows rattling her, the whole island, the ocean. If the bird was to—

Wait.

So focused on the cave, the Cyclops, on fending off airborne death, Sierra hadn't thought of inhabiting the bird, if only to steer it away, get it out of her face. Could she? And how long would she have to command it? Time was precious. For all she knew, time had since been up.

Suddenly, in a fortunate and fleeting movement, she found the bird's throat wedged in her right pincher. Its wings whipped up a hurricane, its beak choked out sound behind a wormy tongue. Its lone talon kicked spastically.

All rubber metal-muscle behind her, she closed the right pincher.

The great bird fell, shivered, then lay still, a heap of wind-tussled blackness. The waves strode toward it.

Sierra scuttled away, faster, down the beach. The cave loomed. She was feeling heavier, feeling more of the crab, like she had put on an oversized outfit and was rapidly growing to fill the sleeves and pants. Still she focused on the Cyclops, driving the crab's rage as the cave twisted and curved. She could see much better in here, too, with crab-eyes.

There was little else she could do. The lair was again in sight and the crab seemed to move of its own volition, swept on by inborn purpose.

She heard the phlegmy cooing of the young Cyclops, shut up in that fortress of a crib, then heard whining that sounded on the verge of blubbering and knew it was KB. Relieved he was still there and alive, she stopped and thought, *Am I there?*

A roar. *The* roar. That eerie mixture of lion and wolf-howl and elephant and other, more alien cacophonies. From the shadows Papa Cyclops appeared, mouth contorted, brow rippling in rancor. It reached into a dark crevice and took its familiar, freshly-bloodied bone-club.

It came toward her.

Go, Sierra thought to herself. *Leave.*

The ground trembled with the Cyclops' approach. Sierra tried to project herself out of the crab but her "movement," her energy, was sluggish, as if she'd sunk too far in and needed a helping hand to pull herself free.

Like a soft cushion, she thought.

Or quicksand.

The Cyclops lifted the club, exposing the redness streaked and stippled across it—the caked remains of her crewmates. How many of them were on there?

The crab hissed, raised its pinchers.

Get out get out get out get OUT!

Then... *snap!*

She opened her eyes, moved her legs, wiggled her toes, felt the rough surface of the grotto beneath her suddenly puny body.

She was back.

The Cyclops sent its club toward the crab and the entire cave shook, the thunder rattling loose the shadows. The crab hissed, barely evading the strike. For a moment Sierra didn't move, entranced with this gargantuan gladiator fight playing out, still sensing she was watching this on a giant blue-screen. The creatures shivered in that unreal stop-motion way, but they moved without any sense of choreography, and so the harried fight represented something perversely natural, gritty and half-made. They were creations orphaned to the elements.

She rose to her feet, scrambled over the rocks. One of the crab's pinchers swept over her. Fragments of hollow stone and bone and metal crustacean flew at her, clattering and slicing over the cavern floor against the walls. She managed to avoid them, struck only once by a small discus of crab-shell that whizzed across her back.

"KB!" she cried, right outside the cage.

KB lay sobbing in the same position where the Cyclops had dropped him. Either he was playing dead or too scared to move. The young Cyclops sat huddled in the far corner, its wail like an alien siren.

At her voice, KB snapped his head in her direction. "Sierra?" His eyes were wide, almost too much so for his sockets. "Jesus! Sierra!"

"Climb over, quick!" she called. She kept one eyes on the battle—the crab-pinchers snipping away like jaws at the Cyclops' wrists and ankles.

KB's gaze crawled up the wall of the cage, easily a fifty-foot climb.

"I can't," he sputtered. "Not now."

"Now's the time! Come on!"

He kept sobbing, paralyzed with terror. In his eyes whirred all the calculations and motions his body was unwilling to make. Sierra was not going to coax him out of there.

An idea struck her.

Through the latticework of the cage she focused on the young Cyclops. Its chaotic mind had kicked her out before, or maybe she just hadn't the tenacity to hang on and assert firmer control. But having nearly mastered the crab, she could try again now.

She concentrated. The push began, the gush of spirit that would take her from Sierra to—*snap!*—the baby Cyclops.

A maelstrom of fear here, instinct obliterating all else. She tried not to let it affect her too much. She was in this thing, not of it. The thoughts rioted around her but would not touch her.

"Sierra?" KB called to her body, which had gone limp. "Oh God, Sierra! Wake up!"

Move, she commanded it. The Cyclops resisted, frozen as it was. She sent the message over and over, slicing through the shrubbery of its primitive nervous system.

And then, when she tried to move its left arm, it moved its left arm.

She wasn't sure how long she'd be able to hold command, so she moved fast, or at least with the speed allowed by its oddly simian bulk. She strode over toward KB, who remained unmoving, lips trembling, eyes planetary in width.

"Christ!" he screamed.

Sierra cupped the Cyclops' hands together and laid them next to him. KB eyed her.

"What... what are you doing?"

I can't answer you!

She offered a singular, urgent grunt. Beyond the cage, the crab hissed and the Cyclops roared and there was more thunderous sparring and titanic cries of anguish and hideous cracking sounds careening about the flame-lit cave.

"What's happening?" he shouted at the baby Cyclops. "What's going on?"

And then KB's eyes drifted to the Cyclops' mouth. She realized her tongue bulged against the inside of her lower lip—her unconscious, longtime habit when she was thinking seriously.

"Uh... S-Sierra?"

With minor effort, she made the Cyclops nod.

He glanced back at her limp, human body. "Umm... "

She grunted again, harsher and more urgent. KB moved, crawled cautiously toward the cupped paws and maneuvered aboard. She lifted him as an elevator and deposited him more than halfway up the cage wall.

I got you this far. Climb the rest.

He understood, clasped the lattice and began to climb. Sierra held her position and would hold it until he reached the other side.

Like a flash flood, the baby Cyclops' native brain rushed upon her. In even greater panic the creature resisted her, she riding this mental rodeo bull as it thrashed and flitted. It saw KB and tried to grasp for him but thankfully he had—barely—climbed out of its reach.

Again he stalled, frozen in bewildered terror at the suddenly shifting moods of the Cyclops.

"What's happening?" KB screamed.

The baby attempted to climb the cage. Best she could, Sierra wrangled it back. *Stop*, she commanded it. Yet she managed only seconds of ambivalence. Its raw instinct won out and she was rendered more a passenger than a pilot. It stretched its arm up toward KB, coming within feet of him.

Keep climbing, KB, goddammit!

Then, a tremendous crash. Under the stumbling weight of the crab, the entire front side of the cage burst inward, spraying dust and shards and spears. Before Sierra could even register what had happened, she experienced momentary blackness, and—*snap!*—returned to her original self, where she could see the baby Cyclops, peer up at it slumped over, a jagged piece of its own cage driven straight through its skull, between its two malformed heads.

Whatever life it once had was now gone. Papa Cyclops, swinging that club with operatic intensity, snarling, lunging, dodging, hadn't seemed to notice the death of its offspring.

"Hey!" Sierra called up to KB, who still clung to his perch toward the top of what was now one of three intact walls. She indicated the gaping hole made by the crab. "That way!"

"You're insane!"

But after a torturous, deliberating moment, KB began his descent. Sierra stayed close to the cage, monitoring the battle in which the crab had but three of its legs, the Cyclops half a stringy hand. The two beasts appeared unstoppable, powered by bottomless energy.

Claw-on-club.

Eyes on the dead baby Cyclops, KB clambered down to the cage floor and ran toward the ragged opening, where he met Sierra. They embraced, though it was less like an embrace than two windblown objects colliding midair.

"Let's go!" Sierra said, taking his hand.

Unable to move as nimbly as the crab, the Cyclops kept a limited radius, roaring, sending hammer-blows with its club, which the crab mostly evaded or deflected. The bone-club smashed against the walls and the floor of the cavern, shuddering earth, and the crab hissed and skittered about on its skeletal prancing, pinchers raised, its legs tickling the ground with the lightness of a master pianist's hand across keys. It caught the wrist of the hand holding the club and squeezed and the Cyclops' mouth roiled in rubbery agony.

Sierra and KB maneuvered past them. The Cyclops unleashed all its might into the crab, smashing and slamming. Hissing. Crying. Desperate. The crab squealed, squishy and anguished. It snapped its pinchers long enough to stave off an attack and to prop itself up but the Cyclops struck again with a splintering crack and the crab tumbled crashing into the wall, its legs and pinchers and eyes quivering in a palsy of death. The giant charged after it and Sierra and KB disappeared down the shadowed throat of the cave and out onto the beach toward the jungle.

#

They ran across the beach, KB ahead of her, arms flailing like noodles in the wind, his feet kicking up sand. Somehow not even an imminent cliff edge would seem to stop him.

"KB!" Sierra shouted.

Could she project or "snap" herself into KB? Sort things out in his head, calm his nerves in whatever small way?

Slowing, Sierra focused on him, blurring all else around him. She tried to channel, to unlock, wield, unleash—however it went—that fluid self, to cast it toward KB.

Nothing.

Real brains are too cluttered.

Maybe.

She thought how "Maybe" had indeed become a defining word lately. Appropriate. What else was there to the illusive fantasy of existence than Maybe? Before God would have said, "Let there be light," He would have had to utter, "Maybe…"

The neural thickets of organic brains would be too easy to get snarled in. These synthetic minds, if, again, they could be classified as "minds," were cleaner. Up for grabs.

Maybe.

But, she knew, there was something else here, too. Each creature Sierra had thus far inhabited had possessed its own, primitive personality. That was quite clear. Some were stronger than others, harder to command, as if resenting the imposing will of a foreign voice. In a creature's mind, there were the creature's "thoughts", and there was her.

In retrospect, though, Sierra was beginning to observe something else: another presence, buried deep in every mind. A Master Presence. It was a kernel of some other self, a stowaway that did not exert itself much, at least not in her experience. It "felt" the same in every animal, a singular energy portioned out equally to those two-legged or tentacled.

Was it the "spark" that had made them? That "animated" them? Some glimmering signature of their God?

Because, she intuited, this Master presence, imbedded as it was, felt… male.

Russell Boylan?

Ahead, KB stopped. He bent at the knees, stumbling, looking like he was about to collapse. When Sierra approached him, he turned and glared at her. His fierce, taut expression, combined with his shaggy mop of hair, made him look lupine.

"What did you *do*?" he said. He looked utterly haggard, all humor sapped, the earth of his flesh salted so that no trace of the old KB might ever again grow there. "What did you do to bring us here? Where are we? *Why* are we? Get us the *hell out of here*."

Sierra wasn't sure how to react. That KB also sensed her connection to this island both comforted and exposed her. Her rightful destiny was visibly here. But what was that? And why had others been dragged here with her, only to be eaten, crushed, destroyed? Maybe KB was just accusing her because she was the Monster Girl. Which made sense. She was doing the same thing.

"I don't know what this place is," Sierra said. "I don't know what's going on. I don't know how any of this is possible. I don't—I don't—"

"We're in a goddamn Russell Boylan movie," KB said. "Like we went right into the screen. Nothing else is out there. Have you seen a single light of a ship or a plane in the sky or a satellite across the stars? Anything? Nothing. We're trapped in some fucking screen."

He was right. There had been no signs that a world existed beyond the island's reefs. The horizon like a wraparound mural, never to change.

"I…" KB started, then hesitated.

"What?"

"I've not been hungry, since I got here," KB said. "Not that I've exactly had the luxury of being hungry. But I've also…"

"What?"

"I've also not had to go to the bathroom."

Sierra took this in. The same applied to her, though she hadn't really considered it. Here, the ordinary demands of the body were moot. As they would be in a movie.

Here, I'm…half-physical.

"We were brought here," Sierra said. "For a reason."

"*You* were brought here, yeah." KB gestured at the rest of the beach, clearly indicating those dead. "All the rest of us are collateral damage."

"How do you know that?" she said, trying to remove from her tone all evidence that she felt the same way.

"Because," he said. "This is your dream, isn't it? An island to yourself, a world of worlds, cut off from the one you always resented. An island of monsters and wonders. Somehow you're making this and pulling me and everyone else into it."

"I'm not making this."

KB shook his head.

After prickly hesitation, Sierra said, "What… what happened to the others? Are they all…"

"I don't know," KB said, as if he'd had that question a trillion times before. "I saw nothing. The Cyclops came after us, roaring and pounding with its thing. Smashing us." His whole countenance quaked with suppressed emotion. "I saw Paul mashed into sauce, Marla belted like a rag doll into the jungle. I fell and I thought I was next. The others scrambled away in front of me. The Cyclops stood over me and lifted me up and carried me back. Put me in that cage with its... god… with its baby… thing…"

Sierra stared at him.

"I don't know where Maxine and the others are, where they went," he said. "If they're still alive."

A roar broke out. Dinosaurian. T-Rex, probably. Not far away.

"We should get higher," Sierra said. "Come on."

They sprinted toward the jungle. Not far in, they found a large, vine-wrapped tree, thick branches splayed toward the sky. Like the one Sierra had slept in the night prior, it made for many possible positions and havens.

Silently and carefully, they climbed. When they'd settled, KB spoke hesitantly.

"What happened to you back there?"

Sierra paused. "I fainted, I think."

"Um…" He squinted, studied her with suspicion but also mounting fear.

One of Sierra's pet peeves in movies was a character who stumbles upon something extraordinary and keeps it to him or herself. The secrecy provides more complex, interesting drama, of course, but given all that could be resolved by just telling another person, she often found herself yelling, *Just blurt it out already. It'll take two minutes*!

So just blurt it out already.

"The baby Cyclops…" KB said.

"I can leave my body," Sierra said. "I can leave my body here."

KB blinked. "What?"

"I don't know how, or why, I can do it." She shifted her position. "But apparently I can project myself into the heads of these creatures. I was in the baby Cyclops, you saw. I was in the crab. For a while."

"What do you mean, 'project yourself?'"

Sierra shrugged. "I don't know. My mind? Spirit? I can move these things, at least for a period of time. There's a push-pull between their brains, and me."

"You can control these things."

"Not too easily, not at first. I think it depends on the creature. I don't understand it myself." Sierra gestured toward her head. "At least my brain doesn't. I feel like some part of me does know more about it. Because it makes weird sense here. I feel looser, less solid. Like I can melt myself down, or rebuild myself."

KB shook his head. "I just don't… I don't know what to say to that. I mean, I can't do it."

"How do you know? You can try."

KB threw up his hands. "I still don't even believe it's possible."

Sierra had a sudden urge to shake him, to jostle back into place the old KB of Dale, of several days ago, who was always so willing to follow her into that dark forest, down all kinds of weird avenues.

"I'm still waiting to wake up," he said.

"Okay," said Sierra. "Then it's all a dream. And you can do anything."

"I could never control my dreams."

Eyes never leaving his, Sierra held out her right wrist, coiled in Elasmosaurus. "Focus on this. Think about nothing else."

KB let loose a long, burdened sigh. Somewhere in it, Sierra mused, floated thoughts of strangling her.

I'm sorry.

He leaned forward and closed his eyes.

"No, don't close your eyes," Sierra said. "You have to look at it."

"Because otherwise it doesn't make sense?"

"I never said any of this made sense."

KB stared at the tattoo. His face took on melodramatic focus, remaining so still he shivered a little, and Sierra was tempted to hit him for not taking her seriously. But he was. She knew him well enough to recognize when he was being condescending and when he was trying so hard that he came off jokey.

Then his face softened, his gaze fell away. "I don't want to be an Elasmosaurus."

"Goddammit." Sierra started to move away, but he clasped her arm and turned her back.

"Let me do it again," he said. "Let me try it with the pterodactyl."

Sierra scrutinized KB's face for the smile she might have once expected, the punch line to his indirect way of asking her to unveil her breasts where the pterodactyl tattoo soared through skin-colored skies.

"I've always wanted to fly, remember?" he said. "I want to try."

Without a word or gesture, Sierra slipped off her still-damp shirt. The air on her flesh felt nice.

Her torso bare, the pterodactyl full and squawking silently up at her neck, she righted herself as KB stared and stared at her chest.

Stared.

"Do I have to flap my arms or anything?" KB said.

Sierra relaxed. Clearly he couldn't do it. His disbelief might have been subverting his attempts, but Sierra in her "excursions" had not had to concentrate too much. Nothing more than a dazed glance at the tentacle tattoo had been enough to launch her into the Kraken. The Cyclops Jr. and the crab had not proven much more difficult.

And before that, she had had dreams, dreams whose images continued to echo inside her, albeit faintly, where she had walked or flown in the massive feet of some monster.

She had not made this. It had found her.

She wondered if it was not so cut and dry as her spirit leaving her body. Perhaps she was more an extension of this island, attached to it at some deeper level. Maybe she was like an ice cube in a batch frozen together, and that, when melted a little, or evaporated a little, some element of her was able to move freely through the cracks of the greater body, and become "stuck" to another constituent.

"I have an idea," KB said. "Why don't you become a pterodactyl yourself and fly us out of here?"

She looked at him. "I'm not leaving my body here."

"Oh. Right." He held up a finger. "Maybe you can just carry your body."

She ignored him as an idea struck her. "Maybe I can fly around, y'know, and look for the others."

KB nodded. There was a hint of shame on his face, perhaps in realizing the selfishness of his request.

"Don't go for too long," he said.

"I won't." She reached out and ruffled his hair before he reflexively pulled away, the faintest glow of a smile on his face.

"Can you..." he began. "Can you get stuck in a creature if you're inside it too long?"

"I don't know," she said. "I don't think so." This was, though, to some degree a legitimate concern. Not a time-limit, of course, but, while in the Kraken or the baby Cyclops or the crab, Sierra could easily envision a dangerous melding of minds, a merging of identities that could result in her becoming absorbed into the head of one of these beasts.

"I'll be okay," she said. "Just stay here. Keep watch. Make sure I don't fall off."

"Okay..."

Though at an awkward angle, she stared at the pterodactyl tattoo, blurring all things peripheral. It started glowing.

Snap!

She had never felt such chaos.

In the crab, her presence had been like a campfire: small, but bright and durable, able to withstand the wind. With the Kraken or Cyclops, two more intelligent monsters, she had perhaps been more of a bonfire.

Here, she was a sputtering match, tiny, fragile, bullied constantly by the fierce whipping gales of this mind, a storm of fear and confusion.

Nothing but blackness surrounded her. She felt enclosed.

Go, go, go where?

Up, up, up! Toward the light, toward the sky, toward—breath.

A cracking sound, and the dark ceiling gave way. Daylight speared her eyes. The world was suddenly a pandemonium of sunshine, broken only by quick, squawking shadows, and a much bigger looming shadow.

Off and on, Sierra's mind surfaced. Mentally, she felt like she was drowning, able to snatch mere nourishing moments of identity before plunging back into the murky rapids of this thing that, in snatches of awareness, she could guess was a baby pterodactyl, just born.

How did this happen? Either she just hadn't refined her projecting technique, or there was nothing to refine. She had wanted an adult pterodactyl. She had expected to see the horizon bobbing afar, the island below her and the wind billowing the leathery tarp of her wings.

There had been baby pterodactyls in *Prehistoric Valley*. The expedition leader's girlfriend, in being kidnapped by the mother 'dactyl, had very nearly been fed screaming and flailing to such hatchlings, if not for the last-minute intervention of another crazed and territorial 'dactyl.

I don't want to eat human meat, was the last thing Sierra thought before her mind went below again, blending her with the squawking infant.

6
THE SACRIFICE

The statues were… him.

What?

Had he an individual body, he would have blinked, recoiled, even gagged a little. The statues were absolutely *not* him.

But they were.

Yes, okay. A deeper part of him knew it to be true, that the carved monoliths, with their hairless scalps, prominent, lumpy noses, the almost comical beady-ness of the eyes, the tiny ears, the wrinkles along the downturned lips, and those aged creases, were indeed who he was. Or, so he hoped, they represented only the idea these misinformed villagers had of him.

That was not his true likeness. He was not like them. He was formless.

He was *everything*.

Nearly every night, the native villagers set a large campfire going, and danced around it and chanted and they would raise up objects in grand ceremony and bow toward the sea and the jungle and "his" statues they had carved, and outstretch their arms in supplication toward the sky and it was all vague and unknowable, except that he knew it was all for him.

They worship me.

"Worship": a new word, a new concept.

One night, he'd hovered over the village, in the body of a young black bird— a Roc, he knew it was called. Torchlight stippled the grounds below, bouncing shadows across the beach. The natives had gathered in a circle, per their usual routine, but the circle was much tighter and they seemed even more energized. The chief of the village halted the ceremony to make a grand declaration.

He did not understand the chief's language.

Then, he noticed something: in the middle of the circle sat one of the young trespassers the natives had kidnapped. The man's arms were tied behind his back, his mouth gagged, his feet twined together. They had brought him out from the hut, where they kept him and the others imprisoned.

He watched all this from above, circling like a dark halo over the beach, and he continued watching as they loaded the struggling tied man onto a primitive gurney. Several villagers broke away from the crowd, two of them carrying the man. The chief visited each member of the party and touched foreheads with them. A sign of brotherhood, he surmised. A blessing.

For what?

For the journey.

Accompanied by villagers with spears and bows and arrows, as well as torchbearers to the light the way, the small party left the native grounds for the jungle.

He hovered over them, kept watch of them down through the trees. The guards were on alert, ready for any obstacle, any ambush. They noticed his presence, or the presence of the Roc. He detected in their eyes a certain veneration. Even comfort.

"He is watching over us," he heard one of the travelers say. For some reason, unlike the chief, he could understand this villager's tongue.

He is watching over us. Were they talking about the bird? He was only in a juvenile body. No, they must be talking about him. Could they see him? Did they know who he was?

He wanted to shout to them, to ask them how they knew, and what they knew, and what exactly it was they were doing. But through the bird's throat it came out only as a tinny cry.

He kept on with the travelers, watched as they crossed two streams and began an ascent toward what looked like the very middle of the island.

For reasons unclear, it concerned him greatly that they should reach their destination. Whatever task they had set before themselves, it was imperative they see it through, and so he expanded his radius, sharp eyes scoping for any oncoming marauder.

So far, nothing but plant-eaters nearby: grazing sauropods, a lone wandering stegosaur, spiked tail swaying, and a restful family of sleeping triceratops. He felt part of them all, as if they were distant phantom limbs, wiggling in breath, in life. And he felt the predators too, even more distant.

The natives' journey climbed higher and higher, vacating the realm of trees for sparser, rockier terrain sloping up into the island's central stone valley, that area serrated with peaks and ruptured by canyons, some of which were bridged by an occasional arch.

And in the center of this center, of course, rose the Volcano, perpetually smoldering, its inner lips pulsing with lava light.

And the bound man squirmed, sinking scream after muffled scream into the gag around his mouth.

In that larger, unseen, multi-creatured body to which he was attached, he felt a tremor. A twinge of interest, not far away. A sensitive beast alerted to the approaching feet of the villagers. In the rocky crevices it dwelt, coiled up tight as a giant spring, acid eyes burning in its dark lair, tongue tasting the breeze.

The travelers were still quite far from the serpent, but the serpent could sense them, just as he could sense the serpent sensing them. He had not dealt much with the snake, and so did not know how obediently it might respond to his commands. Right now, it wasn't a danger.

Another long stretch and they'd made it halfway, thankfully avoiding the area of the snake. As they reached a steep ascent, though, as the bearers of the tied man's platform slowed and glistened with sweat, he sensed many sensations from across the island: a dyspeptic Yeti in the far eastern hills, the pain of a young plesiosaur hunted in the sea, and, at the same time, the satisfaction of its tentacled hunter.

Yet what concerned him most, right now, was the great serpent uncoiling, stretching out into the moonlight, winding curiously through the rocks.

Stay away, he commanded it. *Stay away from the travelers.*

There looked to be no trail worn into the side of the volcano. Often the villagers puzzled over how to circumvent the boulder blocking the ideal path, and they seemed clumsy in their maneuvering. They were not experienced. They had not done this before.

Why were they doing this now? What had sparked in their minds the need for such a perilous excursion? For instilling such fear in the bound man? For even binding him in the first place? Besides the fact that he was not a native.

Up, up, up.

Well beyond range of any creature, they would at least be safe from any digestive tract. It frustrated him that he could do nothing to ease the trek. Sure, he felt the rocks, just as he felt leaves and trees and blades of grass when he wanted to. They were attached to him. But he couldn't bring any influence to the inanimate the way he could to the animate.

Somehow, at some point, the terrain had become fixed like this. He didn't think he'd been responsible for the exact topography of this place, but maybe he had, and just didn't remember. Either way, he couldn't change it.

The caravan reached the very smoldering lip of the volcano. The bound man screamed a muffled scream, hard and loud as he could. The villager whose language he could understand tried to shout over the young man.

"In gratitude for all you've given us," said the villager, "in worship of your greatness, we offer to you this gift."

Then, with a quickness almost too anti-climactic, the villagers deposited the tied man into the smoke. The screams kept on, tumbling down—until they didn't.

And he felt it.

An ecstatic, electrical charge burst through him. All things to which he was connected, every twig or blade of grass, every rock or tree or grain of sand, and every creature fanged or horned, two-legged or four, tentacled or finned, became greater, punched out—*embossed.*

In him, they were all suddenly more palpable, less fragments and more a cohesive body. He was a center. A thing pulsing. He was mighty. He was ignited. He was here.

And he wanted more.

AMONG THE HATCHLINGS

The shutters of her mind went up, went down, went light, and went dark. Sierra panicked. Oddly, the panic appeared to help her, strengthening her presence against that of the chaotic baby pterodactyl's.

But, ironically, in recognizing it, the panic diminished, which lessened her fight which in turn would create panic again: a crashing back and forth of minds.

She tried to focus on the big 'dactyl, directing every ounce of undistracted energy toward it. *Move*, she told herself. *Snap*. The effort reminded her of the few times she'd experienced sleep paralysis and tried wrenching herself out of it.

The crosshairs narrowed, the laser-beam of her attention, energy, homed on the adult 'dactyl, as its wings cut like scythes at the blue meadow of the sky.

And finally… *snap*!

She blinked—then stared at a nest below her. She sat on a nest full of hatchlings. She'd just been there. Yes.

She clenched her much-bigger talons, felt the push of air against her wide wings.

The mother pterodactyl was far calmer to subdue. Sierra could slip herself gracefully into the "groove" of its mind.

She started to fly away, restrained only by the tug of maternal instinct, the notion—unthinkable to the 'dactyl brain—that she couldn't leave the hatchlings for anything other than food. Sierra was able to break through this barrier, however, and rose high, wings trembling in the wind as she took in the vast and versatile spread of land.

Pulsing in the center, ringed by jagged peaks, sat the volcano. In seeing it earlier, she had sensed significance. It was too bright, too *central*, for it to be an accident of "geology."

The volcano is the island's heart, she thought. Or eye—throbbing like Sauron.

She flew down closer, cut over the volcano's smoldering fire-breath. Lava roiled. No one around here. No artifices, no creatures, least none she could see. Absence of evidence, of course, was not evidence of absence. She would have to explore more, see more.

And there was damn plenty to see.

Sierra soared off toward the mountains. The heaves of snow-dappled earth were Himalayan in size. The wind grew cold, crystalline. A thick body of mist frosted the tallest peaks, impervious to the winds. Fitting. Those were the clouds, Sierra figured, behind which *The Crown of the World's* colossal Yeti made its home. One could hardly forget that first glimpse of its arm breaking through the fog, reaching with hungry fingers for the main characters' airplane.

A roar exploded over the mountains. She veered away from the clouds, cut downward. The island stretched far below her, a quilted mosaic of pine forest and jungle and snowy mountains, soupy marshland and Mediterranean scrubland and turquoise-ringed shoreline. All so different, but still a panoramic whole: a family beneath one roof.

Sierra noticed movement on the mountain. A small troop of large, rounded creatures, humanoid but hairless and slick like giant babies, had emerged from a cave. Faintly, she could make out the arid snorts of their dialogue.

She recognized them, but wasn't sure if they were the Mountain Trolls from *The Sorcerer's Pendant* or the Ice Ogres from *The Scourge of Camelot*. She leaned to the latter. Boylan's medieval fantasies had been her least favorite.

One of the ogres stopped and glanced skyward, staring at her.

Then it happened.

ON PATROL

The Rex's hunger overpowered all caution and instinct at the sight of that lone creature on the riverbank, back ridged with jagged gravestone plates, its tail sprouted with spikes. Stegosaur, he realized.

Normally they were too difficult to deal with, too hard to eat. Lately, however, prey had been elusive, and there was inborn hesitance about venturing too far beyond the Rex's kingdom. It feared the island's other tyrants.

He felt sympathy for the Rex, wanted to help it find nourishment. He wasn't sure why he granted special privilege to this spindly-armed beast. It exuded such power, yet in its arms it was plainly vulnerable. Maybe that was the appeal—some endearing marriage between fragile underdevelopment and awesome, gnashing grandeur.

The young Stegosaur squawked and turned tail-out. He considered jumping into and controlling the infant, if only to subdue its fight and offer up a willing entree to the Rex.

Somehow, though, that seemed... demeaning. Even cheating, almost. The Director couldn't or shouldn't manipulate everything on his stage. That he might relinquish some command only sweetened that which he did command.

Jaws wide, the Rex lunged. Another screeching squawk sounded, one far louder with all the panic and terror of bitter existence. A titanic, piercing collision struck the Rex's left side and he tumbled down into the river, bellowing like a felled god.

What happened? Another squawk. Challenging. The *mother*. The mother Stegosaur. He glanced up from the slosh of the river water to see her cresting the ridge. He struggled to help the Rex stand, but pain flared in its leg and its arms flailed. He snapped jaws at the Stegosaur but it was undeterred, issuing its battle squawk.

And the Stegosaur, awkwardly positioning itself on the sloping bank, turned at a lumbering pace and rose its giant mace of a tail. The Rex almost had a foothold, but realized it wouldn't make it in time.

He watched all this happening, half in, half out.

Jump to the Stego? No, that was still too certain, and too easy.

But, not too far away, a Triceratops grazed. He moved to it. To any unknowing outsider, it would appear to have been reacting to the conflict echoing just yards down the valley. It grunted. He oriented its bulk and flung it off, trampling down a new pathway of flattened brush.

The foliage parted, revealing the Stegosaur and the hobbled Rex, now about a third of the way back to its feet. The Trike felt a twinge of fear at the sight of the Rex, but it didn't slow the charge as it rammed the Stegosaur in the side, horns sinking cleanly into its clay. The battle squawk became one of anguish and the baby Stegosaur cried too as its parent toppled over and slid down the bank, tail losing none of its defiant and shivery sway.

He straddled his consciousness between the Trike and the Rex and sent the Trike back to the jungle's green shadows. By his invisible hand, the Rex returned to its feet, though its leg now throbbed from the Stego-strike.

The mother Stegosaur lay sprawled there, crying and flailing in its injury. The Trike horns had truly gouged its side. The Rex approached. The baby squawked a petty warning, but when he swiveled the Rex-head in its direction it recoiled and bounced on away down the river and into the jungle. The mother Stegosaur's legs pumped at air, her tail rising, falling, impaling only earth. The Rex loomed, then stopped.

What is that?

Another smell on the wind. Far more enticing. He tried to coax the Rex into having its fill of the Stegosaur, but its fickle nose had utterly intoxicated it and he went with the Rex's impulse, curious himself what that smell was because it was something different, the scent of some whole other chemistry at work.

The Rex stomped off. New meat. The salty-sweet smell of blood—*real* blood—and flesh filled the Rex. It had sniffed something like this before, and the sensation had left an impression on its fruit-sized brain. It was the smell of the trespassers.

THE MASTER

Soaring above the mountains, Sierra felt pressure against her, the chilliness of an enveloping shadow. A haunted sense of something or someone lording over her. *Get out*, it seemed to say wordlessly.

It was a knowing energy, one seeking to intimidate, to drive her away. The presence grew thicker, stronger. It knocked and hammered at her. Tried to engulf her and squeeze and dominate her, but it could not. She had command.

Then it left. A swirl of confusion in its wake.

Dizzy and drained, she flew down and landed on a rock, collapsing her 'dactyl wings and gathering her "breath," her energy.

It felt as if someone or something had tried to press her out of the pterodactyl.

Someone tried to get in.

Sierra collected herself. The 'dactyl mind buzzed in the background, a restless spectator to her thoughts which now commanded it.

Get out.

Was there another one on the island? Another "essence?" Another projector? Whatever she was, in this form?

The Master presence. The Master.

Get out.

Wanting them for itself, maybe?

The energy was faceless. But again, by virtue of its raw force, by virtue of its determination to take, to conquer, Sierr sensed the presence was male.

And, again, she knew there could only be one candidate, the very maker of these monsters. Russell Boylan.

THE OTHER

Like distant echoes, he felt every beast here, even if he did not yet know them all. Still, he had assumed enough of them, tasted through them, walked and strutted and swam in them, that he could formulate a rough list of favorites.

And certainly a new favorite had to be the Great Dragon: the winged, fire-breathing monster—truthfully, a mere pipedream for the stubby-armed Rex.

Sometimes he fancied pitting two beasts together in a fight to the death, to see which one would win. He would have to shun all loyalties, maybe feel the blows and bludgeons from both simultaneously, or one at a time. Clearly battles broke out all over the island, without his influence. From a distance, he'd felt the Cyclops and the crab. The Kraken and the plesiosaur. Tempers and instincts tumbled and tore in volatile course around these hills and forests and shores.

The T-Rex versus the Dragon?

No doubt, the victor would be the Dragon. He loved donning the Dragon, feeling its heated weight envelope him, enjoyed taking to its limited bursts of flight, the canopy below whipping at his claws.

Only problem: the Dragon itself, left to its own devices, ran on a narrow track. Despite its stature, its potential dominance over every one of its hulking neighbors, it balked at straying too far beyond its native region, a stone castle-tower deep in an evergreen forest. The beast was a slave to instinct.

Which included, apparently, nabbing female trespassers. For shut inside its stone tower, issuing cries of desperation, was one of the outsiders who'd come to his island. A pale, young woman with red hair. He assumed the rest of them had been captured by the native villagers.

Occasionally, he would reach into the tower and snatch the red-haired prisoner in the Dragon's claws. The girl would cower and cry, kick at air and pound his scaly fingers, shriek for him to "Let me *go*!" Her scent was zesty and potent. She screamed and pushed when he brought her close for inspection, probably assuming those seconds her last.

If it had been totally up to the Dragon, they may well have been.

Then, something happened.

He was inhabiting the big two-leggers of the mountains just north of the Dragon's tower, the crooked-toothed things called Ogres. They made their home in a network of caves halfway toward the summit, at the bottom fringe of the snow. They dared not venture higher, not only because they physically couldn't, but also because they knew the mountain summit belonged to a much larger behemoth—the temperamental Yeti.

The ogres slept and fornicated. They ate, too, and had developed a taste for baby sauropod dinosaurs, which with great effort the designated hunters would seek in the forests below.

In casually glancing skyward, he noticed through the ogre a strange flying creature, one he hadn't been too aware of before. It was sharp, un-feathered, and appeared graceful though it seemed to move in fits and spurts. Almost like a miniature Dragon.

He forgot about the ogre and tried to enter the flying creature—this *pterodactyl*. He extended himself toward it.

It rejected him. He bounced off, just as surely as he had from the villagers. He tried again—no dice.

Worry rose in him. He tried once more and this time wedged in. Then he felt it: another presence, an *Other*. He could not get any decent sense of who or what this alien force was, before he was sent reeling away from the pterodactyl.

Through the ogre's eyes, through a nearby sauropod's eyes, he stared at the flying creature.

Already occupied.

It was *his*, though. *Everything* was his. This was impossible. He had made the vessel, but someone else was controlling it.

Who was this Other? On this island he was emperor, emperor and maker. Why should he not have absolute reign of every grain of sand and every stumbling or racing or flying beast? Unthinkable, that there should exist minds or places he could not fill with himself, that belonged to something—someone—else.

The Rex followed its own course now. He sat complacently behind its yellow eyes, trundling along the fine track of a blood-scent through the bushes. The smell grew riper, thick enough to bite. He emerged at the base of a large tree. Paused.

Up.

The Rex craned its neck and there it was: a creature much like the villagers, a young person, no, two, sitting frozen and staring at him from the wide perch of a tree branch. A male and a female.

Only the male seemed to be aware of him. The female sat limp in his arms. He noticed odd designs on her limbs, colorful images that took on increasing familiarity the more he peered, until the male-youth turned her body away protectively. His eyes widened at the Rex. The male-youth's body heaved with breath. His leg dangled over the side of the branch.

He stepped forward, all muscles meshing, all bones locked and loaded.

"Get back!" shouted the male. His scrawny arms wrapped around the unmoving woman. Between the thunder of the thing's fear, the Rex could discern whiffs of acrid hormones, the stink of incomprehensible feelings.

"Get the fuck *away*!"

On its own volition, the Rex gave another demanding bellow.

Then they came—shooting sparks that slit the air, fiery pinches across his flesh and again he roared and roared louder as the heat and the pain increased.

More sparks shot down, striking the ground and his legs. His breast.

He looked all around and saw them, tiny creatures that'd emerged from burrows and nooks in the tree, their beady eyes all narrowed on him, their stubby hands clutching bows that flickered a constellation of flaming arrows.

The name came to him: Wood Gnomes. The island's smallest creatures.

In a chorus of tinny cries, they unleashed another barrage of arrows. The Rex recoiled. He restrained its urge to attack the tree, to rip loose all its life. The arrows were small, leaving blackish pockmarks on his flesh and an unpleasant burning smell.

Not worth it.

As the Rex, he strode away into the jungle. He jumped to the gnomes, expecting difficulty with their size. He discovered, though, that inhabiting one meant inhabiting all; they operated in hive-like unison. Easy to manipulate.

Through gnome-eyes he had a better vantage point on the boy and the colorful girl. The female remained silent, motionless. Nevertheless, she intrigued him. Her painted pictures resembled some of the very beasts he commanded. What did that say about this place?

Behind the designs, he sensed the distant vibrations of a power not unlike his own. It unnerved him, and he thought of the pterodactyl that had just rejected him. Did she represent the Other?

The boy leaned in and muttered something to the girl in his arms. The voice was low, but harsh, audible to gnome-ears.

"Goddamn you," said the youth, "you did this to me. To us."

You did this?

The male then turned incredulous eyes to the gnomes. "Um, thank you," he said. "Thank you."

The gratitude would not last long. He moved the gnomes accordingly, lowering every arrow into place. Whimpering, the boy scrambled down from the tree, collapsing most of the way. The girl rolled out of his grasp, but he quickly took her again and sprinted away, a flaming rainstorm spitting after him, the gnomes chittering in triumph.

He flexed the Rex again, brought it lumbering after them. The male screamed. He answered with a roar. Surprisingly fast, especially as he carried the female, this small creature managed to stay ahead of his three-clawed thunderclaps. Yet the Rex was undeniably less agile itself, weakened by hunger and Stegosaur spikes and a brief storm of flame-tipped arrows. He was losing momentum.

The Triceratops, though, was still within range, and in one locomotive push he rocketed the Trike back into the fray, picking up the Rex's trail as the meat-eater trickled off and he left it to wander at will.

He barreled through the trees, snorting, the Trike's powerful pounding gait no less than a metal-boned attempt to hammer the whole island below the waves. Somewhere in its brain, the Trike itself was confused at its own motives, wondering what had possessed it to give this chase.

He centered the horns on the skinny bulls-eye of that backside.

Then, like a quick gasp for breath, a thought hit him.

What are you doing?

"Oh Christ!" the youth cried, as the horns neared, even poking at the fabric of his rear. "Oh God oh Christ oh shit—!"

The Trike began to reassert itself, subverting some of his command. Its fear grew, he noticed, as the environment gradually transformed from fern-choked jungle to drier scrubland, to slopes of chaparral and precipitous sun-baked cliffs.

Warning signals rose in the Trike—it knew its territory, and this wasn't it. The beast quickly became unreliable.

It didn't matter. The ground abruptly fell away beneath the sprinting boy, who yelped as he and the colorful girl he carried tumbled out of sight into deep, deep darkness below.

THE DRAGON & THE DAMSEL

In flying over the jungle toward the spires of the evergreen forest, something caught Sierra's eye—a thread of smoke, pushing up into the sky or the tree line. It was distinct, seemingly located on the coastline opposite the one where she and the others had washed.

A campfire?

Just then a scream, female and young, erupted below. She angled down toward the forest, scouring its shadows but could scarcely make out anything for the heavy pines.

Then the trees opened and she saw it, the enormous wings collapsed together, the arrowhead tail curled along a heaving scaly body, the swaying head and the sharp smoldering snout.

The very *Scourge of Camelot* itself, squatting on its castle tower proper, which, in the film, it had usurped from Merlin the Wizard. The fire-belching, damsel-nabbing Great Dragon. Except in lieu of British B-movie actress Betty Hemsworth, with her princess costume, red hair and capacious scream-queen lungs, it had taken perhaps what amounted to a consolation prize.

Maxine!

The girl kicked and writhed in its grasp, red hair thrashing. The Dragon seemed unsure whether to eat her.

"Let me go already!" Maxine cried.

The creature reached into a tower window beneath it and deposited her back there. A short roar pulsed from its mouth.

Without much thought, Sierra veered, flew straight at the dragon.

The monster saw her instantly and bristled, all muscles in rippling dialogue with one another. Its mouth yawned wide, the beast looking almost ready to laugh, the jaws working with automatic precision.

A hideous scarlet glow pushed up the back of its throat. Out spewed a geyser of flame. Sierra barrel-rolled away from it. She buzzed close, squawking. The dragon tried to snap at her. Its wings remained folded like a horned shell over the rest of its body, concealing armaments it was not yet ready to employ. The dragon—possessive, territorial, maybe even paranoid—did not want to leave its perch unless it had to.

Sierra curved back sharply over the beast, fixed in a tight and loopy holding pattern. The dragon bellowed, shifting its position on the tower. It sent flames at her but she was too fast, unbroken in deploying her only two defenses: irritation and disorientation.

She drew closer and closer. Anger shuddered across the dragon. With a defiant cry Sierra landed atop its back. Finally its titanic wings extended, flapped. The ridge of its spine quivered. She rode a scaly earthquake. The tail lashed the wind, swinging like a manic and desperate serpent.

Sierra squawked and squawked. The dragon thrashed its head, sent fire-tinged roars curdling the wilds around them.

As Sierra turned back from another loop, she saw the dragon rummaging inside the castle tower.

"No! Stop!"

Maxine, screaming. It had taken her once more.

The dragon rose at last. Sierra lifted from its back and began circling it once more, evading the lightning-snaps of teeth. She had to be careful of its wings, those huge angular tarps that could slap her into submission.

Like an upward cyclone they ascended from the castle tower, Sierra the pterodactyl whizzing in tight loops toward the sky, the dragon at her heels (or talons) aching now to squash this pest as Maxine struggled in its grip.

The pterodactyl's native instincts began to boil up again, insisting she escape while she could, but Sierra managed to subdue them.

Can't leave. Can't leave.

Once she found an opening, Sierra folded her wings and divebombed straight at the dragon's forearm, the one holding Maxine. Her beak drilled in its wrist, harsh enough its fingers loosened and Maxine slipped from its palm and fell, screaming.

Sierra folded her wings and dove like a hungry pelican, a feat impossible for the grandly cumbersome dragon. A roar followed her to the tower. With one talon, she caught Maxine by the leg, then swung her away in a wide arc from the dragon before securing her second talon around Maxine's waist.

"Holy *shiiiiiiit!*" the girl shrieked.

An idea struck Sierra. She angled away toward the mountain range.

The dragon's following.

The tide of fire lapped at her, heating her wings and rear. The pterodactyl itself screeched in pain, pain that Sierra, the longer she occupied the 'dactyl, began to feel more potently. And just behind the bursts of smoke and fire the dragon itself loomed, slashing its demonic wings twice the size of her own, its terrible form a hybrid of all powerhouse feats both industrial and natural: a T-Rex in a train. A flying vessel mixed with a volcano.

How did a pile of clay and metal shoot *fire*? It didn't, of course. But neither did synthetic material conspire to produce life. Whatever accommodating principle ruled this place, it had allowed for fake fire, movie fire, to act as rubber did for skin, metal for bone—a stand-in for the real.

The medieval forest segued into snowy mountains, bosomed along the island's edge. Sierra curved upwards, buzzing over foothills and cavern mouths. She tried glancing down at Maxine but the 'dactyl's musculature prevented it. She relied on Maxine's constant squirming and wailing as indicators she was okay.

Lashings of flame behind her, scorching coughs and snorts between roars of frustration. Her advantage: the pterodactyl's size and agility, its fighter plane to the dragon's cumbrous jet.

The dragon sped up, putting its smoking snout within snapping distance of Sierra and Maxine. Sierra evaded it swiftly, relying on her instinct as well as the actual pterodactyl's as she turned and sliced like a leathery machete through gathering shrubs of mist.

Snug in her talons, Maxine sobbed.

The dragon's roar assumed a forlorn tenor—one of fear, she thought. Even panic. It was uncomfortable at leaving its territory. But by rule of its cinematic genes, it would not—could not—allow its maiden to be snatched from it. *That* couldn't be had.

It was those cinematic genes that Sierra now relied on, as she continued her whistling ascent up the mountain, unsure exactly where she was going but hoping her theory might play out. She kept alert for a shadow in the fog, and a colossal forearm that might break the clouds in punishing reach for the airborne incursion, as it had for the low-flying plane in *The Crown of the World*. It was the famous first appearance of the Yeti, its hand, to the gaping horror of actor Rhodes Reason and the other main characters, growing ever-larger upon the windshield before sending their plane whizzing down into these white terror winterlands.

The air grew colder. Sierra worried Maxine might freeze. The girl still squirmed, but less energetically. For several moments the world was unmade by clouds.

The monster was gaining.

A new concern presented itself: accidentally dashing Maxine against an invisible rock face. Sierra rose higher.

Then she heard it: that imperial *roooooaaaarrrr*. Fear exploded in the pterodactyl but Sierra could manage it, though it was getting more and more difficult.

The Yeti's roar itself, that thunderous sound, dispersed the mist before its forearm, which rose like some hirsute whale breaching a gray sea. Its clawed fingers rippled, grasped. Maxine screamed. Sierra did, too, but again it came out in 'dactyl-speak.

Sierra spun deftly past those abominable fingers. She kept on, not daring to look back as the mist closed like curtains behind her, visually censoring what she could hear—the titanic clash of the Yeti and Dragon, two monsters separated by a decade of Boylan's career, whose celluloid worlds had never touched, but whose fateful meeting did not bode well for the dragon as it uttered hoarse gasps, its cries choked by those clasping paws, the enveloping mist faintly aglow with reddish flares of its breath.

#

His focus elsewhere, his feelers were nonetheless everywhere. As the conflict with the dragon escalated, the more he became aware of it. Like a bruise on his body, he could feel the heightening throb of its rage.

He'd inhabited the dragon the moment it had entered the clouds. Vaguely before him: the apparition of the pterodactyl, the one that wasn't him. The one from which he was absurdly barred.

And then the gargantuan arm had reached out for him, grasping the dragon by the throat and pulling him down and away from the pursuit. He knew the attacker. It was called a *Yeti*. He'd inhabited it once before, but to no significant control.

He entered the Yeti for a second time, which was like stepping into a massive, mostly-vacant warehouse. It had much room for intelligence, though possessed little.

For a while he'd wrangled with the Yeti, trying to quell its temper against the dragon barely half its size. It wanted to asphyxiate the creature, throttle it to death. Lame snorts of flame sputtered from the dragon's snout. He'd had to gather every rein of the Yeti's instinct and calm it down, restrain it.

Eventually, the Yeti released its grip, and the dragon, shamed and weak, retreated in broken flight into the mist.

As the Yeti, he roared.

He would not have the luxury, he realized, of much wandering, discovering, of fattening himself on sacrifices. More important business pressed. There was a blight on his body. He realized he had to truly begin claiming everything now, asserting his presence in every rock and tree and grain of sand and animal. To consolidate his power. To amass an army of him.

#

Sierra cut down over the canopy, winding and zooming with her kicking, red-headed cargo across the upper spires of jungle.

"Help me!" Maxine screamed.

You're being helped.

The damn girl continued to writhe. Sierra couldn't tell exactly what Maxine was trying to accomplish, as falling would kill her—though considering what happened to Kasey, maybe in her mind falling would be preferable.

She came upon a stream and followed it, passing over clusters of wading Parasaurolophus—those crest-headed herbivores—and bypassing two sipping sauropods, much of their bodies shrouded in forest.

Further downstream stood a lone baby Stegosaur. She couldn't see Mama and Poppa but knew they had to be nearby. The primitive 'dactyl alerted her to movement in the trees. It was small. Two-legged. Lumpy-looking. No, wait. A person. Carrying another person.

Carrying *her.*

KB!

She veered a sharp right. Maxine yelped again. Sierra slowed her speed, wings pregnant with wind, hovering over the area she'd spotted KB. What was he doing out of the tree? Why was he scurrying across the open jungle with her body slumped over his shoulder?

Something had happened. She vacillated between terror and frustration, blaming herself and blaming Boylan then KB.

She couldn't see him. The canopy blotted all trace of his movement. She squawked, hoping he might look up and see Maxine, whom she gathered had not yet spotted KB herself.

Squawked again. And then—

A tremor of movement! Something big jostled the trees like a loose wig. A low ominous grumble issued from the larynx of deep prehistory.

And she heard a voice squeak:

"Shit!"

The adult triceratops charged, parting the jungle long enough to offer glimpses of what was taking place.

KB what the hell are you doing?

Sierra spotted herself down there, limp and half-naked over KB who, for someone out of shape and carrying another body, maneuvered with surprising agility. Sierra motioned to intervene but remembered Maxine. She wouldn't set her down before she could have a chance to explain.

"Hey!" Maxine shouted down at KB, though in vain.

She had to do something. KB was going to be impaled. Killed. Her own body easily soon to follow. And where would that leave her?

The Big Dumb.

The triceratops halted, crying out in what sounded like fear and disapproval. Sierra noticed they'd neared the edge of more tropical topography, where the land became rougher and rockier and dotted with Ancient Greek-like architecture.

The lands of Sinbad and of Ulysses, where Perseus had encountered his many Perils, not the least of which was the memorably ghastly Medusa slithering through those gray-lit, earthen chambers.

She saw KB, and her limp body, carrying her body over the final stretch of jungle into this new land.

Beneath KB's feet, lightly camouflaged, was a square structure.

A ruin?

And then, like a fastball at her brain, she remembered Russell Boylan's much earlier "ancient mythology" film, the one he later regarded as a throwaway effort, one of several on which he cut his teeth: *Theseus & the Labyrinth.*

"I did always love the design of the Minotaur," Boylan had said. "I just wish that I'd had the chops at the time to do it justice."

For years thereafter, rumors had circulated of a remake, which Boylan didn't dismiss. There was much to improve upon, that was agreed, but little doubt existed that in this theoretical remake would remain one of the original's more popular scenes.

"When the ground opens beneath Theseus and he falls right into the Labyrinth," Boylan had said, "and he hears the Minotaur's roar for the first time. I thought we did that well. It still gives me chills."

7

LABYRINTH

The 'dactyl's wings parachuted as far as they could go, fat with air and she drifted down, down toward that newly created hole through which KB had fallen with her body.

The Labyrinth. She screeched, her descent slowing, Maxine wriggling to free herself more confidently the closer the ground rose up.

Dammit! *Dammit* KB! Why had he moved from the tree? There were probably a thousand possible explanations, all legitimate though not so right now.

She circled a holding pattern fifty or so yards above the hole, spiraling down.

"Jake!" Maxine cried. The girl's squirming grew so fierce that Sierra was tempted to just drop her.

Instead, she set Maxine down calmly and fluttered to a rest, wings folded. Maxine's concern for KB appeared to diminish as her confusion grew over the behavior of this flying dino gently depositing her here. Cautiously, the redhead approached the edge of the open shaft, sending rocks pitter-pattering down the steep slant cascading into shadow. Weeds and roots ringed the perimeter.

"Hello?" echoed a thin voice up from the dark below.

Relief softened Maxine's demeanor. "Hey!" she called. Sierra squawked herself, for emphasis. "Jake! Jake, are you down there? Are you okay? It's Maxine!"

"Maxine?" came the timid reply.

KB's hopeful call was met instantly by a resounding subterranean roar: a terrible sound both predatory and admonitory.

"Yeah!" Maxine called back. "Are you okay?"

"I'm okay, I think," he said.

Another roar. Echoing. Closer.

Sierra squawked again. She shimmied closer to the entryway. The 'dactyl's eyes were surprisingly adept in the dark. KB was down there, bruised but okay. Okay but trapped.

As was her body.

"Jake..." Maxine said.

Slowly, KB rose to his feet. He strode forward, mindful of each step.

"Maxine!" Jake cried. "I'm down here!"

"I can *see* that." Her voice trembled.

"Did Sierra bring you here?" he cried.

"Huh?"

"Sierra. Did she bring you here?"

"Uh... no... I was... this dinosaur thing carried me —"

"*That's* Sierra."

"What?"

"The pterodactyl. The dinosaur bird. That's Sierra. Sierra's *in* that bird!"

"Huh?" Maxine glanced at her, and Sierra made the 'dactyl nod. Rather foreign to its anatomy, the gesture was mildly painful.

"Never mind," KB said.

Sierra extended her wings, ambled toward the opening. Maxine ducked out of her way. The entry was thin, the slant sharp. It could be navigated, she thought, with some inhuman adroitness.

She began squeezing itself through, sidling with tentative ease, talons splayed across the ramp as she made her clambering descent.

Another roar. Sierra kept on.

"I don't know where you are," KB said to her. "I mean, I don't know where your body is…"

"Jake, what is that?" Maxine called above. "That horrid noise?"

She drew closer, closer. As did the bellows. KB began crawling up the slant on his stomach to meet her halfway. The incline was slick but he managed. When they were near enough, he reached for her.

She encircled both his forearms in one firm talon-grip and, in strong pulses of her wings, she brought him back to light. She dropped KB next to Maxine, who sat watching the whole process in a rapture that to Sierra looked just plain short-circuited.

KB embraced Maxine.

"You're okay?" he said.

"No," she said. "But I'm still here. I don't know how. I don't—I don't—"

He sobbed. "I don't, either."

HEATHENS

Closely, and through aerial eyes, he kept watch of the villagers. For the most part, they persisted in their proper worship, paying homage to the carved stones bearing what could only be his likeness.

As the village sat dark and sleeping, he flew as the Roc over the coastline, circling wide, floating as a huge taloned blotch against the moonlight.

Below, beads of traveling light caught his attention.

Torches. Some villagers were awake. More, they were going somewhere. There seemed only a handful of them. Was this at all custom? Sanctioned? Though nothing stank of any obvious impropriety, suspicion flickered in his breast—or at least the great-feathered beast he presently occupied. Instinctively, he wanted to swoop down and scare them but thought better of it. Not far away from them hung the webbed colony of spiders. They were darker, quieter.

They were more effective at spying.

The spider filled his mind, and suddenly, he filled the spider, four legs jutting from either side of him, body fastened to the sprawling silk on which dwelled hundreds of arachnid brethren.

He crawled from the web, scuttled through the forest that he now took in through multiple glassy eyes.

He hadn't appreciated how much easier it had become, since his Awakening, to inhabit and to animate all life here, to steamroll all other aspects of natural minds, to fully make them *him*. While not certain, he mused that it had something to do with the sacrifices. Somehow, they helped him become. They thickened water into blood. They were taps of a fairy godmother's flesh-granting wand against wood.

Except... the pterodactyl.

Don't think about that.

He pondered the native sacrifices. Regardless if they served him, regardless if all this, every sprout and every breath and every movement, were sourced back to him, the actual logistics of the sacrifice eluded him. How often were they going to haul a person up to the volcano? And, whatever the timeframe, why that timeframe? The village kept prisoners, those assumedly destined for sacrifice. Could he not just ransack the village, maybe as the Dragon, scoop them up and deposit them in the volcano himself and be done with it?

What were the rules?

Calm down. He had to stop thinking so... wildly. He had to have faith in the villagers, who knew what they had to do, even before he had. He couldn't presume to suddenly know better. He would allow them recourse to continue as planned, provided they remained devoted to him.

Hell, maybe dumping ten bodies at once in the lava would overload the system, fill him with so much... so much... what? Life? And make the volcano erupt, effectively wiping him out. Maybe it would give the island a heart attack.

A seizure?

Moving fast, he reached the stray villagers. About five or six of them, he reasoned. High flames snapped at the dark, obstructing their faces. They moved cautiously, covertly, though purposefully. He grew anxious. In a community so worshipful of him, any deviation concerned him.

Increasingly, it frustrated him that he had no control over these villagers. The frustration was compounded by the obvious fact that he had, by unwitting presence alone, made some tremendous impact on them. They devoted themselves to him. How did they know to do that? How had he reached their intuition, how had he touched their hearts and their souls, and, most importantly, most maddeningly, if he'd had their hearts and souls... why had he let go?

All this, of course, had occurred before his Awakening. It had taken place in some forgotten, pre-natal era, when the island had been created.

But that was yet another quibble: if he had made the island, why did he not remember that? And, voluntarily or not, why would that memory have left him?

The small group of straying villagers set upon a clearing, where they buried their torches in the ground, steadying them as a loose ring of braziers. They huddled within the circle, and in hushed tones began chanting. He couldn't make out what they said; whether a failure of the spider's ear or his own ill comprehension, or both, he wasn't sure.

He scuttled closer, toward the dim light. Watched through the marbled spider eyes as these villagers bowed their heads in rhythm, petitioned the heavens with raised arms, much as their greater community had done just before the sacrifice.

Except... they're not petitioning me.

Then they dug, scraping up the soil between them. To get a better vantage point he crawled up a nearby tree.

The villagers' shallow excavation yielded flat objects with faces on them. Masks.

They buried them there. For secret use. They've been coming here.

He grew fearful.

They've been coming here and I didn't know.

Each mask bore the same face. It was clear, though, that it was not his face, or, rather, not the bald, lumpy visage they'd so arbitrarily assigned to him. On each mask a variety of smaller designs surrounded the main face, silhouetted illustrations he could barely make out but which appeared, at his distance, to be symbols of the island's creatures.

The villagers put on the masks, took turns chanting. He studied those painted expressions. Unique beauty there. The big brushstroke eyes, the small pointed nose, the lips. It was all so... fertile. Life-giving. Though still a murky notion to him, he thought: *Female.*

Life-giver.

Other.

He knew something of a twinge in himself. He felt betrayed. These beings were to serve and worship him. They existed on him. Who did they think they were? And what—who—was it that might exert itself against him, who had set foot on his terrain, popped up like a cancer on this flesh of his?

The female-youth. The girl. Yes. The skin painted with beasts and creatures. *His* beasts and creatures. From what he remembered, she looked somewhat similar to the icon now worshipped by these traitorous deviants. But she had been limp, silent.

He remembered that distant sense of power emanating from her, that deep whiff of kinship he'd felt.

These traitorous villagers sensed this power, too. Enough that they questioned, even abandoned, their loyalty to him, which made him question himself, whether he truly deserved such worship. Was he the trespasser?

Who truly possessed this place?

No matter. This Other would have to be driven out, before it took from him all his worshippers and all his creations.

Because without them, he would be nothing. A final exhale to the wind.

MINOTAUR

Sierra maneuvered down the shaft, beating her wings about the dark. The pterodactyl itself surged with terror, but under her control it was more like a contained storm. A pterodactyl had never been here before, of course—probably little to nothing else had. And even though she could fly out, Sierra felt increasing panic at being forever trapped in this maze of night.

The hallway left or right yielded nothing. Her body was nowhere in sight. She supposed she could return to it, so she might see that it was intact, even inhabitable, and to glimpse its surroundings. But that entailed risks, of course. What if she'd be returning to something broken or mangled? Arrive into squealing, thunderous pain?

Then—you can always leave. Snap *somewhere else.*

Well, sure. She might be anything, apparently. *What do ya wanna be when you grow up? When you leave the nest of* you? A Cyclops. A Kraken. A Tyrannosaurs Rex. A Yeti. A Medusa (*was there a Medusa here?*). A Roc. An Ogre. She could be the buffet. But she needed her body; in almost twenty years with it she'd become rather attached. While perhaps not her most ideal or truest form, it came closest of all to whatever that truth was—whatever it was to which the name "Sierra Nevada Smith" referred.

A growl trembled through the corridors. The pterodactyl's prickly wave of terror pulled her in multiple directions, wanting to be any place she wasn't, but Sierra remained put. She squawked, but couldn't tell how much of that was her and how much the pterodactyl.

Sour wind wafted over her. Breath, she realized. Rancid breath. The 'dactyl's prickly wave of terror became a flood, sweeping her on instinct down the hallway, fluttering and sputtering beyond Sierra's control. It whirled around corners, shrieks of claustrophobic horror emptying from its breast.

Where am I? Every thought ablaze. *Christ where am I?*

She tried to remember *Theseus & the Labyrinth*, but in the 'dactyl's sensory rush it was like trying to read Dickens in the middle of a riot. What did this maze look like? Obviously, set construction had not called for a full-on labyrinth. But this wasn't a set; this was the world of the movie, completed. All imagined gaps filled. Question was, how perverse a trial had Boylan conceived his Theseus braving?

Calm down, she told the pterodactyl. She could feel its thoughts, almost like they themselves were made, as synthetic as the rest of its form.

Calm down.

She fluttered to an intersection—four passages leading off into pregnant dark. The growling persisted.

Still powered by instinct, she took off in one direction. *Dammit.* She had lost her footing utterly. Any orientation obliterated. Who knew where her body was. The thought of no exit, of being forever ensnared in this network of stone (the density of which actually felt like stone) now frightened her more than running into the Minotaur.

The pterodactyl said: *Go! Go, go, go! Go anywhere as long as you go. It's coming.*

She said: *Wait.*

Sierra tried to recall the route she'd taken in those blind bursts of panic. Only snatches came to her, islands of blurred imagery. She did not know east from west or north from south. Come to think of it, she couldn't discern these on the outside, either.

She wanted to cry.

Then—the breath. Again. That heated breeze, rank with the smell of death, of hunger. A hunger so strong it would allow no development of mind.

All muscles in the pterodactyl, all its clay-made reaction, pulled at it, but this time Sierra was able to restrain it. She leapt forward, opened her wings and turned and there it was.

The Minotaur: half-birthed from the darkness, at least a dozen feet in height, demon-eyes burning, head and limbs waving and wrinkling and jittery in the torchlight.

It roared.

Its right arm was still in shadow. When it came into the light, when Sierra saw what hung from its grasp, she steeled. The pterodactyl squawked.

The Minotaur held *her*—her body, that inked-up human skin now sagging from its hands like some steer carcass on the rock. Black hair curtained her face.

Sierra focused on the Minotaur. She pushed forward, but the effort was heavy all of a sudden, like moving through mud. Her vision wobbled. Fleetingly, she saw herself—her 'dactyl self—through the Minotaur's eyes before snapping back. She looked with longing upon her body. She panicked.

The Minotaur leaned its snout close to her human body, ruffling her hair with puffs of that foul, foul breath. She shivered. The beast looked at her with a glint in its eyes, half maliciously playful, half pure hunger. It wanted to taste her flesh.

No. No, no—

Sierra tried to project again. The heaviness had lessened, but she still couldn't drive herself fully into the head of the Minotaur. Was it too dense? Certainly no more than the damn giant crab.

I'm losing it, she thought, panic flaring hotter. If that were the case, she had to get back to her original body. There was no way she was going to stick it out as a stop-motion pterodactyl.

Snap!

Her human body felt light, unexpectedly agile. The Minotaur held her in one yawning grip, grubby fingers cinching her waist. She tried in vain to pry them loose. Its breath curdled over her, rot-scented and as foul as she imagined. Slowly its mouth broke open, tongue peeking out like a cautious red worm.

No, fuck you!

In the frenzy she hadn't even noticed the liberated pterodactyl, now fluttering and screeching and bouncing around. It saw the Minotaur and went straight for the snorting beast, streaking claws-out and plowing into the hardened torso with enough force to loosen the Minotaur's grip.

Sierra fell to the ground, took in two lungfuls of dusty stone. The Minotaur bellowed behind her and the 'dactyl shrieked and she clamped her hands over her ears. She looked. With mounting agitation, the Minotaur was about to swing its club at the 'dactyl that stuttered all over it like the shadow of a confused bat. She focused on the 'dactyl.

Snap!

There was no heaviness this time. In fact, she gained control much faster than ever before, immediately pumping the 'dactyl's wings backward just as the Minotaur arced its club, nicking her talons. Then it roared and charged with all the fury of some hell-spawned linebacker, its hooves barely missing her sprawled human body.

Hovering there, she focused on the Minotaur... pushed forward... moved...

Come on!

Snap!

Success! And there she was, across the hallway, encased in this myth-creature. She commanded it to halt and it did, though not without inertia. It swung the club anyway, slamming the wall, then collapsed to its knees. Grunting. Mucus-gurgled breathing. The pterodactyl was now little more than a lump of scales. The Minotaur's two horns bracketed her vision.

In its mind, the Minotaur resembled the Baby Cyclops, except this time it actually seemed easier to find her place within it.

She raised the Minotaur to its hooves again and stared at the 'dactyl, waiting for it to attack her now that she'd left it to its own devices. She was ready for it. But the flying dino barely moved. In fact, it didn't move.

As if it awaited input.

Suddenly, Sierra became aware of a grandness about her, a strength and a capability beyond that afforded in the rubbery sinews of Minotaur muscle. It was like discovering two or three new perfectly usable limbs. She existed not only in the Minotaur, but...

—focusing on the 'dactyl, she flexed a wing—

She was *also* in the pterodactyl!

The heaviness, she thought. I'm growing.

Could she inhabit three things? Why would it stop her at two? Could she feasibly become Lord and Master here, the Puppet Master from whose palm all such grotesque marionettes were strung? Could she dance them across the jungles and sands and mountains however she saw fit, act as a demiurge child playing in her eternal sandbox across one bright eternal Saturday?

Never had she known such a seamless blend of childishness and godliness, the "god" in her feeling right at home in nothing but play.

Maybe, upon reaching god-stage, upon validating the child's suspicion that truly anything was possible, childhood could have its renaissance.

Then came the grim reminder: *People are dying.*

People are dead.

The more Sierra became aware that she existed in two animals, the more her perspective shifted. She could peer through the Minotaur's eyes only, if she wanted. She could peer through the pterodactyl's eyes only, if she wanted. But she could also assume the position of a watchdog seated before multiple security screens, peer through both simultaneously.

Except—she still had to relinquish control of her body. Her original flesh, it seemed, really was a prison. Beyond its parameters, movement and experience might well be limitless. But inside her body, only "Sierra" was possible, only Sierra's abilities, only Sierra's thoughts.

The Minotaur's eyes here were well-adjusted, vision clear. The labyrinth pieced intuitively together in her mind. The passage before her, past the 'dactyl, split in three, the right toward a bed of lava, the center toward eventual wall-spikes, the left toward the tunnel of bats that had enveloped Theseus in a spectacular display of dubbed, pre-blue screen special effects.

None of those things mattered to her now. She was Lord and Master here.

She knew the way out.

With the Minotaur's knowledge of the labyrinth, it was no longer a labyrinth. Sierra strode along in the Minotaur's hooves at the same time she flapped alongside the 'dactyl's membranous wings, twisting, winding, fluttering through the corridors. She held tight to her limp body.

In straddling the two creatures, Sierra bobbed in a state that felt increasingly exalted. Her left arm was a Minotaur, her right a pterodactyl. More arms to come: a kind of Vishnu and a kind of Krishna, slipping into the gloves of all this life.

Finally, she saw it—a light. An exit. She ran and flew toward it, quickly realizing that it was far too small for the Minotaur. Perhaps it was never meant to leave these walls.

As the 'dactyl, she took firm hold of her body, grasping it by the torso, and fluttered toward the daylight. She looked back at the Minotaur standing there neutralized, a perpetual snarl on its lips. She kept herself inside it until she was fully out of the maze. Then:

Snap!

She contracted to only the pterodactyl, ascending over a nearby canyon where massive hammocks of spider web hung.

From below, the Minotaur roared its confusion and belligerence and frustration, likely realizing it had somehow allowed intruders to come in and slip away. But, and Sierra knew this was just speculation, filling that roar also was the desperation of a prisoner.

THE REST OF THEM

Sierra noticed Maxine and KB watching her entire descent, staring up at her as one might a UFO about to land. KB stood behind Maxine, his arms around her waist. Sierra was struck by just how vulnerable a unit they were—two like-beings in a world that was nothing like them.

She flew down. Maxine stiffened at her approach. With his other hand, KB rubbed her forearm. Sierra heard him say, "It's all right."

"Sierra?" Maxine called, directing her attention to the inanimate lump of skin held by the pterodactyl.

KB rubbed his face, massaged his eyes. It was almost like he didn't want to look.

Sierra deposited her body in front of them then flew off. As she did, she saw KB and Maxine rush to her body, probably wanting to rustle her awake. She would return to her body imminently, once she set the pterodactyl down a healthy distance from them. As soon as it regained its native faculties, there was no predicting the flying beast's behavior.

Alighting on a treetop, Sierra focused on her body.

Snap!

She awoke to a universe dominated by the faces of KB and Maxine, both strained, their eyes a few sights away from total delirium. She blinked. She coughed. In her body, her glorious, limited body, she sat up.

"Sierra!" KB said, going in to hug her. She put a loose arm around him. Maxine stared at her with some mixture of wonder and terror and a trace of contempt.

"Are you... okay?" Maxine said.

"I'm okay," Sierra said. "What about you?"

"What happened down there?" KB said. "How'd you get... you back?"

"Doesn't matter right now," Sierra said. Addressing Maxine, she asked, "Where are the others?"

Maxine and KB glanced at one another, recapping in a second whatever sad saga Maxine must have divulged to him.

"They were taken," she said. "The ones not killed by that thing on the beach... they were taken."

"Taken."

"By people."

The word 'people' had an edge that prodded her breast. What people? Other people? Sierra remembered the thread of smoke she'd seen from the air, on the far coastline—just before Maxine's scream brought her snout-to-snout with the dragon.

KB said to Maxine, "Tell her."

Maxine nodded, exhaled.

Sierra listened.

"Back at camp, we heard that roar, when the giant came," Maxine said, "and we just started running, even though we were all sick. It didn't matter we were dizzy or exhausted. We just… fear gave us back our legs, I guess." Maxine closed her eyes. She held up her hand over her brow, shielding her face like a visor, perhaps trying to block out other comments or thoughts. "Okay…"

"It's all right," KB said, rubbing her arm.

"That giant two-headed thing came running down the beach," she continued, "we thought it'd maybe gotten you, Sierra. None of us knew where to go. We ran and looked for some kind of hill to climb. Most of us fell down. The monster roared. It was graceful and ugly and terrifying all at the same time. It loomed up behind us and started swinging its club around—"

Tears now drenched Maxine's cheeks, her story half-sobbed. Hiccups and sniffs between words.

"—I think it got Marla first. I heard her scream, cut off sharply by the club against her body before she went flying into the forest. Blood flew. Everyone else screamed. The club came down again and slammed the ground like an earthquake and I think Paul was killed. Tom and John and KB and Michael and I kept running toward the forest. I was sure I was gonna die and honestly there was a bit of me that didn't care. Anything to get me the fuck out. I was gonna throw up. I fell again. Waited for the crush. Then I heard KB screaming. I look back and now I'm screaming because the monster is dangling him upside down. I thought it was just gonna eat him.

"Maverique came back and collected me, helped me up," Maxine continued. "We made it into the jungle, and found a little empty cave not too deep but deep enough where we didn't feel we'd be exposed. We were gonna have people trade shifts in watching out for stuff. We stayed there that night… and, by the way…"

"What is it?"

"None of us felt hungry," Maxine said. "Or needed to go to the loo. Or drink."

KB and Sierra shared understanding eyes.

"We tried to trade off watch duty," Maxine said. "But Tom fell asleep. And then we were woken up around dawn by… people. There were people there, just outside the cave, watching us."

People here—a timid brightening of hope. Yet, inexplicably, at the same time Sierra felt violated. How had other human feet found this place before hers? A strange possessiveness, tinged with jealousy and resentment, stirred in her. This was *her* island. This was her backyard. This was her new Dale and her playpen and her—

And again, in stony repetition, came the thought, *People are dead. People are dying.*

Sierra wasn't sure why, but she'd begun to assume a kind of ownership of this island. Even in the limited container of her body, she did feel a heightening expansion of herself. It felt like an immersion, similar to being underwater, except the water extended from her, a previously-unknown tissue of energy that encased her, existed around her and had always existed around her. And she, now aware of it, could grow *into* it.

"Who were these people?" she asked.

Maxine sputtered a laugh, which in any other context might have sounded mocking.

"They were natives," Maxine said. "They wore loin-cloths and head-dresses and these boot-things and they had spears and bows and arrows pointed at us."

"Natives," KB said. He looked expectantly at Sierra. "Natives?"

"What did these natives look like?" Sierra said, even though a picture had formed in her mind, and even though said picture derived heavily from movies like *Terror B.C.* and *Dino Island.*

"She just said what they looked like," KB said.

"No, it was weird," said Maxine. "They were... they were really diverse. Ethnically, I mean. There were white people and black people and Asians and Pacific Islanders and Indians and... I mean they looked like those... it was strange. None of them really looked alike. They looked like people now, only dressed up. And they had these sort of glazed, dumb eyes. Like they were brainwashed or something. Like..."

"They were playing a part," Sierra finished.

"Maybe," said Maxine. "I don't know."

Obviously, somehow, Sierra and *The Wanderer* had stumbled into the confines of a Russell Boylan movie.

Or, they'd been brought to it, reeled in as if by a person tugging decisively on an invisible tether.

757 Crashes In Pacific—208 Estimated Dead; Legendary Effects Artist Russell Boylan Among Them.

Sierra of course wasn't sure of where exactly this island was, or if it "was" anywhere in the usual sense, but... was it possible that this island occupied the very coordinates of Boylan's plane crash? Had he stared down the gaunt visage of Death, gleaned its merciless agenda, and, speaking over it, said, "I've actually got some ideas I want to run by you"?

And had Death... listened? Granted him some exception in a quasi-life among these creatures of the imagination?

If so, where was Russell Boylan himself?

She thought of the other presence, the energy that had tried to drive her out of the pterodactyl's body. That conquering, domineering, needful energy.

You don't know. You know nothing.

But she was starting to know. It was part of that bigness she felt. That godliness. Systems, rules, possibilities, potentialities and eventualities were stepping forth from the haze of her mere human understanding, all clarified by some grander lens through which she could now peer.

"These people," Maxine continued. "These... natives, whatever they were, told us that we were trespassing by being here, that—"

"They spoke English?"

"The one who spoke English did," said Maxine. "But he might as well not have. We tried to tell him who we were, that we'd been stranded here, that others had been killed and that we needed help. We said we didn't want to cause trouble and that we weren't trespassers and that we did—do—want to get out of here."

"And?"

"And... his eyes were still dull, dumb. Like he was a puppet, someone reciting lines. As I said, he might as well not have spoken English. And it was good English. He was a white bloke. Sounded American. I didn't understand it. A white American with war paint and feathers and carrying a spear. What the hell? He told us, 'By coming here, you have angered the Great Kundo.'"

Sierra's gut flopped. KB looked at her.

"Isn't that a Russell Boylan thing?" he said.

"No," she said. "It was his mentor's, John Terwiliger. It's what got Boylan started, though. He saw it as a kid."

"Saw what?" Maxine said.

"*The Great Kundo*, it's a movie. One of the first big monster movies."

Many more erudite than KB had erroneously given Russell Boylan credit for *The Great Kundo*, understandable since Boylan's filmography and ambitions so exceeded that of his mentor. It was a perfect example of the oft-misunderstood mantra that "Good artists borrow. Great artists steal." They didn't steal the actual work. They stole the spotlight. They dethroned their former king. Or queen.

"So apparently they worship a movie," Maxine said. "All right."

"What happened?" Sierra asked.

"They rounded us up, told us to go back with them so that we might begin appeasing this Great Kundo. They seemed kinda afraid themselves—like they never could have imagined other people would be here. They surrounded us. I could tell Maverique and Tom were itching to get on them but didn't cuz of the spears and arrows they had pointed at us. They led us through the jungle. Any moment I expected some creature. Almost wanted it. The native-people were on high alert. We passed by a herd of those brontosaur things. They blotted the sun for a while.

"We asked where they were taking us. They didn't respond. It seemed like they only addressed us when they needed to. They took us through the jungle and it started becoming cooler and the trees changed until the jungle was no longer the jungle but like a pine forest, like in the English countryside. I grew up a few miles from Sherwood Forest. It was like that. I didn't know what was going on. What had happened. The change was sudden, but not."

All made of the same fake stuff, Sierra thought.

"They seemed to try and hurry us through this forest. I got the sense that this was a shortcut they'd avoided before. Maybe they were trying to get us back to their village or whatever as fast as possible. I heard them mutter the word 'dragon' and, well..." Maxine looked up at Sierra. "Then it came. The *dragon*. Swooping down on us. It was so big yet we'd barely heard it until it was right over us. Everyone shouted and started running and one of the people held a spear at me, barking at me in Spanish, I think. He kept one eye on me and the other on the dragon, and it was like he didn't want me to go with them.

"The dragon seemed only interested in me," she continued. "It wouldn't stop, wouldn't stop until it got me. I tried to hide in a tree hollow but it tore up the whole tree until I was exposed. I couldn't do anything. It grabbed me and just... just took off."

In describing the ordeal, Maxine entered a countenance plain and detached, her eyes in a thousand-yard stare.

"I was delirious," Maxine said. "In and out. Screamed but it didn't feel like me doing the screaming. It kept me in that tower, would pick me up and look at me every once in a while like it couldn't decide whether or not to eat me. I started to wish it just would. I didn't know what to do. My only thought was to scream and hope I might alert someone, somewhere. Anyone. And..." Maxine lowered her head. When she brought it back up she appeared almost agitated, like she was having trouble working a thought through her brain. "Sierra."

"Yeah?"

"Jake," Maxine said, "Jake said you were... you were..."

"The pterodactyl?"

Maxine nodded, slowly. She bit her lip, her eyebrows raised, slanted, her demeanor one of exasperation, weary anticipation.

"I wasn't the pterodactyl," Sierra said. "Just in it. I can move throughout these creatures, become like a puppeteer from the inside..." *Inner animator*, she thought. "That's all I know, though. And I can be..." Sierra laughed, but it was loony laugh, a sputter of madness, "...more than one."

KB stared at her. "At once?"

"Yes."

He blinked.

"Every creature is different," Sierra said. "Some are smarter, dumber than others. Some are easier to process than others."

"How the hell?" Maxine said. "How the *hell*!"

"Think of me as a bird who's just discovered it can actually fly out of its nest and see other trees."

KB studied her. "So, what are you supposed to do?"

A dull sting of embarrassment. Sierra couldn't really answer that question. She'd come into a supreme ability. A supreme *power*, really. And she was still learning it, settling into it, beginning to glimpse, at this elementary stage, the vistas she might yet reach.

I can become the whole island.

Can I?

Right now, beyond the immediate concern of finding the rest of the crew, no distinct purpose existed for all this. It had begun to feel almost like a savage game, a form of brutally artful entertainment.

"That's something I have to find out," she said.

The electric breeze of a thought wafted between them. KB was the first to voice it.

"The others," he said. "If they've been captured by people on this island, natives or whatever, could you... well, could you get them back?"

Sierra, of course, knew what he was insinuating, because the idea had already occurred to her. She could don the body of the pterodactyl and dive bomb these natives' village, wherever it might be. Could, at the same time, storm their grounds as the Minotaur—if it could venture beyond its home Labyrinth—or the

Cyclops, and pluck from their grasp the remaining crew of *The Wanderer*. If they were still alive.

"I can try," Sierra said. "But…"

"But?"

"There's a force on this island," she said. She almost said 'another force'. "A presence. It also controls these creatures."

"What kind of force?" KB asked.

Sierra looked at the ground as she spoke, pacing back and forth within a small space. "It's a force that exists throughout this island, I think. It was weak at first, in the background, but it's getting stronger and stronger. I've felt it deep in every creature. And it's growing in them, like water filling up a well."

She paused, studied the two wearied faces in front of her.

"It's almost like it's trying to claim everything for itself," Sierra continued. "To mark its territory. I think he knows about me, too, that I'm here. That I'm trespassing."

"Did you just say he?" KB asked.

Sierra stopped.

"It feels male," she said. "The force feels male."

The next two words sounded pushed from KB's mouth. "Russell Boylan?"

Yes. Yes. Of course. He made himself god here. This is his realm. We got caught in it, snagged like a fly in a spiderweb. Food for his monsters. Food for him.

"Feed them your dreams," she mumbled.

Feed them to *your dreams.*

He drank blood. Yes. Not literal blood, of course. Boylan was more the energy vampire, siphoning all he could from the world, from others, and pouring it into his work. He'd gained a viral reputation for commanding control, for throwing himself into creative sparring with colleagues, regardless of their rank or esteem. He'd been a demiurge, shuttered away inside mortal skin. And now he'd found a new imaginative sparring partner in Mother Nature.

But what was she, Sierra Nevada Smith, doing here? On his territory? Living and tasting and wearing his masterpiece? If she were honest with herself, past the fog of questions Sierra felt perversely honored.

"I can't say either way," Sierra muttered. "It's resistant to me. It wasn't really at first. But it's taking, or trying to take, the creatures for itself."

"Then what?"

Maybe once he wrangles back control, he'll go storming the doors of the real world, transcend the movie screen, bite and claw and stomp down all dimensional barriers.

"I can't say," Sierra said. "But… I can see which monsters I can take. Which ones I can get into."

Neither KB nor Maxine said anything.

"We'll save them," Sierra said. "And we'll get out of here."

She listened to the rest of the jungle, the cries and roars emanating from the trees. A sense of mission heightened in her, noble and ominous, much as she imagined might have filled the knight or the lord or the general on the eve of war.

And she fixated on that word, as if it were newly learned: *war*.

III
CLASH OF THE TITANS

1
TRIBAL STRIFE

Violence had broken out—villagers loyal to him had discovered the clandestine sect brewing in their midst, the traitorous worship that had drawn an unsettling number of adherents. He still commanded the majority, including the chief, but he felt this issue could no longer be ignored. If these deviant villagers, these deserters of him, weren't the source of the Other, then certainly they encouraged it—strengthened it.

In a burst of spears and arrows, the deviant sect had been driven away, permanently. It seemed inevitable, and they were prepared for it—they'd begun erecting rudimentary shelters farther up the mountain, had carved for themselves statues and idols of whatever deity it was that had hijacked their dreams and their souls.

On several occasions, he'd contemplated taking action himself, maybe storming their rogue village as the Tyrannosaur, send them scrambling in fear back to him. But he held off—for, with every piece of artful homage, the deviants appeared closer to formulating a more concrete image of this Other, just as his worshippers had (somehow) conceived him as a beady-eyed bald man with a small mouth. He had to ensure who or what it was, if it was indeed the painted female-youth he'd glimpsed earlier.

And then, in the center of their puny village, they'd put up a tall stone statue, maybe eight or nine feet high, the largest thing they'd made. Though he did not exactly know the meaning of it, the term "totem pole" came to him: it looked like a totem pole, yes, a column of stylized-though-recognizable creatures, from the Kraken to the Cyclops to the Tyrannosaur, all framed in the body of a humanoid female whose own head rested at the apex.

Her face, curtained by waves of black hair, was sharp with beauty, far more delicate and glorious than the ugly image of him that filled his village below. He was struck not only with anger but envy, a new emotion for him.

In forest shadows he strode as a Stegosaur, keeping just beyond the fringe of his village. Three breakers out to sea, he cruised by as a Plesiosaur. Overhead, he soared flat-winged as the Roc bird.

From all such eyes, he monitored the village closely. The women sat in large circles, sculpting and whittling new deadly points on new spears and arrows. Men, primarily those younger, trained into the night. Preparing a battle. A conquest.

These worshippers recognized the blasphemy of living adjacent to another god, of idling by as it was massaged, exercised, asserted into greater and greater *there*-ness. It was their duty, then, to him and to themselves, to snuff it out.

In the center of a ring of torches, they also readied another sacrifice: a sturdy-looking man with a mustache, who fought spiritedly. If vainly.

As much as he could, he salivated. This ultimate privilege—the ritual sacrifice—appeared his and his alone. Those who worshipped this feminine Other did not participate in any sort of sacrifice. That was because the island's ultimate meaning was him.

But then, he wondered—maybe there was some other source from which she drew power?

STRATEGIZING

At some point, Maxine's hand had found KB's, and held it. They sat there, eyes on the ground, avoiding Sierra who stood collecting breaths and herself.

"I don't know if I'll be able to do this," Sierra said.

"We have to do something," KB said, not breaking his focus. "I don't know what we can do." He looked at Sierra. "But apparently you can do something."

Sierra nodded, slowly. "We'll see."

You're going to save the day. Save them all. How? Where will you go, anyway? How will you get out?

Sierra knew she could not exist in her own body at the same time she existed in any other creature, or creatures. But, free of the constraining capsule that was her original physical form, she may be unencumbered. A liquid ghost.

Yet didn't she need some visual cue in order to project herself into a specific creature? Maybe if she concentrated hard enough, she could hop from one creature to another. But how would she control them all? How could she go from little league to the majors in so short a time?

They needed some kind of a plan.

"I can be the Minotaur," Sierra said.

Maxine and KB snapped back to the present.

"What do you mean?" KB said.

"I can control the Minotaur," Sierra said. "And I can guard you both and guard my body. I can't be—" she gestured to various sections of herself "—*in* me when I'm taking up other creatures." In a lower voice, she said, "I don't even know how many creatures I can be. Or how to be them." She glanced at the Kraken tentacle on her leg. It started to glow. "That's why I have to move fast."

\#

He could feel her growing, in him, on him. He had the advantage, that was certain. He had the worship and the presence but she could well be operating in places of which he was not aware, had not yet mined. He had to cut off, stomp, smash, snip any source of power feeding her.

The traitors had already begun to scatter out of their huts when his brontosaur arrived, screeching, swaying its long neck and stomping upon the small patch of earth they'd carved for themselves. Beneath its thunderous legs, their dwellings crumbled into kindling, their painted feminine idols and statues were ground into pulp, some of the villagers themselves mashed into red pudding.

One sauropod was enough to get the job done—he had gauged correctly. The dragon and two Rocs circled the perimeter, picking off via claw or flame any pesky straggler deserter trying to flee.

He was stretching, settling, twisting tight around the metal bones of his rightful offspring. Not offspring, he thought. *Selves.* Variations of him. Dino-claws. Talons. Hairy eight-legs. Snaking bodies. Tentacles.

RUMBLINGS

Once again, everything became blue, the aquatic world scattered with rocks and phony wavering kelp and little else. The tentacles stretched before her, thick rubbery batons conducting silent music across the sea. The Kraken mind enshrouded her—it was coolly calm, practically ambivalent to her presence.

Then, like an energetic Mac truck, the Master rammed its way into her space, pushing at her. With as much metaphysical muscle as she could muster, Sierra resisted. The Kraken seemed to react to this sudden conflict behind its eyes, thrashing its tentacles at nothing. But it couldn't escape. Its essence, whatever gave it the spark of life, was now the rope in an outlandish tug-o-war. To anything or anyone else it would probably appear that the Kraken, groaning in confusion, had become diseased.

All Sierra could do was hold her ground in this mental fog, focus her energy as well as she could on filling the rest of the Kraken.

A sudden thought struck her: *Can I talk to the Master?*

An obvious idea, sure, but one that hadn't even occurred to her in all this whirlwind.

Focusing, Sierra thought: *Who are you?*

She waited. She had claimed at least three tentacles, but had lost two, leaving about seven more, plus the main cockpit of its mind.

Then came another force, a wind of sensation that above all seemed to say one thing.

I ... am the island.

It was not a clear voice. More a spitball of the subconscious, launched with gooey precision.

I am everything, came another.

Yes, the force that underpinned everything here.

She thought back: *Russell Boylan?*

Her "tone," if such a word could be used here, was neither accusing nor inquiring. The name came out like a strong breath.

She waited.

The singular word came back:

Who?

#

Elsewhere, Sierra stirred. She spread far and quick across the pterodactyl population. Her own leather-winged Air Force, squawking and consolidating across the clouds. They were muscles, ready at the flex. Hers to command.

As was the Tyrannosaur—or one of them, at least. There were many here. She had found a young one to occupy. She was able to spread to an adult one, as well. She tried on a Triceratops, and it fit. Slipped through the long-necked, stumpy-legged sleeves of a sauropod. The dinosaurs were plentiful, the bulk population of the island's interior. The plesiosaurs were more difficult—there were only two she could find, and both resisted her.

Like a spider unleashing lines of gossamer every which way, Sierra shot herself across the island, attaching to whatever she could. The more bodies she added to herself, the greater grew her arms, legs, heads, teeth, wings, the more she sensed some graduation to a new level of being, an Every-thing. Her original body became some old ramshackle home, a puny starter easily forgotten, her connection to it waning in the incredible feed from all sensory channels island-wide, all of which heightened her awareness.

There was an assurance of supreme capability, a constant and silent ego-stroke. She felt loved, in a weird way. Believed in.

She felt worshipped.

By whom, she didn't know. Occasionally she heard what she thought might be distinct whispers, a susurrus of voices filling the back of her mind, like draughts blown through her ears. Sporadically, she would pick up a word of English, but it never made sense. And then, just as soon as it came, it would leave.

And, increasingly Sierra felt like she was coming into that largeness she'd been sensing, that divine expansion of her. Except it wasn't an expansion, she realized—this was the state of being always intended for her, the one that in her old life on regular ol' earth she could only faintly scent but whose source, whose actuality, now stood within tangible reach. All along, that old earth-life, full of nothing but symbols, had been a demotion, a restraint on her natural inheritance.

And now, something else, this Master, sought to restrain her from reaching in full this divine largeness. She wasn't sure why, why it was so belligerent. What was it she'd thought earlier, about this place? That it betrayed an amateur artist's premature efforts on his own Sistine Chapel? This artist, Russell Boylan—he had died an old, wise man, but he was a teenage god.

What are you, *then*? she asked herself.

She really couldn't answer that question. At this point she was three Tyrannosaurs, half a Kraken, an army of pterodactyls, a Triceratops, four winged skeleton swordsmen, and one mountain troll. She sought out other giant crabs and found only two, one of which was a juvenile. She took the adult one. The two-headed Cyclops also seemed available, though, temperamental as always, it resisted her presence within it. With so much energy unspooled so fast across so many creatures, she wasn't sure she would be able to keep the Cyclops in line, but she had to try.

The Master was claiming more and more: the Yeti, the Dragon, multiple dinosaurs, Medusa. She bounced across the island seeking available creatures and would strike these as a bird on a glass pane—deflected.

And then there were creatures like the Kraken, where hers and the Master's influence seemed about level, sparking battles within the beast itself, which felt like a crashing together of two different fluids.

She came to fit five T-Rexes, two of them juveniles—Sierra counted herself lucky to have gotten those. Many of them were taken, and she didn't know the Rex well enough to try and control it herself. Tyrannosaurs seemed a favorite of the Master.

She sought out the herbivores, quite a number of which she found available—the Brontosaurs, the Styracosaurs, the Stegosaurs, the Triceratops, the hooting hordes of paraseralophus. There were smaller carnivores, little raptor-like creatures from *Terror B.C.* that she was able to claim.

In jungle clearings, her Triceratops' feet scraped the soil, readying to charge the Tyrannosaurs lumbering toward her, whose heaving chests knew only the flimsy protection of their tiny arms. The Rexes roared. She sent her own Rexes after the Master's, gnashing at their necks, knocking them down where they would be prime meat for the hungry horns of the Triceratops.

A maelstrom of fangs and claws and scales, thundering across the jungle. Trees crumbled and smoked into debris against the dino-weight crashing into them. Rexes tore in two the paraseralophus, wrestled her Stegosaurs to the ground even as the spiky tail slammed their rubbery skin.

Her pterodactyls were a rain of knives from the sky, tearing, pushing, clawing. She lost a number of them in Rex's jaws. A death was a limb lost, another video screen gone blank.

Sierra had some sauropods, but not many, not enough. A tsunami of them came charging through the jungle, barking and stomping her own dinos. She sent her brontos after them, ramming the horde, bulk on bulk, lifting some of them on their hind legs, swinging their tails and crushing under those pillared feet the heads and necks of those fallen.

Meanwhile, in the sea, she was winning the Kraken, running the Master into a dark corner. With the creaky heaviness of steering a battleship, she hauled the Kraken toward the beach and propelled it forward, tentacles flowering.

The village was in sight. By hazy glimpses she could tell they'd seen her and were running, scrambling, screaming. Closer. Closer. The Master fought back but she elbowed him away. The Kraken was responding more and more to her. She wondered if it was ultimately up to the creatures themselves which of them (which god?) might command them.

As the Kraken, she was the closest to the village. Her dinosaurs, her other beasts, were still a distance away. A few pterodactyls had gotten through the airborne resistance of Rocs and winged skeletons, most of which were commanded by the Master, but there was little a few 'dactyls could really do anyway, before getting an arrow in the chest, or being set upon by those larger beasts.

She sent her tentacles into the village, sucker-slamming the canoes, the campfires, pulling up huts like so many vegetables from the soil. She could see Maverique and Tom, tied and squirming, fevered.

Braver villagers hurled spears at her tendrils, to effects no worse than toothpicks on a python. She flung the offending natives into the jungle, or plucked them screaming from their warlike stance and tossed them aside.

— *something's there!*—

The Kraken spotted it before she did: an enormous, streamlined shadow, torpedoing toward her, toothy mouth wide. Flippers hammering at the current.

A full-grown Plesiosaur.

She tried to turn in time but it had the jump on her, sinking its fangs right into the glassy bubble of her eye, ripping and gnashing in a frenzied tantrum smacking not of indifferent hunger but spite and revenge and war, the Master filling its long sleek frame.

And then, from the air, from over twenty pairs of keen pterodactyl eyes, Sierra spied the behemoth coming down the mountain like an avalanche of fur. It appeared born of the mountain itself, the snowy earth given legs to crush, arms to pound, teeth to chew. It howled.

It was coming.

DESCENT OF THE YETI

Increasingly, his doubt grew that he would be able to totally banish the Other, in all her forms. He could destroy every creature she had taken, nestle himself comfortably into these stolen beasts, but there was never a guarantee that she would be completely gone. There was the prospect that she could spread, potentially obliterate him. Always he would spend his days searching, a neurotic eternity of someone scouring their skin for suspicious moles. What kind of peace would that be? He was desperate.

Maybe I can co-exist with her? No. He refused. He could not allow her to co-opt the power which was his right. They were his creations. They were him. And a suspicious mole was not a good analogy. For she had not grown out of him. She was a splinter, an outside incursion. She had pierced some membrane, opened his private dream to the light where others lurked.

Her source was here, and within reach. The T-Rexes she possessed, the Stegosaurs and the Triceratops, the Cyclops and the pterodactyls, the Minotaur and whatever else, all funneled within these sandy parameters to a source: a tower from which she broadcasted her signal.

Vicious and voracious as they could be, no other beast or dinosaur could accomplish what he now sought: a thorough ransacking of the island, a turning of it inside-out, all stones lifted, all shadows banished, all corners rinsed and lit. To cleanse her from all his pores.

The Yeti. *Yes.* The Yeti. By far the biggest thing on the island. It exceeded the height of the biggest dinosaur. It dwarfed the Cyclops, could observably strangle the Dragon with one hand, and could probably rip into it like a chicken wing. Its roar could challenge the elements.

As far as he knew, his energy was not limited in scope. He could portion himself out to an infinite number of entities. There was no maximum. So saying one creature required "more" of him was not entirely accurate, even if it felt true, as in the case of the Yeti. He stretched long and luxuriously through the corridors of its tissue.

He could flip the island.

Down below, he fought what seemed an increasingly losing battle for the Kraken, snapped his Tyrannosaur jaws at an unceasing horde of Stegosaurs and Triceratops, scuttled in spider-legs upon giant crabs, slapped bat-wings at the wind as he clashed midair with squawking pterodactyls, prowled sauropod feet on pesky mountain trolls.

He did all this and much more. The bites and bludgeons and black eyes reached him from every direction. Up here, though, housed in the enormity of the Yeti, he was detached, some target in a rolling white empire.

He strode from his mammoth cave, into the constant rush of a blizzard. He roared, an instinct that came mostly from the Yeti itself. He thumped his chest. Across the snowy fields he left huge slushy footprints, leading a path down the mountain.

The wind softened. The cold diminished. The heat was new and the Yeti grunted in displeasure, but he had control and kept it moving.

The clouds thinned and he could see the rest of the island laid out like miniatures, where the jungles and forests shook in ripping and clawing and tearing by all predators and their prey within those canopies and on those hills.

As the winged skeletons and Roc birds, he tried to keep the pterodactyls at bay, but a squadron of them broke loose and zoomed toward his Yeti, crying, knifing in taloned unison toward him. He was on a slope on awkward footing—the Yeti was rather cumbersome in this respect, especially now that it was no longer in its home terrain.

He roared, swatted, and swiped at the pterodactyls, but they were too agile. The flying dinosaurs used their beaks to snag patches of his hair and tissue, focusing on his wide giant face, trying like pesky insects to have at his eyes and cavernous ears. All of them flung at him by the Other.

He came upon Mountain Trolls not of his control. Hairy and long-faced, sporting banana-shaped noses and wide shoulders and long curved claws; they were like miniature Yetis—hardly a match. He trampled them, kicked them rolling down the mountain. The rest scampered.

He moved faster, quivering the earth. Persistent pterodactyls still followed. Some he managed to snatch, rip apart, chew into oblivion. The air grew warmer, the wind lessened. The Yeti could function down here. He would make it.

Again he roared, announcing a new arrival to the fray.

LABYRINTH II

While Sierra knew KB's parents had dragged him to church as a child, and while Dale's Pastor Hawkins fiery rhetoric often made it so anyone couldn't not listen, she wouldn't call KB's denomination Christian. It was far more worldly and specific.

Pathetic it might be, and however egocentric for her to say, KB's real religion had been Sierra Nevada Smith, a walking altar, a moving target of worship. She'd lost some of this power as they grew, but not much.

Never was there a more twistedly apt representation of this than down here in these corridors, where she stood as the nine-foot sentry of the Minotaur, club slanted over shoulder, every breath a lordly muculent purr, its nipple-ringed front bathed in sickly light from the surface.

Just behind her, KB sat with Maxine against the wall. Sierra could feel his stare.

She was a monster to keep out monsters, those rousing unseen forms now thundering and screeching, pounding and howling across the island. The Minotaur, she noticed quickly, was a feisty one—Sierra had to assert extra effort in keeping it under her thumb. Every once in a while she swung its head toward KB, Maxine, and her own body that lay there like a discarded dummy.

Once, she saw Maxine crying, and watched KB entwine their hands.

"How are we ever going to get out of here?" Maxine muttered. "We don't even know where we are, or how we're even here."

"If there's anything this place tells us, it's that anything is possible," KB said, "including us getting back."

"Even if we do," she said. "How will we fucking live? Knowing... this exists?"

With the Minotaur's honed hearing, Sierra caught what KB said under his breath.

"It doesn't exist," he said.

Maxine sniffed. "What?"

"Nothing."

Sierra could tell he tried to avoid looking at her own limp body, slumped against the wall opposite them and blanketed in shadow.

The next time Sierra looked, she saw KB and Maxine in a prolonged kiss. KB was the first to withdraw.

"Sorry if that was weird," he said.

Maxine snorted. "Are you joking?"

Something's here.

Sierra righted, growled, backed up a few steps. From the surface above issued a sound like escaping gas, except there were words in it, windy and incoherent but taunting. A hiss.

Yes, it's...

She readied the club.

The intruder stopped. The whole climate fell cold with predatory curiosity. The hissing was breathy and flinty, feminine in a way. A shadow fell upon the lighted wall: a human-like torso, curved parenthetically. A pair of breasts. The profile of a human face, atop which swarmed a gangly nest of serpentine forms.

Both KB and Maxine stood and moved further down the corridor, hugging the wall, bodies heaving.

"What is it? What is that?" Maxine whispered.

Sierra, of course, knew exactly what it was, though it was not Russell Boylan that had introduced her to this particular grotesquerie. He'd only perfected it.

She'd known the creature since her dip into ancient mythology in Mr. Paulson's 6th grade history class. The textbook illustrations had made the monster look classy, even exotically alluring. A demonic seductress. Boylan, however, in *The Perils of Perseus*, had injected into his version his every knack for unruly, herpetophobic nightmare.

MEDUSA

He liked the fluidity of this creature, its flexible, streamlined body. Its arms held two long, curved blades. It smelled by tasting the air. Rudimentary language and intellect whistled through its mind. But he controlled it, this snake-thing called Medusa.

He steered it down the incline, where he heard the growling. Where in the blackness two orange eyes burned back at him.

The *Other*. Another tongue lash—he could smell this beast, but beyond it wafted that scent of fleshly terror that had attracted the Medusa.

He knew this terror. Had sensed it before. He remembered the chase through the jungle, the male-youth with the colorful limp female, the frightened Trike stopping just before the ground opened, spilling the youth and his silent companion into the land's dark bowels.

Something significant was down here.

Swords up, he sprang hissing down toward those fiery eyes, barely evading the arc of the club the Minotaur sent back at him. Only a few of Medusa's scalp-snakes caught the blow, screeching on impact. He swung the right blade at the Minotaur, cutting open its torso. It groaned, pained but still defiant and again it launched its club but he moved defter and encircled his slithering bulk around the beast's hoofed legs.

Then something caught his eye.

Farther down the passage sat a body, human like the villagers. It was the painted female. He could see more of her illustrations now. There was a Pterodactyl. A Yeti. An Elasmosaurus. The Kraken. And more—much more.

Not far behind the body lurked two other persons, that same male from before and a red-haired woman, the very one the Dragon had kidnapped. They watched with swollen eyes. They were the source of the fear he'd smelled.

But it was the illustrated woman that held his attention. He had seen her incarnation in stone and wood, in crude icons large and small. It was her. Yes. He felt it.

The Other.

Two blows found him, slamming his hips where the snake-body began, the other landing by his neck. The scalp-snakes squealed, a seething, writhing storm above his eyes. He fell to the ground, quickly unraveled his body from the Minotaur now towering over him, its snout crinkled in snarl. In the repose of a medieval executioner, it lifted its club and brought it streaking down. He met it with one of his swords and sliced the club in two, and, overcoming his daze, he sprang at the Minotaur, squeezing the Medusa body around it, tighter, tightening, coiling up and up, managing to trap its two arms. The beast sank its canines into him but all he could do was keep on, hissing all the while his inevitable triumph.

The Minotaur was finished. The Other tried to enter the Medusa, tried to pummel him out, but he had too tight a hold on too many of its reins.

At the instinct of the Medusa itself, he centered its gaze on the Minotaur's. An eerie green light washed over the bullish face. He realized it was coming from him, that the Medusa's eyes were glowing and the longer the glow held the harder the Minotaur's skin grew, coarsening, cracking, until the beast became an enormous mound of granite.

The Medusa unraveled, peered down the hallway where the two other humans now scrambled away into the maze, the male one carrying the body of the Other. He straightened out and slithered after them, pouring through the corridors like a slick scaled river.

"Its eyes are glowing!" cried the red-haired girl.

"Don't look!" said the boy carrying the Other. "Don't *look* at it!"

The Medusa was fast. Strangely, even though the male one carried a whole other body, he seemed to able to outrun the red-haired girl. One slight stumble and it was all he needed to whip his serpentine body forward and catch her by the ankle.

"Oh God!" cried the red-head.

The male looked back with horror. Confused. Disbelieving. Conflicted. He set the Other's body down and rushed toward him.

"Maxine!" the male cried.

The red-head struggled as he dragged her closer. He slid a coil around her torso, then another, trying to hold her still though her movements were too chaotic. He sensed, however, that the Medusa's eyes would not work on these creatures, as they were of a different make than the Minotaur.

And so, he alerted every creature in his command to where he was. Where the Other was. He would be able to squeeze her out. To feed her body to *him*.

To absorb her power.

From every nook of the island, his army of all sizes and anatomies began their unanimous march, pumping and pounding, flapping and stalking, racing and bounding toward that sudden center that was the Labyrinth.

Only those creatures commanded by the Other stood in his way, but she did not command as much as he and so there was nothing she could do to prevent him from surrounding her. Every passage out of the Labyrinth, he would be waiting there, jaws at the ready.

Squeeze her out. As if in anticipation, he tightened his coils on the red-head, who gasped.

From the air it was a beautiful thing to watch, this closing radius of his offspring, slicing through the shrubbery, all homed for the first time on one, singular, explosive point.

2

AWAKENING II

The Minotaur was gone, another limb severed. Sierra tried to squirm her way into the Medusa but the Master's command was very near total—she couldn't seep through. She had her creatures collected, though they were a sad cavalry compared with what the Master had amassed around the area of the Labyrinth: fortifying layers of sauropod, Rex, Stegosaur, spider, serpent, Roc, winged-skeleton, dragon…

And, now…

The entire corridor shook, the whole Labyrinth trembled. A series of collisions rained from above, accompanied by a howling, bellowing roar.

The Yeti, newly-arrived, pounded upon the roof of this place, massacring the maze, crumbling it into earth. As pterodactyls, as Rexes, as brontos, Sierra did all she could to try and stop it but the colossus proved too colossal, able to squash Rexes like mice, kick away the brontos like they were pesky, runty dogs.

The Medusa set Maxine against the wall and uncoiled her. She collapsed, dazed. KB lay sprawled on the floor, as did her own body which laid limp and vulnerable. But there was no way she could get at it, having no control over the Medusa, and prevented from the outside by all the other creatures.

The Labyrinth caved in, daylight finding new depths. Both KB and Maxine cried out, huddled together. The Yeti seemed to destroy around them, careful not to actually crush them. The Medusa whirled a coil toward KB and snatched him by the leg, dragging him into dusty shadows.

Maxine scrambled to her feet and tried to run, tried to clamber over the chunks of debris when, in a great heated gust, the Dragon swooped in and reclaimed its prize. She screamed, rising high in its fist.

Wood Gnomes appeared, lifting Sierra's body on their backs and delivering it to a clearing, where the Yeti stopped immediately, its purpose fulfilled.

Through giant crabs, through pterodactyls, through Rexes, Sierra tried to get at her body, but it was no use. The Master had control. The Master was master, and as the Gnomes he deposited her like a sacrificial offering atop the smoking rubble.

As the Yeti he bent forth, a monstrous face pressing down from the sky, and he reached down a hair-tinseled arm and took her body in its paw.

There was nothing else she could do. She threw pterodactyls at it, but with its free arm the Yeti easily deflected them—at least those that made it past the swarm of sword-lashing winged skeletons.

Then, in continuing this creature-to-creature choreography, the Yeti lifted her body in its palm, where a Roc swooped down and took her cleanly in its claws, pumping its midnight wings toward the center of the island. Toward—

The Volcano.

There was no real decision to make. Her body had been taken. In the Roc's curled claws, she hung above everything, sailed limp toward the center of the island. The friggin' volcano. Sierra still didn't totally understand why the Roc or the Yeti themselves did not just swallow her, or tear her to pieces.

The volcano is special. The raw open orifice.

The eye.

The heart.

The generator.

She would not abandon her body. She did not want to be anything if she could not be Sierra Nevada Smith in her original form, that first temple which had allowed her almost two decades of the world's sights and smells, tastes and sounds and touch, in which she had stored her darkest thoughts, filed away every fetish or fantasy stupid or noble, cried every tear, laughed every laugh. She had not always been very kind to it: marking it up, putting poisons in it, but with that body she'd created a universe.

And then—*Snap!*

Snap!

Snap!

Snap!

Snap!

Across the island, from every ravaged battlefield of jungle or desert or water, Sierra withdrew herself, contracted back to her, disrobing the dinosaurs, sloughing off all wings and tails and claws, tossing off all teeth and terrors, her many invisible limbs retreating into two human arms and two human legs, her many minds mingling once more under one skull.

She was Sierra once more, powerless. Caught in the Roc's metallic clasp. She couldn't resist and didn't try to. She barely moved, just gazed at the wilds below.

The Roc descended. The fiery maw of the volcano widened closer, closer. A meditative peace filled her. Sierra closed her eyes as the talons loosened, then opened. Gravity took her and she fell, though the fall did not feel like a fall, more like she was being lowered on a soft platform. She opened her eyes and saw nothing but lava.

No, she thought.

Not lava.

#

She was submerged not in heat but in cold, frigid cold. Like the illusion it was, the red-amber flame cooled instantly to somber blues and grays, and Sierra knew the closeness of two things: water and death.

A long chamber stretched before her, partitions of seated people divided by narrow aisles. Windows black with abyss lined either side. No one moved. Small, strange fish flitted about. Debris drifted lazily, particles organic and mechanical. Every face was a different expression frozen in time, images of death peeling away in rot.

757 Crashes In Pacific

This was it, the place where, after over seventy years of fateful turns and twists and meetings and visions and adventures, after finely crafting the chemistry and the person called Russell Boylan, the cosmos had chosen to lay him down.

She did not see him immediately. But she felt him. Knew he had to be somewhere amid this array of bobbing heads. Sierra was uncertain what she herself was. She did not have trouble breathing, nor was she affected by any currents or pressure. Only the cold reached her. She began to think maybe it wasn't an elemental cold.

Moving down the aisle, she passed grandmothers and grandfathers, some whose hands were twined in that final moment. Passed boys and girls, who looked as if they'd slept through the disaster and now would sleep forevermore. She passed men and women of numerous ethnicities, in whom culture and nationality and age and color had vanished in the face of the vulnerable Human confronting death.

Some, she recognized.

She remembered the comment from Boylan's producer, Errol Maybury.

"Russell was always in charge," Maybury had said. "Even if no one really knew that, even if he didn't really know that, he always was. He drank blood."

Of the island natives, Maxine had said: *None of them really looked alike. They looked like people now, only dressed up. And they had these sort of glazed, dumb eyes. Like they were brainwashed or something. Like...*

Like they weren't totally in control.

They were Boylan's fellow doomed passengers. He'd cast them, as if in a film. Snagged them by their ankles on their ascent to the Big Dumb, wrangled them into the role as the obligatory natives inhabiting this island, the El Dorado of his imagination that he in his prohibitive flesh could never truly realize.

She found Boylan, slouched in an aisle seat toward the middle of the plane. A faint nimbus of light shown about him, a beacon of sorts, drawing her to him. His eyes were closed and he looked peaceful. Sierra moved closer and noticed something striking: he wasn't decaying, not nearly to the extent of the other passengers. It was as if his spirit clung tenaciously to his flesh, preserving their marriage of seventy-three years.

Sierra approached him. If measurements existed in whatever place this was, she would only be feet now from Russell Boylan.

Yes, Boylan had resisted death, had thrown a lighted punch at the dark. The plane had crashed, and Boylan had been eviscerated, not of his physical vitals but of his mental, his mind turned sloppily inside-out, unfolded like a game-board of which he was master. A fugitive dream.

Yes, a dream. One cultivated, fed, in that fertile band of all possibilities. A dream caught in the purgatorial windpipe. A dream made on the canvas of fixed time—in a seizure of natural law.

Sierra touched him, shook him.

Russell Boylan's eyes opened.

#

He opened his eyes.

Suddenly, he was not himself. Or, at least not the self he had been moments ago, the self spread throughout everything he knew to exist. He was another self, a self that, in quick escalation, was feeling more and more right, more and more true, than anything he had known prior. All eyes and ears, all instincts, had shrunk back to him, collapsed to his singular identity.

Haze all around him. Before he could even see where he was, images and memories came flooding back, each one another weight upon him, a piece of clay packed onto his sculpture, a bone or joint rigged into place. The ultimate scaffolding that housed all else. His own grand cinema show illumined, he the son of *The Great Kundo*, the student of John Terwiliger, the creator of twenty-nine visions, the celluloid life-giver.

He was not one thing or another. He was all things and that all-thing had a presence and a name and it was Russell Boylan.

As if watching from a theater, he saw the life of this Russell Boylan strung out before him, a seventy-three-year-long reel of sensation and creation, none of which would have been possible had not every moment of every day of every year played out as it had, all those moments that upheld and made him.

He felt the fulfillment of reunion.

He blinked, realized there was someone in front of him. A young woman. Very familiar. Her. Yes, *her*. He remembered. Realms of Magic Convention in San Francisco. Sierra Nevada Smith. He remembered her movie, *Ancient Apocalypse*. He remembered thinking, feeling, that on some level she was like a part of him that had broken away.

"I know you," he said. "Sierra?"

She didn't seem to know how to react. Confusion, tinged with a bit of torment, tugged at her pretty face.

"I'm Sierra," she said.

Except for her, everything else was starting to blur away—Russell hadn't even been sure where he was, exactly, until this happened. He had been sitting down, next to many others. He began recalling the last moments of his life, the screaming and roaring and smoking tumult of a final descent. How deliriously he had been ripped from this world.

That's not your world anymore.

"What happened?" he asked. "What have I done?"

"You're Russell Boylan," Sierra said.

He sensed more and more the tether that bound him and this Sierra. He had used her. She had never left his thoughts.

He started to remember more. He'd been on an airplane. The plane had struck the ocean, water engulfing the cabin. A great liquid blankness had overcome him. He had resisted it. Tried to beat back whatever had awaited him. His vision, his grand and ultimate vision, had risen in him, around him, palpable, his ultimate dream, his paramount expression, suddenly and mysteriously possible. Like an embryo of imagination, of a world bobbing and seeking nourishment to grow.

More nourishment than he could give it, in fact, and so in that very moment he had called out, reached out over the endless expanse of all connections formed, fleeting or formal or familial, seeking the light of those he could draw from, the minds that knew him and that had sustained him, and in that timeless moment he had been most drawn to the pulsing beacon of a young woman, unlike any young woman he had ever encountered, of any generation, one painted with his creations. He had culled from her living energy, recruited her as the accelerant that kindled this Promethean flame of his, rendering her complicit in this touchable vision that had stirred for so long in their shared souls, absent of all divides cultural, generational, even temporal.

"I'm sorry," he said.

He could think of nothing else to say.

#

Sierra was taken aback by this apology. *Sorry*. It seemed so petty, yet also so freighted with despair, the only thing, perhaps, that could be said. Except suddenly it did not seem necessary. Boylan's spirit had thrown a tantrum, that was all—a riotous exploitation of sudden capacity. A teenage deity testing his limits.

Sierra hung there, unsure herself what to say. Then:

"You're the master," she said. "Masters never apologize."

Boylan's eyes closed, a long blink. He turned his head, gazed out the window. Rapidly his skin was beginning to decay, death carving out new trenches in his skin as it shriveled toward bone. His eyes more and more crater-like. Tiny pieces of flesh breaking off and drifting through the murk. His spirit was still holding on, refusing to join the strong current pulling him to the other side, toward the unknown of the Big Dumb.

"You need to let them go," Sierra said, indicating the other passengers. "You need to let go."

Boylan returned his gaze to hers. He understood.

Sierra reached forward and touched his hand and their hands conjoined, except they weren't folded into one another but actually combined, meshed like two clumps of plasma. Suddenly, she felt like she was going somewhere with him, like she had hitched her wagon to his.

The environment of the airplane became a fragmented illusion, breaking away into another space that was more like a non-space. Neither she nor Boylan were solid. Nothing was solid here. Nothing was fixed. All future creation quivered here, next to all things created and all things that might have been created, mingling indistinguishable from all things imagined, or to be imagined.

God's sound stage, she thought.

She looked at her hand melded into Boylan's, lifted her eyes to his. His gaze proved the hardest object in this space, even if behind it there pressed a young child, palms splayed upon glass, looking into the home of another and asking, in muffled tones, if she might want to come over and play.

Now fused up to their forearms, the growing sensation became harder and harder to resist. The coarse edges of her own self were being dulled by this meeting with Boylan's. There was a supreme rounding out, a harmonious click, a wholeness long in coming and they knew themselves and they knew one another and they now knew a greater thing the fruit of their... union, was it?

They knew a potential power that existed between them, which had, either by natural discretion or oversight, been cut in half and spaced generations apart, buffered by decades, mediated by TV and movie screens. But these two halves had circumvented that nature, left it for this one, this greater Nature that, all their lives, had throbbed its absence in the deep center of their breasts.

"I need to go," said Boylan. "But you need to stay."

"What?"

"You need to go back."

Go back where? Where am I?

Just then, the texture of this realm began to change, grow denser, like a cloth slowly being soaked in water. Oddly, Sierra sensed a growing fragility to it, as well, as though she could grab a piece of Boylan and tear at him as easily as one could a wet tissue.

She was becoming heavier, while Boylan was growing lighter.

And then most of the tissue was pulled away, and Boylan was gone, absorbed into mist. Pressure swarmed upon Sierra, the density becoming almost unbearable, until she realized she knew this density—this was the world to which she belonged, at least for a while longer. It was the thick, hard sand beneath the much lighter, shifting grains on which she and Boylan had been dwelling, and out of which the island had been constructed, and which had now been blown somewhere else, to go where winds might dictate.

All slipperiness, all lightness, was gone. She was back.

Where?

3
AWAKENING III

With every blink she peeled one hazy veil away, until the colors became objects, the round edges sharp, her surroundings shaped into what looked like a small white room. Toxic deja vu rose in Sierra.

Her body ached, felt loose. She imagined someone having hollowed out her organs and stapled them back in wrong places.

She lay in a cot, beneath thin white blankets. She wasn't alone. Sitting in a chair at the front of her bed, just as he had almost ten years prior, was KB. He looked haggard, drained, and stared at her as if knowing any moment she would awake.

Sierra wasn't sure if she were unable to speak, or didn't want to.

"God," he said. "Sierra."

A tremendous image retreated from her, scrambling away from her immediate grasp toward some forever precipice. She reached for it, but it was a dream dissipating, ebbing to only a specter of experience on a faraway vista across a big sea. A big, dumb, blind sea.

Big Dumb.

Dully, her head throbbed.

"Do you remember anything?" KB asked. His voice was hick with skepticism. He had never addressed her this way before—so reprimanding, so parental, so adult. A story swelled behind his eyes.

The Wanderer, she thought. For a moment she assumed she'd spoken aloud. Wherever she'd just been, thought and speech were one. Now they were distinct again.

They watched Ancient Apocalypse. *I...*

This time an image splashed upon her mind: Kasey. Kasey had been swept away. As had others. Taken off into some dark oblivion. It had been night and there had been much water. Everything tattered and shadow.

"What," Sierra said. "What's going on?"

KB's sigh was long. There had been something terrible that had happened. An elemental upheaval. Everything had been fluid and changing and so many forms had become formless, primed for reshaping, for transformation.

For death.

"We're in Darwin, Australia," KB said. "Those of us who're left, anyway."

The words cut at her stomach. Her eyes widened. Across some murkier part of her memory a large dark shape rose up, like an island silhouetted on the horizon.

"We hit a big storm," KB said. "It came pretty much out of nowhere. They called it a squall. Nature's tempter tantrum."

Sierra swallowed. She could feel the tears beginning to boil in her breast, pushing up, tingling behind her face.

Yes, the storm. But it wasn't a storm, was it? It was something inside the storm. The Eye. Like the Bermuda Triangle, some hidden world inside the clouds. Yes.

For reasons inexplicable, Sierra longed to be enveloped by that storm again. Longed to be overwhelmed by it and to disappear into it and to become it.

"Who..." she began. "Wait..."

KB stared at her.

Why is he looking at me like that?

"You ran from the crew room," KB said. "You ran outside just as we were about to enter the squall. The clouds were gathering. It was starting to rain. And... you slipped on the stairs."

Shit...

"You'd been drinking, hadn't you?" KB said. "I could see it in your eyes, the way you walked. I think I could even smell it."

Sierra closed her eyes, inhaled.

"Maxine and I followed you outside," KB continued. "Just in time to see you slip on the wet staircase. You hit your head on the railing and fell halfway down the stairs. It was surreal. Brought back too many bad memories. Your eyes even fluttered, like they did that night back in Dale."

Sierra sniffed, the hospital room becoming a hot liquid glaze. She tried to avoid eye contact with KB.

"The ship died soon after the storm hit," KB said. "Navigational equipment, electronics, all just blinked off. It was almost like the storm knew we were coming, that we were easy prey."

"My God..."

"We were freaking out every which way. What to do. How to go anywhere. You were woozy, in and out. Maxine and I took you to the clinic. Michael also watched after you."

'The clinic.' The term for *The Wanderer's* little medical facility. Mentally, Sierra groped for the very things KB was describing, for the images in between when all this had happened, but they just slipped around her.

"With the ship dead, we couldn't call for help," KB said. "We were sitting ducks. One huge swell in particular hit us hard, flooded the crew lounge. Paul, Marla, Anna, Jenny... hey were all... well... they were... Kasey made her way out, I think, but not for long."

KB studied her with an expression she couldn't read. All this news hovered over her now, dripping its acid into her.

"I stayed with you in the clinic," KB said, quieter. "Maxine and I did."

"How did we get here?" Sierra said. "Who made it?"

KB shifted in his chair. "Maxine made it. So did Michael. And Tom." He mentioned several others and the names wafted over her, Sierra sinking into melancholy. "When the storm started to pass, the boat came back to life. It was weird. It was like the life of the thing had gone into hiding and then suddenly, it was back. We were able to radio for help. It ended up that we were actually only a few hundred miles outside Darwin."

Sierra closed her eyes. The tears fell, tickling her temples and cheeks. "Jesus."

"I got a bit banged up, obviously," KB said, lifting his arm cast. "When they brought us ashore I got sick, too. Came down with a fever. Still kinda getting over it. They thought it was pneumonia. Or some infection from the boat's broken septic tank when it flooded."

They held eyes. She had tumbled to the rim of consciousness, it seemed, where something had reared up from the other side and grasped hold of her, tried to pull her down, down into that big dark dumb sea. Through her, it—what was 'it?'—had tried to reach its tentacles to KB and the others, pull them down with it and with her.

"I hate fevers," KB muttered. "I get dreams. Crazy dreams. I don't remember them, but they're always insane." He looked away. "But you wake up, right? You wake up and you get better."

#

In her dream, she was in an airplane, face against the window and peering out upon the white meadow of clouds. She tried to crane her neck to peer higher, to look up and up and to see if she might grasp where sky became space. But she couldn't. She never could. And then she resumed her seat and glanced around the suddenly empty cabin and knew that she was alone, the only passenger hurtling through this sunny limbo between earth and heaven.

And then Sierra awoke, and sat up in the hotel bed, a fine layer of sweat on her skin. It had been two days since she'd left the hospital, but she still felt sickly and hollowed out, a container that would need time to refill.

She rose from the sheets and went to the window, where the scattered lights of Darwin glittered like tiny souls huddled against the dark. Moonlight drizzled on the ocean, offering the only hint of a horizon dividing the sea and the night sky. The owner of *The Wanderer* had arranged for every survivor a week-long stay at a nearby hotel here by the Darwin shore.

Sierra had already put in for her formal resignation. In four days' time she would fly to Melbourne, from which she would then fly to California. She couldn't help feeling responsible for everything that had happened, even, strangely, the lunatic weather. She felt like something had escaped her, slipped her grasp—a rebellious child, say, or volatile pet—and had made an irrevocable mess of everything.

She turned on the bedside lamp and went to open her suitcase. From deep beneath her clothes she unearthed the remaining Irish whiskey. She retrieved a plastic cup from the bathroom, poured and sipped, soothed by the crackly warmth down her throat, the amber peace now spreading through her.

She returned to the window. An eerie sensation came over her. Sierra stopped, tried to identify it. It felt familiar. A faint charge to the air. The feeling of another presence gathered around her, like mist. Enclosed her.

Not alone.

She downed the rest of the whiskey in her cup. Something in her softened and the presence strengthened, its permanent energy now emanating through whatever passage had opened within her.

"I know you're here," she whispered.

There was a kind of pulse to the energy, an uptick, as if it — *he?* — were pleased.

A number popped into her head: *18*. Sierra sensed urgency behind it, repeating in a soundless voice.

18.

She glanced around, perplexed. Movement caught the corner of her eye, as quick as a flitting bug. The TV? She waited, watched the screen. A brief line of static flickered across it and she understood.

Grabbing the remote, she turned on the TV to channel 18, happening upon a panning shot of monster armatures arrayed across a workbench. Next came clips of spear-toting cavemen fending off a snapping T-Rex, the claw-on-club battle of the two-headed Cyclops and Giant Crab, the Dragon laying siege to Camelot castle towers, the Yeti arm reaching for the intruding airplane.

"Throughout the middle of the twentieth century," said the narrator, "Russell Boylan was the face of Hollywood monster movies, of special effects." Next came a photographic montage depicting Boylan as a suspender-wearing child in the 1930s and 40s. "It is not surprising that, early on, he became a devout worshipper of monster films, particularly the classic *The Great Kundo.*"

After a muted clip showing Kundo's metropolitan rampage, the footage cut to what looked like a theater stage, backdropped by a black curtain, with both the slick-looking host and the featured interviewee—Russell Boylan, as she'd known him—seated in director's chairs.

"I guess I never properly worshipped God," Boylan said, smiling. "I just played him on-screen."

"Or off," the host quipped.

"Both!" said Boylan.

"Any lingering projects you still want to tackle?"

"Well, my head's always full of monsters," he said. "They haven't stopped visiting me, trying to get out even if the flesh isn't as cooperative as it once was."

Sierra poured another cup of whiskey, took a drink. Academic Sierra knew she was in the throes of an extraordinary moment, in extraordinary company, and yet it was so intimate, so right. Like a relative had dropped by. With each intoxicating sip her tether to this world seemed to lose another thread, and she felt like she could recede into this presence enveloping her.

Yet something else came out of the mist now, a form molding before her mind's eye, silhouetted initially but donning shade and dimension beneath the meticulous fingers of an unseen author. It was a wonderfully grotesque thing, a marvelous monstrosity and though Sierra did not recognize it, she did, in a small, revelatory flash, glean similarities between it and her made-up drawing of the Dale Devil that she'd given to Dwayne all those years back.

I'm being consulted, she thought.

Pitched to.

A heightening sense of approval grew in her. Moving fast, she set down the cup and took up a pen and the hotel notepad and began to sketch.

In putting down the first few lines, she noticed immediately a feeling of… demotion, was the only word she could dredge up. There was a time she'd not been this 'separated' from her creatures, with her here and they there. Right? Somehow, sometime, she'd practically been on the page with them. As such, everything she did now came off slightly wrong, a chronic artistic near-miss. Whatever in her had previously signaled that 'click' of creation had since broken.

Or so it first appeared. Her hand remained fastened to the paper. *Keep going.* They were still there, the visions. Waiting to live. She felt guided, an unseen force moving her hand across these stilted attempts.

Two pages later and she was beginning to truly feel it again. *Nice wings.* She carved out the eyes she saw in her head. *Bigger, make them bigger.* She did. Yes. Sierra drew and drew. Soon, the process overtook her, and she was there again the page, dressing her devil-thing like any good parent.

#

It was no longer home, Sierra realized in returning to Aunt Grady's house in Sacramento. She wasn't sure it had ever been home. Though her aunt embraced her, the house did not. She was beginning to think it never had.

The Question had already been circling her mind long before Aunt Grady, over mushy meatloaf and watery gravy, asked it herself, with obvious hesitation.

"What do you think you'll do now?"

Of course. One always had to be *doing* something. Not that Sierra necessarily wanted to ignore the future, which she saw as a cloud bank harboring adventure.

But with adventure, of course, came unknown terror.

She had been so restless, probably because she had never really settled long enough into one place to call it "home." From her dad's trailer to Gran-Jo's to Aunt Grady's house to a bunk on *The Wanderer*. The world had sculpted of her a nomad.

Yet Sierra did not feel much that she did the wandering, more that other forces passed her around like a bad Christmas fruitcake.

"I'll find something," she said.

"Well, you know you can stay here as long as you need to," said her aunt.

Sierra did not so much live her days as watch them, gliding by them as though they and all their players were exhibits, voyeuristic curiosities to be taken in, dismissed. She knew at some dimmer level that this world was not real, that in fact it was all fakery and that so many of its inhabitants participated so willfully and unwittingly in it.

They're dead, Sierra would sometimes think. Such a reminder would inevitably come with an equally unshakable notion.

Because of me.

Some mornings she sprang from bed, ready to forge another path, ready to cram the world into something manageable. Other days, she would awaken and find utter futility in rising from the sheets, her body made of concrete, her mind weighted with stony indifference.

Yet the dreams and the creatures were still there throughout, amassing in various corners in her skull, waiting, as if biding their time for the right moment to assert themselves.

She considered her occasional indifference an indicator of how deeply she truly did feel. It was a coming-down period, a respite between the high and the low. She had felt something high, very high, and her spirit now just needed time now to re-gather itself. To drift in amiable calm.

Or, perhaps, to prepare for the next big thing.

Approaching midnight, the rest of the house ticked on dark and silent. Sierra stood in the glow of the refrigerator, parting items as quietly as she could—the slightest noise could disturb Aunt Grady, even if the woman wore earplugs and closed her bedroom door.

In the very back of the lower shelf she happened upon a lone bottle of her namesake ale. She reached in and took it, then made her soft-footed way to the garage at the end of the hall.

The door squealed when she opened it. She turned on the light and lingered in the doorway, sipping from the bottle, eyes cast over to the corner shelves where shadows and dust had heaped themselves upon the several boxes her aunt had labeled "Sierra's Stuff."

No doubt one of them held her creatures from *Ancient Apocalypse*, all of them crammed together, craning their necks, howling and roaring and snapping their jaws in stationary protest at their purgatory.

What to do with her creature-creations? Sierra squeezed past her aunt's Honda and took the two bigger boxes down and set them on a nearby table. She opened them both. Her monsters, drowned in cobwebbed shadows, stared their dead eyes up at her. A small spider scurried over the brontosaurus. She took a long sip of ale.

Suddenly, increasingly, she did not feel alone. The presence eddied into her. Around her. The electric snap to the air. Her flesh pliable once more, like clay. Capable of anything. Being anything.

She felt urged forward, her spirit caught up in a mounting wave. Purpose thickened in her blood.

She reached into her jeans pocket and unfolded the best sketch she'd made at the hotel in Darwin of the New Monster, the thing almost the Dale Devil that was partially her own and partially someone else's.

It's time.

"I'm gonna need your help," she said, taking another sip.

She put down the bottle and picked up the Tyrannosaurus she'd made, noting its crude deficiencies. She bent the tail, wiggled the arm, opened the jaws. She smiled, pretending to animate the beast and moving it about as a child might a toy, stomping it around her dark dusty corner, this prehistoric terror of the garage.

Gingerly, she placed it back among its creature-family, then rooted through the other box. Old, creased issues of *Famous Monsters of Filmland*. An issue of something called *Eye-Lands*, a publication about movie special effects with Boylan's two-headed Cyclops on the cover. She sensed disapproval when looking at the magazine, as if it were something she shouldn't be keeping. She remembered, then, that it was *Eye-Lands* that had first spoken of Russell Boylan "going extinct."

Elsewhere in the box were comic book adaptations of *Cretaceous Crater*, as well as an illustrated anthology of H.P. Lovecraft. Small clay figurines she'd made about a year before hurling herself head-to-toe into *Ancient Apocalypse*.

At the bottom of the box was an old videotape in a clear plastic container. She popped it open. The label read *Sierra's Birthday Bash*, scrawled in Gran-Jo's trembly handwriting. It had been her first birthday since her father died, and her first since going to live with Gran-Jo, who'd insisted on a party. A bunch of Dale kids, most of whom Sierra knew only by face—including KB, then—had been invited, and their neighbor, an excitable man forever pregnant with a beer-child, had been recruited to film the celebration with his then-new JVC camcorder.

She felt urged to watch it, and so took the video to the living room TV and popped it into the still-working VCR. She made sure to lower the volume.

A blank screen, licked by static. Then—an image of herself, little Sierra Smith, party hat strapped to her head and seated over a crumbly piece of cake. Behind her, other, unknown kids shouted and ran and played. She seemed to be ignoring them.

By the video's date, stamped in the lower left-hand corner of the screen, Sierra realized it'd been taken the very year of the Night of the Terror. In fact, if she remembered correctly, only a few weeks before it. The Sierra before her on the screen was another person, lacking all that had come to make her. The Sierra before her had no idea that in so short a time she would graze the Reaper's robe, that she would soon be driven from her skin to make room for another Sierra— the Monster Girl.

The video stuttered to a new shot: Gran-Jo's trailer, taken in early dusk from the backyard, porch light burning that sickly orange. In the center of the grass sat the rusted ashy fire pit where she would often convene with KB and roast weenies and tell scary stories. The camera wobbled, and she could hear excited child-like breaths. That was me. She was the one now holding the camera.

A memory began to emerge. She had 'borrowed' Gran-Jo's camera, snuck it outside. As it was well past the Night of the Terror, when Gran-Jo had really begun to crack down on her roaming, she must have been breaking all kinds of protocol.

From the left side of the screen a huge shadow descended, a wave of dark sawtooth jaws that clamped down on the trailer, swallowed it into rubbery oblivion. She chuckled. It was her T-Rex toy. She'd held it close to the camera, pretending to have it eat the trailer.

She watched as this newborn Monster Girl lowered the T-Rex, the waning light catching the dinosaur's dumb plastic eye that now peered at her across the years.

Then the video cut to black. Sierra watched and waited for something else to come up, but the screen showed nothing, only flickering static until even that, too, was gone.

4
6 MONTHS LATER

TINSEL TOWN

She did not know Los Angeles well at all, but its infant metro system, covering essentially downtown and Hollywood with maybe a finger or a toe into the Westside, proved none too complicated to navigate. She rode it to Hollywood Boulevard and Vine, where she filed off with many other closed-up faces and ascended the steps toward the bloated Southern California sun, and the urban mania where the sidewalk broke into star-shapes.

Her first stop, of course, would be that famous Chinese Theater, what used to be Grauman's. She couldn't remember the "new" name.

As she walked, Sierra observed all the others around her, and she wondered where they were going, wondered if they knew where they were going, wondered what movie they found themselves the star of. What movies in which they guest starred. Which ones they were merely cameos. They were all extras to her movie. Every stranger was an extra to your movie.

She thought about KB and Maxine, the very reason she was in Los Angeles right now. In two days they would be getting married, in a small ceremony in Malibu. They were moving forward.

Except maybe they weren't. As far as Sierra knew, neither had a real passion or prospect. They were just getting hitched. Maybe marriage was the way people tided themselves over with the illusion of moving forward. At least you'd have a companion in your cluelessness.

She noticed some people staring at her, understandable given that her tank top and cutoff denims unveiled more of her colorful monster-laden skin. Sierra felt oddly vindicated, too, drawing attention in an area where tattoos were like birthmarks, where the eye had options like enormous cleavage and hipstery man-boys.

Waiting at a corner for the crosswalk, she had a sudden urge to look down. Thus far she'd paid no attention to the names she'd walked over, but there was no mistaking the significance of the one now directly beneath her sandals.

RUSSELL BOYLAN

She brought out her camera and snapped a picture of Boylan's star. It was the only picture she took that day.

Another quarter-mile or so and the Chinese Theater loomed—Mann's Chinese Theater, that was it. The building's exuberant facade dominated the block. Was there such a thing as a positive haunting? It had a spirit of dreams made, and dreams beginning. Every glitzy premiere, every spark of inspiration ever had in one of its seats, still thrived here.

People clogged the courtyard of hand and shoe prints from celebrities, their cameras biting off moments and memories. They took pictures with the costumed superheroes. A gel-haired Superman posed with a couple Japanese children. Batman put his arm around what looked like a European teenager. There was Chewbacca and Thor and The Terminator and Wonder Woman and all other fanciful shavings from the imagination, all grouped here.

Sierra stood at the fringe of the crowd. In her mind's eye, she parted the mob, cleared them all away. The scene for her took on a monochromatic tint, almost black and white, silly as that might have been. Mann's Chinese Theater again became Grauman's. And the only people in this illusory diorama, the only ones she saw, were three children, two of them faceless, one very recognizable. It was a face she'd seen in photographs, from documentaries and books.

The leading child was Russ Boylan, ten years old, emerging from the cinematic lair of *The Great Kundo* a changed soul, his wide eyes pregnant seeds of his future, of the coming years that would make him *him*, that, in turn, Sierra realized, would make her *her*.

Who would *she* be, after all, if in 1942 this ten-year-old kid had decided to stay home from the movies?

She raised her camera, prepared to take what would have been a second photo of the day, when from her blind spot a figure approached her. His voice, kind but assertive, left no doubt that he addressed her.

"You're quite a show," he said.

She looked at him. He was a few years older than she, thin, sallow faced.

"*Prehistoric Valley*, right?" he said, gesturing to her pterodactyled chest, and to her wrist. He then pointed at her leg. "The Kraken. From *Ulysses*. Right?"

"You got it," she said, with a faint smirk.

"Awesome. You're like a walking multiplex of Boylan."

Sierra snickered. "Guess so. They're my pets. Never mind the dog." She lifted her tank top, exposing the giant furry menace by her ribs. "Beware the Yeti."

The guy smiled. "I actually met Russell Boylan."

Sierra's focus was so quick and so fierce upon him that the man seemed to deflate a little, pricked by a guilt, perhaps, that he'd over-spoken.

"I shouldn't say I met him," he said. "But I used to write for *Variety*. I went to the premiere of *Cretaceous Crater* and he was in the audience. I was five seats down from him, in the same row. The whole movie I kept looking over at him. His expression never changed. I had to know what was going on in his head—"

"You were the one," Sierra interrupted, "that he made the 'People want to dream' remark to?"

The guy nodded reluctantly. "I always felt bad about putting that in print. He was a hero of mine, especially as a kid. I have all his movies. I guess I just felt a little slighted. But I had to understand where he was coming from. And I probably didn't have the most tactful approach. I still don't. Look at how I just bulldozed you."

"It's fine." Her smile felt more inwardly genuine than it did on her face. "He was able to put in his two-cents. I'm sure he never regretted it."

"I guess. I felt like I added something curmudgeonly to his legacy. People gave him shit for that quote."

"I don't think he's too concerned about that now."

The guy sighed. "I can't imagine he is. I'm Andrew, by the way. Andrew Slater."

She took his hand. "Sierra. Sierra Nevada Smith."

"Like the mountains?"

"Or beer, yeah."

"Cool." After a brief interval of surveying the crowds, Andrew turned back to her. "I quit my job at *Variety*, by the way. I run an online magazine now."

"Good for you."

"I like to write about older films. I got tired of the new stuff. Everyone knows about the new stuff." He gestured to her like a magician waving something into existence. "And, I gotta be honest—I can't help but look at you as a feature post. 'The Ultimate Russell Boylan Fan,' maybe? Right? Right?"

Monster Girl, she thought, but kept quiet. "What would I need to do?"

"I'd want to interview you, if that's okay. Snag some pics of your tats." He leaned toward her. "That's tats, by the way. Tattoos."

"I know, I heard you. You can snag pictures of my tits too, if you want."

Andrew laughed. "One thing at a time. You're just way too quirky to pass up. I mean that in a good way. You're a living tribute to the man himself."

Sierra's only hesitation came from having her solitude so unexpectedly ripped from her, from having her expectations of roaming and wandering dashed. But she had done enough of that, maybe. At least for today.

"Sure," she said. "Let's do it."

"I can give you my card," Andrew said. "Or, actually, if you have time now…"

"I've got time now."

"Sweet. There's a Starbucks down the street here. Let's pitch camp there for a little while."

They started to walk. This abrupt, surreal twist on her afternoon had yet to fully sink in, but Sierra acclimated. She started to feel grateful for it.

Without fully deciding to, she found herself blurting out, "I'm also an animator. Stop-motion."

"Really?"

"Yeah. I guess," she hesitated, clawing at the ether for words, "I guess I'm trying to keep it alive."

"What've you made?"

"Well, I was working on a way-too-ambitious project a while back. But then I switched gears to another one now that I'm doing. Still too ambitious, probably, but I'm bleeding it out of me. I gotta."

Andrew made an impressed 'huh' noise. "I only ask because I actually know a couple producers who love that sort of stuff," he said. "They're big sci-fi and fantasy fans, and big on Russell Boylan. Tanya and Josh are their names. I can probably try and arrange a meeting, if you'd like."

Sierra smiled, tentatively. Everyone in Hollywood seemed to "know a producer" or a director or actor, but it couldn't hurt to say yes. "That would be cool. Not yet, though."

"Of course." They paused at an intersection, where the destined Starbucks awaited on the opposite corner. "For starters, they're called Miskatonic Productions. How's that for a name?"

Sierra laughed at the repurposed name of H.P. Lovecraft's fictional university. "That's awesome."

She thought of Dwayne, his Cthulhu fishing hat, how Gran-Jo had always pressed her to be 'pure' and how she had taken the wish to heart, aiming herself to be nothing less—even if her personal idea of 'purity' differed vastly from her grandmother's.

The light changed and they crossed the street.

"So, you from L.A?" Andrew asked.

"Not from L.A.," Sierra said. "Place called Dale, in Northern California."

"A town, I guess? Never heard of it."

"Kind of," Sierra said. "It's a splatter of trailer and mobile homes. It looks like the droppings of a giant seagull."

#

Perched on an ocean-view cliff, Sierra sat and watched KB fidget at the altar, his wide-spaced teeth spread in an anxious grin. The music played and mothers and fathers and flower children and the flower dog and the groomsmen and the bridesmaids trickled down the aisle, through a blooming garden of watchful eyes.

Sierra watched with them, but was actually pondering what the earlier version of the Tyrannosaurus Rex's arms had been like, before evolution had defunded that particular project.

Then, Maxine appeared, drifting angelic toward her fiancé. Cameras went off. She reached the altar, the music stopped, and KB and Maxine took hands and the reverend spoke.

And spoke.

They exchanged vows.

Sierra fixated on the backdrop of the Pacific Ocean. The sight overwhelmed the new married couple, and the altar. And the reverend. It didn't escape her, the irony of KB and Maxine having chosen an ocean view setting. One might think they'd never want to glimpse the ocean again.

She knew, though, that despite his neuroses, his insecurities, his darker imaginings, KB was ultimately more of an optimist than she. Once he'd had mentioned how the Night of the Terror had strengthened their friendship, because "I saw you almost dead—how many people can say that about their friends?" Likewise, she could imagine him saying to Maxine, "We survived a sea wreck together—how many couples can say *that*?"

Now KB and Maxine were setting sail again together, where? Toward what shores? There were no shores, they might say, because marriage was about daily reveling, not an endgame. Not about seeing or even finding it all, whatever all that was.

From the main table, the ornate KB and Maxine watched her as she stood. The raucous boil of the reception simmered. Three glasses of wine and one champagne in, and urged by the sheer attention of so many eyes, Sierra put extra energy into articulating every word.

"It's quite surprising," Sierra said, glass in hand. "I still don't know if I believe that I'm seeing KB, or Jake, here in this tux, next to a bride. He and I used to run around the woods together when we were kids. He saved my butt. And more than once, too. I owe my life to this kid. And he'll always be a kid, because I'll always be a kid." She looked at him. "Right?"

Tepidly, KB nodded. By his expression, he was curious where she was going with this.

"Just as he'll always be KB, at least to me," Sierra continued. "Sorry, Maxine."

Maxine shrugged. She pecked her new husband on the cheek.

"I know some might be wondering why I actually call him KB," Sierra said. She paused, suppressed a burp. "You ever notice his teeth? Those black gaps between them make them look like a piano keyboard. Hence, KB."

Scattered laughs.

"I remember hearing," Sierra said, "or reading, that we should always marvel at the good things life throws at us, because it has no obligation to do that. We know that too well, right?"

The couple nodded.

"KB and Maxine, you both have found each other. But KB, you could just as easily have been a Viking, dying by the sword a thousand years ago, and Maxine, you could have been born next year, in some rat hole somewhere in Beijing, and so the two of you, while perfectly compatible, would never have met or even known about each other. Right? You know what I mean?"

Confusion thickened the air above the crowd, but the general demeanor was politely indulgent.

"Life threw you guys a big bone. And you recognized it. Maybe that's the ticket. Recognizing it. Maybe it throws all of us a bone, and most of us just suck at seeing it." Sierra felt tears welling in her. She raised her glass. "But I'll shut up now."

For only a half-hour after dinner, Sierra sat and watched the festivities, the people mingling and dancing, before calling for a cab and heading to the curb just outside the Santa Monica hotel, where she waited. She lost herself dizzily in the night sky, its stars threatened by a slow wave of coastal fog.

"Sierra," said a voice behind her. Tinny. It was KB, standing there in his tux. "I saw you leave. Are you okay?"

Still gazing at the stars, half-consciously Sierra said, "Do you remember what we went through?"

"What?" he said. "Of course—"

"You were in my dreams," she said. "Weren't you?"

"What do you mean?"

What do you *mean, huh?*

She blinked, lowered her head, the earth and all its heaviness returning to her. She didn't know what she meant.

The cab arrived, headlights drilling up the U-shaped driveway.

Sierra turned to KB, opened her arms for a hug. "Congratulations again."

KB returned the hug, but snickered. He glanced behind him as if to confirm no one was within earshot. "Sierra, come on," he said, "you hate the whole marriage thing."

"Hey, fuck you." She went to punch him on the bicep, but he pulled back and she stumbled, very nearly falling. He went to catch her, but she maintained her balance.

"Sierra, Christ," he said. "Watch yourself."

She chuckled. "Why? I'm okay."

"Well, for one, your dad…"

"What about my dad?"

"I remember some of the stuff you'd tell me about him," KB said. "About him drinking and all. Just be careful."

She stood there, studying him, the ground wavering.

"I can come with you, if you want," KB said. "Just to make sure you get where you're going."

"Are you kidding? You're married." She pointed to the hotel behind him. "Go be a husband."

"Maxine will understand. I'll just run in and tell her. I can just take the cab right back after."

"No," Sierra said, pointing an index finger at him. "Go back. Seriously. Just go back. I'll be fine, man. I will."

With extra caution and focus, she climbed into the cab. KB watched her. She closed the door, the window of which was down a few inches.

"Bye, Sierra."

She put up her hand. "Congrats again, Jakey."

A wan grin pushed up the corner of his lips.

In a squirt of words, Sierra told the driver her motel and where to go, and the vehicle pulled away into traffic and the hotel was lost to dusk and headlights.

KB was right about her view of marriage—kind of. Marriage was merely the symbol. Symbol for what? Sierra, somehow, knew that answer, though she couldn't articulate it. She knew she had felt the actual thing behind the symbol, the supreme end of many a sad attempt, of so many bumbling, contrived efforts undertaken by people who did not realize that union, true union, transcended pastors and overpriced rings and licenses and identical surnames. That was all bullshit, really. True union couldn't be had in this world, where heavy things constantly bumped into one another.

Maybe this world was a symbol for another, the way, say, films were for this world.

How do you know this?

How had she known true union? Sierra wasn't certain. The details had left her, but the feeling had stayed, the feeling and something more, something deeper and beyond feeling — along with the assurance that that was what was most significant, and most rare.

NIGHT ON TERROR ISLAND

"That's not the real title, right?" asked the narrow-faced blonde woman named Tanya. She wore a smirk, playfully patronizing.

Night on Terror Island, it read on the flat screen in front of them. Sierra chuckled a little uneasily. She shared a glance with Andrew who sat with his chin resting on his palm, looking at her over his knuckles.

"No," Sierra said. "It's a temporary title."

"I like it," said the man named Josh, a mid-thirties bohemian-type with a bushy ponytail and a new-looking black shirt that read 'Miskatonic Productions.' "In a kind of SyFy Channel, bargain-bin kind of way."

"Okay, shhh," Tanya said.

Sierra closed her eyes for a long second, nerves in a laundry cycle in her stomach. Doing this. *Actually doing this.* The intensity of the work still lingered in her bones. The preceding days and weeks and months she'd become fused to the routine of animating, swept up in the life slow-dripping from her fingertips into the creatures. The outer world banished, sleep demoted to a suggestion, food to an afterthought.

"You've lost weight, it looks like," Andrew had noted when she'd re-emerged, and returned to L.A. "I gave it to them," she'd replied, indicating the demo film and its creatures.

The four pairs of eyes watched, quiet and thoughtful, as her winged devil did swiping, fluttering, gnashing battle with a giant octopus that stutter-thrashed its rubber tentacles in a twisting, gyrating rage. She'd deliberately chosen an octopus, as an homage to Boylan—his own test reel, the one that had wedged his foot in the door with Errol Maybury, the one he'd produced at twenty-five in his own garage workshop, had featured an oversized cephalopod. The tradition of the 'test reel' stretched past Boylan, too. His own mentor John Terwiliger had excited studio suits in the early 30s with his short showcase of what would evolve into *The Great Kundo*.

"You did this all yourself?" Tanya asked.

"She did," Andrew said. "Isn't that crazy?"

"This seriously looks like something out of Russell Boylan," said Josh. By his incredulous expression Sierra for a moment wasn't sure if he was impressed or oddly offended. "Though... maybe it's because I haven't seen one of his movies in a while, but I think this looks better. I mean, his films were pretty big productions—"

"Some of them," Tanya interjected.

"Some, yes. But this has a kind of homemade, indie quality that I like. It exists totally within its own world, done and done and through and through."

"Thanks," Sierra said, her whole body aflame with excitement.

"The creatures seem like extensions of one personality," Josh said.

"Goin' a bit deep for this, aren't ya?" Andrew said.

"Sorry, this is just cool. Brings it outta me."

"I actually wonder if we can get this in front of Joe," Tanya said.

Josh raised an eyebrow. "Cranston?"

"Yeah."

"Wait," said Andrew. "Isn't he the Cretaceous Crater guy?"

"Yeah, but he's a big Russell Boylan fan," Tanya said. "We have a couple possible connections to him." She turned back to Sierra. "I think I speak for Andrew and I when I say we're excited to pursue this further." Smiling, she added, "To help bring Russell Boylan back from the dead."

"Not to diminish you," Josh hastily noted. Turning toward Tanya, he said, "This is Sierra's baby."

And Sierra thought, *It's half mine.*

GENESIS

All lights dimmed in the single screen of the Arrow Theater, and for a long moment—interminably long, for Sierra Nevada Smith—sounds of the crowd rose like streams of bubbles in the dark: the popcorn-munching, the mostly-inaudible mutterings edged with playful cynicism, the shifting and scraping of bodies and feet for the right position in which to spend this next eighty-seven minutes.

She tried to avoid looking at the people around her—they were predominantly young, or young-ish, many eclectic-looking, many poised, so it felt, to strike their critical matches. The screening had sold out, unexpected for the debut.

What would happen next, though? After the exhausting blur of the production year, the gestation and the labor and the delivery and the fine-tuned meditation beside the monsters, after whatever had come out of all that had been ingested by all these eyes, what then?

Sierra took a quick sip from her flask. Then another. She noticed furtive glances her way, but didn't mind.

Then the screen illuminated, the dark obliterated, all possible worlds in the minds of the crowd washed away, supplanted by this one—her own.

Not wanting to be ensnared in the exiting rush, Sierra left the screening minutes early, maintaining her balance well enough. She filed out and hurried toward the bathroom, thinking maybe she might vomit. Then the Arrow's wide-paned entrance, dark with night, called to her and she made a beeline for the door. She exchanged distant smiles with the young ticket-taker.

Outside, the chilly evening rushed upon her. She took several deep breaths. Fog had crept close and thick around the theater. She could barely see the parked cars and the little side street not thirty feet away.

Steadily, a calmness settled over her, a fulfillment that felt larger than herself. She wasn't alone here. A heartening affirmation filled her, and Sierra had a brief vision of herself, as if she were looking at her own reflection. Someone was beside her, this presence so close, even protective, an apparition of familiar form with a firm hand on her shoulder, squeezing his approval.

And, inside, the screening room doors opened, the people emerging.

#

STOP MOTION STILL KICKIN'
New Film Carries Old Methods Into 21st Century
by Andrew Slater

It was hard to gauge the initial mood of last night's screening of the new independent horror-adventure film, *Terror Summit*, produced by Miskatonic Productions, a film that proudly—and, perhaps quixotically—resurrects the noble-but-brief tradition of stop-motion animation for its special FX (for those uninitiated, Google the name Russell Boylan, for starters). There was palpable anticipation, certainly a piqued curiosity among those old souls (or, in some cases, those simply older) but also a snickering caution from those no doubt set in the belief that stop-motion is the VCR to computer animation's DVD.

But *Terror Summit*, and, in particular, its surprisingly young and colorful primary animator, 22-year-old Sierra Nevada Smith, appeared to silence all premature snickers with last night's debut screening at Santa Monica's Arrow Theater.

The audience walked away with what I can only describe as fanciful fulfillment, the older matinee-attendees treated to reunions with their younger selves, those less familiar acquainted with what might as well be a new art form. Terror Summit represents a rediscovered treasure, lost beneath wave after tidal wave of hyper-realism. It is like a glimpse between the frames, at the very dreams that begin and beget movies, at some kind of purer cinema.

The deserved focus of *Terror Summit*, its cast of stop-motion beasties, all tweaked into painstaking existence one frame at a time, returned to the screen an escapist surrealism not seen in generations. The creatures, and, in particular, its monstrous 'mascot,' the bat-winged devil lording over its Lovecraftian island, move with a life and a vigor wholly unique. Though the tradition of stop-motion is not new historically, it's new here—it's difficult to even pinpoint why, too, the reasons no doubt lurking deep in the subtleties and nuances of Sierra's style, and what she brings to her creations. That such craft and vision came from someone as young as she is something remarkable, if not miraculous for us monster buffs, and will no doubt be the talk of creature-town once *Terror Summit* acquires wider distribution.

Sierra Smith, covered in the artful, tattooed representations of Russell Boylan's filmography, is somewhat demure when asked about her achievements.

"I leave room for the dream," she says of her process. "For mine. For yours."

THE END

CHECK OUT OTHER GREAT DINOSAUR BOOKS

PRIMORDIA
by **Greig Beck**

Ben Cartwright, former soldier, home to mourn the loss of his father stumbles upon cryptic letters from the past between the author, Arthur Conan Doyle and his great, great grandfather who vanished while exploring the Amazon jungle in 1908.

Amazingly, these letters lead Ben to believe that his ancestor's expedition was the basis for Doyle's fantastical tale of a lost world inhabited by long extinct creatures. As Ben digs some more he finds clues to the whereabouts of a lost notebook that might contain a map to a place that is home to creatures that would rewrite everything known about history, biology and evolution.

But other parties now know about the notebook, and will do anything to obtain it. For Ben and his friends, it becomes a race against time and against ruthless rivals.

In the remotest corners of Venezuela, along winding river trails known only to lost tribes, and through near impenetrable jungle, Ben and his novice team find a forbidden place more terrifying and dangerous than anything they could ever have imagined.

PANGAEA EXILES
by **Jeff Brackett**

Tried and convicted for his crimes, Sean Barrow is sent into temporal exile—banished to a time so far before recorded history that there is no chance that he, or any other criminal sent back, has any chance of altering history.

Now Sean must find a way to survive more than 200 million years in the past, in a world populated by monstrous creatures that would rend him limb from limb if they got the chance. And that's just his fellow prisoners.

The dinosaurs are almost as bad.

CHECK OUT OTHER GREAT DINOSAUR BOOKS

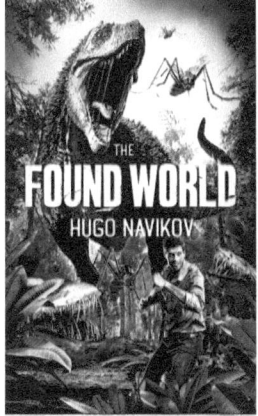

THE FOUND WORLD
by Hugo Navikov

A powerful global cabal wants adventurer Brett Russell to retrieve a superweapon stolen by the scientist who built it. To entice him to travel underneath one of the most dangerous volcanoes on Earth to find the scientist, this shadowy organization will pay him the only thing he cares about: information that will allow him to avenge his family's murder.

But before he can get paid, he and his team must enter an underground hellscape of killer plants, giant insects, terrifying dinosaurs, and an army of other predators never previously seen by man.

At the end of this journey awaits a revelation that could alter the fate of mankind ... if they can make it back from this horrifying found world.

HOUSE OF THE GODS
by Davide Mana

High above the steamy jungle of the Amazon basin, rise the flat plateaus known as the Tepui, the House of the Gods. Lost worlds of unknown beauty, a naturalistic wonder, each an ecology onto itself, shunned by the local tribes for centuries. The House of the Gods was not made for men.

But now, the crew and passengers of a small charter plane are about to find what was hidden for sixty million years.

Lost on an island in the clouds 10.000 feet above the jungle, surrounded by dinosaurs, hunted by mysterious mercenaries, the survivors of Sligo Air flight 001 will quickly learn the only rule of life on Earth: Extinction.

Check out other great

Dinosaur Thrillers!

P.K. Hawkins

THE LOST ISLAND

Scientists Dr. Eccleston and Dr. Lerner have done many routine expeditions for the Skurzon Corporation in the past, helping the company search the ocean for newly available resources freed by melting ice. They're expecting to maybe find oil at the bottom of the Arctic Sea. What they aren't expecting is a lost island that defies all scientific understanding. When something comes out of the sea and destroys their research vessel, the scientists and the rest of the crew are forced into a game of survival against forces no human being has ever seen alive. If they can survive the giant insect swarms, the man-eating plants, and the dinosaurs, they might be able to live to tell the tale. But when each passing moment reveals murderers in their midst, their survival starts to look less and less likely.

William Meikle

THE LAND BELOW

A treasure hunt into the deepest cave system in Europe takes a turn for the worst. Now rather than treasure it is survival that is at the forefront of the spelunkers' thoughts. But their attempt to escape out of the dark deep places is thwarted. Men are not at home in the depths. But there are things that are, pale terrifying things. Huge things. Things red in tooth and claw.